Kristel Thornell was born in Parramatta and, outside Australia, has lived in Italy, Mexico, Canada, Finland, the United States and France, where she is now based. She has degrees in Italian Studies and English, and a PhD from the Writing and Society Research Group at the University of Western Sydney. Her first novel, *Night Street* (2010), co-won the *Australian*/Vogel's Literary Award and won the Dobbie Literary Award and the Barbara Ramsden Award. It was shortlisted for the Glenda Adams Award and the Christina Stead Prize for fiction in the NSW Premier's Awards, and Thornell was named one of the *Sydney Morning Herald*'s Best Young Australian Novelists. Her second novel, *On the Blue Train* (2016), has also been published in a Chinese translation.

the sirens sing

kristel thornell

FOURTH ESTATE

Fourth Estate
An imprint of HarperCollins*Publishers*

Australia • Brazil • Canada • France • Germany • Holland • India
Italy • Japan • Mexico • New Zealand • Poland • Spain • Sweden
Switzerland • United Kingdom • United States of America

HarperCollins acknowledges the Traditional Custodians of the land upon which we live and work, and pays respect to Elders past and present.

First published in Australia in 2022
by HarperCollins*Publishers* Australia Pty Limited
Gadigal Country
Level 13, 201 Elizabeth Street, Sydney NSW 2000
ABN 36 009 913 517
harpercollins.com.au

A catalogue record for this book is available from the National Library of Australia

ISBN 978 1 4607 6266 0 (paperback)
ISBN 978 1 4607 1525 3 (ebook)

Cover design by Lisa White
Cover image by Tommaso Tuzj / stocksy.com / 732633
Author photograph by Massimo Municchi
Typeset in Bembo Std by Kirby Jones
Printed and bound in Australia by McPherson's Printing Group

FSC
www.fsc.org
MIX
Paper | Supporting responsible forestry
FSC® C001695

I

THE BLUE MOUNTAINS
1993–1994

1

KATOOMBA STATION

She tended to be alone, an air of shyness or social reluctance about her – but perhaps he just wanted to imagine they were alike. Heather was a year younger than David, in Year Eleven when he was in Year Twelve. He'd glimpsed her in hallways, assemblies and on the bush track that wound up to where buses deposited and collected students. He saw her in the school production of *The Importance of Being Earnest*, in which she appeared tense and slightly breathless yet pulled off her ditzy character remarkably well. He was mesmerised when she had to kiss one of the male leads. It looked like perfect kissing: careful, warm and consuming. He wondered how choreographed it had been, how much spontaneity was involved. Was Heather going out with that guy in real life? If not, he had to have a wild crush on her. David was sitting near the stage, close enough to observe the unbelievably pretty twin ridges of her upper lip and her pillowy lower lip, as well as her mottled dark-blonde hair that faintly brought to mind a tortoiseshell cat.

A week later, on a bus, he overheard two girls from Heather's class discussing her, insinuating that she didn't have a boyfriend and was almost certainly a virgin, because she was up herself. The meanness and jealousy were of course standard for school gossip. David was relieved not to have to imagine Heather kissing her fellow actor off-stage.

One day, he arrived early at his French lesson and there she was, having lingered after hers to chat with Yvonne, the teacher. The classroom was full of the bluish-grey afternoon light that percolated through the mist and gum trees outside, along with the usual smell of plastic chairs, newish meagre-pile carpet and whiteboard pen. The school was a small, Steiner-inspired New Agey place that David's mother struggled to pay for. Though the fees represented a considerable sacrifice and an ongoing stress, he'd been a student there since his second year of high school, a decision prompted by some uneasy experiences he'd had at state schools (to do with his reliably good marks, bad performance at sports and probably also his lack of social nerve).

Now, three-unit French was his favourite subject and, as he was the only one taking the course, Yvonne sometimes prepared coffee for them to sip during the lessons. French felt closer to daydreaming than studying, and even learning verbs and vocab by rote was relaxingly hypnotic. Yvonne had long, force-of-nature auburn hair that she wore loose; she'd no doubt in her younger years been a hippie or some other variety of free spirit. Her complexion had a greenish tinge, as if she were standing in an arbour, her freckles a dappling of shade. The veins on her hands were very evident, foreshadowing grandparent hands, but she was a rare older person for whom you could nearly imagine sensuality without disbelief or revulsion, giving as she did an impression of living among revered books and other sensory rituals. She kept her notes and pens in an endearing brown leather satchel, was passionate about French and had a soft spot for David, seeing that he was too. He felt privileged to be sipping her rather gritty, heart-pleasing coffee while conversing in French. On and off, it seemed they could have been in a café somewhere else in the world, could have been strangers, relatives, friends, even lovers; those hours felt nicely bendable.

The day he arrived early and found Heather and Yvonne together, he noticed coffee cups on the table between them and understood from their absentminded body language that they were even more bonded than he and Yvonne were.

'Oh hello, David,' Yvonne greeted him in French. 'Do you know Heather? She's studying Italian by correspondence, like you. She's just started.' Few students took correspondence courses. 'David's doing his second year. Perhaps you two could get together sometime for conversation?'

They mumbled vaguely, covertly assessing each other.

Later, he thought he'd said, 'Yeah, that would be good.' Though he wasn't certain if he actually had or Heather had been anything but politely noncommittal.

It must have occurred to Yvonne that David would consider the prospect of studying with a more junior student boring, because she added, 'She'll learn fast, very fast.' Her tone was stern; she meant it. 'Heather's one of the most gifted people for languages I've encountered. Ever, in my career.' She quickly tried to rectify the implication that David was an averagely good student in comparison with Heather, the star. 'You two are among the best students I've had. I've been lucky with both of you.'

The following week, crossing over from Blackheath Station towards the shops, he suspected he saw Heather in the distance. Far off, but coming in his direction. He accelerated, thrashing around in his mind for what he could say to her. What strange bit of grammar could he mention? The use of 'the impersonal *si*' that somehow called for a plural adjective when the verb was singular (*si è contenti* – one is happys)? Or some word that sounded like jokey baby French? Could he ask if she felt her French and her Italian helped each other up to a point but also sometimes mutually interfered, leaving the two languages wobbly? This might lead to them bringing up Yvonne's suggestion that they meet for conversation practice.

It *was* her. Willowy in black jeans, bulky black jumper and brown Blundstone boots. Without seeing him, she turned into the fruit shop and he continued straight on, blushing fiercely. He couldn't follow her into a shop.

Often over the next months (both when he was doubting his own aptitude for Italian or slightly high on an inkling of it), he wondered how fast Heather the prodigy was progressing. He strove to be as impressive as she was; remotely, she was lifting his game and he enjoyed the idea that being students of correspondence Italian sort of made them members of the same club.

One afternoon a problem on the train line, something involving a wombat, interrupted his journey home from school. He had to wait at Katoomba Station along with the other peeved passengers for a promised bus. He was leaning against the mustard-coloured timber of the old station building, the backpack at his feet heavy with stuff he should have taken out to study. But he was utterly sick of all the drawn-out apprehension of looming assessment tasks and exams, and he hankered to goof off, just slide around in time without having to desperately finish or feel guilty about not finishing anything. He wasn't great at taking it easy: for as long as he could remember, he'd been used to the tightness of tension in his stomach; when he was nine or thereabouts, during his parents' custody battle over him, a doctor had told him to eat yeast so he wouldn't keep getting ulcers on his tongue from stress. He tried to picture himself the following year in an after-school life of untimed time, lounging around in pyjamas over cups of tea and buttery crumpets, or settling in his perch in his favourite cedar tree to read something for fun. Did adults live like that, though, if they weren't rich? Anyway, he'd be at university, wouldn't he?

Heather was coming towards him.

He looked away, and then at her once more. As she got closer, he saw that her cheeks were pink from the cold and her hair was up in a high ponytail, austerely classy. She was carrying a butcher's-paper parcel, probably from the milk bar. She was so absorbed by whatever she was listening to on her Walkman that it was likely she wouldn't notice him. But she did, out of the corner of her eye at the last minute, and took a step back.

'Hi. Hang on a tick.' She removed her earbuds. Her Walkman was a white Sony with grey details and rounded edges. 'Chip?'

He was starving. They were in the glum slump in his mother's pay cycle. Hours earlier he'd demolished the lunch he'd packed – cheese sandwiches and a banana – and there'd been nothing else to get him through the famished wastes of the afternoon. Five more days to payday, when his house would be jolly with treats to get stuffed on, Tim Tam and Mint Slice biscuits, little frozen cheesecakes and the like. The proximity to salt and deep-frying made him salivate. She smiled and tore off a piece of butcher's paper with which she fished him out a generous cluster of chips. There was a freckle beneath her lower lip, like a tiny smudge of chocolate.

'Sure you have enough?'

'There's heaps.' She thrust the offering at him.

He took it, his excitement flaring insanely as their hands touched. While they ate, she leaned against the wall beside him.

'I hate having to get buses,' she said.

'I know, it sucks. I really hate getting buses back from Sydney. Massive drag. I get nauseous on coaches.'

'Me too. Just seeing the colourful carpet on the seats. And the way they move – sort of smoothly, but vibrating. Do you go down to Sydney often?

'Every fortnight, custody weekends with my dad.'

'He lives there?'

'Yeah.'

'Cool. Can you finish these?' She passed him the whole parcel. 'My dad isn't around. Where in Sydney does yours live?'

'Newtown. I can't take all your food.'

Was she giving it to him because she'd had enough, or was she just being well-mannered? She had a kindly poker face that made it hard to tell, and nor could he tell if she wanted him to ask about her dad.

'Please, really.' She brushed salt from her fingers.

He began to hunt through the soft folds of the package for chips, which were floppy and wickedly addictive with chicken salt. 'Thanks.'

'We lived in a lot of places in Sydney,' she went on. 'Glebe was the last one.'

'Oh? We used to live in Glebe, too. What street?'

'Ferry Road. We had a Housing Commission flat. Marianne – my mum – loved living there. She's from Adelaide, but she says Glebe is her spiritual home. The city was getting too expensive for us, though. When they told us we'd have to leave our flat, we thought we'd try living up here.'

He didn't know that road. He liked the neutral way Heather had spoken (it reminded him of the detachment with which he himself tried to think about money stuff, house moves and the like) and the information she'd given made him feel a tad more confident. 'We were in a squat on Bridge Road. And then in a shared place on Arundel Street.'

'Cool. Do you have any brothers or sisters?'

She was taking down her hair; it became voluminous and wavy. He focused on the chips, the lethargic pale-blue sky and the crisp air that suddenly brought a wild, snug smell of woodsmoke.

'No. Only child. Single parent.'

'Me too.'

They smiled at each other and it was exhilarating.

Gesturing at the station building behind them, Heather said, 'You could live in this if it was in the middle of a field or moor, somewhere isolated. I wonder if I agree with Sartre about hell being other people. Most other people, at least.'

She seemed to watch how he was taking this. He nodded. Then she showed him what she'd removed from her hair, a purplish-black ribbon.

'I got this from the second-hand shop on Katoomba Street. Mum got paid, so we're in the money. I shouldn't be blowing my allowance straightaway, but I couldn't resist this because it's French.'

'Can I see?' he asked.

He liked that she was sharing the lurching around of her mind. But maybe she was talking out of discomfort – that only-child responsibility to fill the deep space with companionable sound. He wanted her to talk to him because she chose to, not because she felt she had to. He cleaned his hand of salt as best he could in order to hold her new ribbon, and it was dreamlike and intimate to grip something that had just been wrapped around her hair. The texture was faintly fleecy and the edges had a fine wire in them; he fancied it warm from her heat. He considered what she'd said about other people being hell and how this might confirm she was a loner like him. He might have preferred to feel more comfortable with others, and certainly to be madly loved and desired by a girl. (How long would he have to wait for that? *Would* it happen? Would someone truly recognise and need the crucial parts of him?) Oh what to say that wouldn't be try-hard flirty? How to impress this complex girl?

'Nice. So how's your Italian going?'

'It's going. Actually, I'm pretty obsessed with it. I wish I could wag school all the time and just do that. Spend all day watching the Italian movies I tape and listening to corny Italian music and reading stuff aloud to myself. I suppose I should be talking to real people, which is sort of the point of learning a language. Yvonne keeps asking me if we're practising together.'

It was funny to think of Heather and Yvonne mentioning him. He had to concentrate now, because this was an ideal segue into proposing they meet again.

Their bus was announced over the loudspeaker in a tetchy tone, provoking groans and elaborate sighs from some of those waiting on the platform.

Trying not to sound desperate as the moment dissolved, he said quickly, '*Mi piacerebbe.*'

She responded that she'd like that, too.

But someone was calling her. 'Heather, over here!'

A guy, waving largely.

It was the first time David was ever jealous of Robbie, as Heather waved back and said, 'I should go. That's my friend Robbie. He goes to Katoomba High. He's an artist.'

She was slipping away. He didn't have her phone number or any guarantee of running into her again.

'See ya round,' he said like a sad dickhead, following her towards the bus.

When he climbed into the dense coach air – synthetic upholstery, unventilated breathing and sweating, the queasy hint of a fermenting banana – he saw Heather approaching the back seat, where Robbie was. He had the bravado of guys who take over back seats on buses, did he? He wore a black-and-maroon-checked flannelette shirt over a black T-shirt and was kind of dashing, unfortunately. Lean, long and broad-shouldered, his hair a glossy, glamorous black. With a touch of Mark Seymour and maybe of Chris Isaak, too. Fucking *hell.*

David sat alone a few rows back from the front, in the uncool, close-to-driver region, and realised only then that he had her French ribbon in his fist. He couldn't go and give it to her now. Had he made it sweaty? Guiltily, jubilantly, he buried her possession in his grubby canvas backpack, on which he'd refused to write his surname in keeping with the embarrassing convention, and pulled out *Wuthering Heights*. He needed characters to slide into and the thought of moors. Had Heather's reference to a moor meant that she'd read and loved it, too? I should have asked, he berated himself. And what music had she been listening to?

He wouldn't see her again for almost a year. Meanwhile, the folded ribbon sat in the drawer of the desk in his bedroom. He let himself touch it only rarely and with clean, dry hands. His fingertips lightly exploring the softness and its wiry boundaries.

*

Decades later, living in America, David would very occasionally dream of Heather. Around the time of his marriage ending and his nostalgia for Australia peaking, he dreamed of them both as children in Sydney. Not meeting, but going about their lives in parallel. Heather roller-skating along a footpath in a Choose Life T-shirt. (In real life, she once confided to having been a nervous roller-skater in those years and to having proudly owned such a shirt.) David being taken to Hoyts Cinema to see *Can't Stop the Music*, sporting a studded belt he was happy to consider punk. (He had fallen asleep early in the movie, after having insisted to his mother that he was *really* sure he wanted to see it.) Waking from the dream, he felt overwhelmed by a sort of warm sadness.

He had been dwelling on his and his mother's life back then and now he reflected that Jan would probably have crossed paths with Heather's mother frequently. They might even have attended the same yoga class (where the blue mats gave off the grungy tang of previous users' feet) and they would have walked past each other during expeditions to buy biodynamic bread from Demeter or dried fruit and natural peanut butter from Russell's. He imagined Jan and Marianne passing each other on Glebe Point Road, Marianne singing a track from Talking Heads' *Remain in Light* that she'd been listening to earlier with Heather. And Jan in turn getting the song in her head and singing it quietly later at home, while she tried making chai for the first time with spices from Russell's.

There was a true memory in there: David lying on the floor in front of *Monkey* on telly and the bar heater he got so close to it virtually singed him. The aroma of what was simmering on the stove reaching him, cloves and cardamom like ancient forest medicine, the honeyed heat of cinnamon and ginger. And every so often, the words of that song. He came to associate the track speaking of wind in your heart with the transcendence of spicy steam and foreign TV. With endless long walks through the Inner West, all the pungency of the Sydney of his early childhood. With Heather. He hadn't known her then, lying in front of the heater, but each of the sensations that made up that mental scene was leaning towards her. And those dreams he had in America left a longing in their wake, as if he had heard the echo of his name being called.

2

BLACKHEATH MEMORIAL PARK

It was late in September, close to dusk, and David was sitting by the pool that was closed until November. He was impatient for it to be open again, for the feeling of leaving the world above the water behind. There was usually hardly anyone else swimming there when he was. And if there *were* other swimmers, there were quite a few possibilities as to the kinds of people they might be. Blackheath was like that. For example, it could be an athletic elderly lady like the ones he saw heading home from the shops with a don't-mess-with-me attitude, who tended gardens ambitious with roses and rhododendrons. Or a sporadically fast guy, who was possibly scary and might have lived in a run-down weatherboard box or a redbrick one behind which all the trees had been mercilessly razed. Or a relative of the gruff but friendly Greek couple who ran the milk bar. Or a Sydney yuppie with a renovated homestead on Shipley – if not a brand-new place all fancy with skylights and decks – where they only stayed on weekends; coming up from the city to potter around antique shops in jodhpurs and stylishly rustic riding boots and indulge in Devonshire teas, ploughman's lunches and pricey meals at the Hydro Majestic and the Paragon. Or a leftie who tended to be broke like David's mum – maybe one of the classic former, late or eternal hippies who'd moved from Sydney to the Mountains in search of some sort of alternative lifestyle involving Buddhist temples, clean air and the rare fun of waking in winter to find the bush icing-sugared with snow.

A girl said his name, sounding slightly surprised.

She looked like she had been lost in the rhythm of her walking, her face bared and opened by exertion.

'It's Heather, from school.'

'Of course.'

Of course. This apparition, when he'd given up hope. For a moment, he turned away from her face, the touch of inky violet in the skin under her eyes, the muted plum of her lips, the hair that she was sleeking back with one hand. He noticed that the trees had darkened as if the oncoming night were emerging from them.

'It's been ages.'

He half turned back. 'Yeah, hasn't it?'

He had the impression of having lived a short life since their last meeting, of needing to concentrate to recover the person he'd been then, to be sure he could identify him.

'You at university now?'

'No, I decided to have a year off, try to save some money – so I hopefully won't have to defer paying all my fees. Apparently, they charge you interest if you do that. Anyway, I'm working in the pub at the hotel opposite the station. It's all right.'

He didn't say that as he'd been poised to move to Sydney, his mother had thought she had breast cancer; the tumour turned out to be benign, but the incident had made her appear more delicate and unready for David to leave home. Then not long after he'd made the decision not to, having had no romantic relationship in years, his mother had started going out with Carole, the therapist she'd been having sessions with, and David became the third wheel, wondering if he shouldn't have moved out, after all.

'Is it allowed, getting together with your therapist?' he'd asked when she announced the news to him.

'Well,' she'd hedged, smiling. 'This is the Mountains – things can get a bit incestuous, can't they?'

Heather said, 'It must be nice to be out of the machine for a while.'

'Yeah.' But actually it had felt more like falling into a crevice.

'By the way, congrats on your results.'

'Cheers,' he said. 'Unexpected.'

'Hardly. Yvonne told me you were at the top of the state in Italian.'

'Second place. You'll probably come first.'

'Yeah, right.'

She would though. He changed to Italian. 'So, how's Year Twelve been?'

And her Italian was unleashed on him. 'I'm doing my best not to get too stressed about the exams coming up, which is why I'm trying to do lots of exercise. I wish the pool was open already!'

'Me too,' he said.

'Anyway, thank God for foreign languages. I'm not really having fun with anything else.'

He was a perfectionist himself and had been expecting her to be excellent, but perhaps not so smoothly, authentically. He was dazed, as if new half-envisioned possibilities were suddenly fanning out before them.

He asked, 'Do you want to sit for a bit?'

'Okay.'

There were smells of pine and rhododendron and the air felt like it might have been carrying imminent rain.

She sat down beside him and, considering his knees, he said, 'I've been missing Italian. I haven't spoken it since the oral exam.'

'That's a long time. You'll do it next year, at university?'

'Definitely. I want to major in it. Even if it doesn't get me a job.'

'Me too, I think. You'll go to Sydney?'

He nodded. 'You?'

'Probably.'

'Your accent is incredible.' *And your grammar, your comprehension, your everything.* He was blown away by how she seemed to have simply allowed herself to fall backwards into Italian like in some trust exercise, knowing it would catch her. She had the mystique of unquestionable skill.

'Really? I never talk to anyone.'

Because there was nothing to lose and he might never see her again, he said, 'We could talk together sometime?' The words came out lopsided by nerves.

'We were going to do that before and we never got around to it.'

'No.'

'Well, I don't know if you'd be interested, but I'm about to start conversation lessons with an Italian woman who lives on Shipley Road. I've been teaching Robbie – my friend Robbie – a bit of Italian and he's thinking of coming. Would you want to, as well?'

'When would that be?' he asked cagily.

'This Thursday afternoon.'

'I work Thursday night, but I'm free in the afternoon.' He remembered her implying, the last time they'd met, that she and her mother were sometimes short on cash, as he and his mother were. 'I'd pay half.'

'Don't worry about that. I got money for my birthday to cover the lessons, one a week till the exam.'

'I have a job, though, and I'd want to contribute, if I came.'

'We can talk about that later.' She rubbed her shoulder beneath the strap of her singlet top. Her arms were pale and long. 'The first … how do you say?'

'Mosquito.' This lingered in his mind after he said it, and he sensed it lingering in hers: *una zanzara*.

'Nice – it sounds like the noise they make.'

'It does, doesn't it? I like it, too.' Staring at the ground in front of him, realising she had barely sat down, he added, 'Do you want to walk for a bit? Maybe through Parklands?'

He glanced at her and she was nodding.

As they set off through Memorial Park, he learned that she lived quite close to him, on Fourth Street. They were moving fast, loosely.

'Do you swim much when the pool's open?' he asked. 'I come a few times a week.'

'I'd like to do that, swim regularly. I don't usually come here so late in the day. It's pretty now.'

'Yeah.'

Now was perfect, rich and ripe because of her company. The pool they had left behind them was glowing in his imagination as if it were open and illuminated, eerily beautiful like some sci-fi liquid jewel. He thought about her bitchy classmates calling her a virgin. Was it true? David was, more and more self-consciously. They passed the old-fashioned kids' play equipment, the big boot and the rocket that could bring on wistfulness but didn't with Heather there, not in a doleful way. Soon, they were entering the grounds of the former Parklands Hotel and it was clear that she was as used to the trespassing as he was. He'd never shared the place's mood of genteel haunting with anyone before. They kept away from the foundations of extinct buildings and were mostly quiet until crossing the perimeter of big old pines and up onto Govetts Leap Road.

In English she said, 'There's a party at Robbie's place tonight. I wasn't going to go. I'm not very into parties and I don't drink or smoke dope. But would you want to come? You could meet Robbie.'

He was thrilled that she was inviting him to her Italian classes *and* to go out that night, but almost equally put off by Robbie's inclusion in both activities.

'Um, I wouldn't be gate-crashing?'

'No. He's cool. I think you'll like each other.'

'Okay, I'll come.'

They made a plan to meet an hour and a half later, where they were standing, and he headed away from her up the hill at a rapid clip, marvelling at how there could be nothing, barrenness, and then something extraordinary arrived to shake you awake, fill you, utterly change everything. And it was nearly too much, too gleeful and unsafe, not knowing what exactly it was, imagining what it might become. He'd thought of Heather very often, but it was that evening after walking together that she began to devour his mental time whole, truly occupy him, all the inner reaches, so that it was impossible to separate thinking of her from thinking of himself.

3

PARKLANDS

After agonising over his very few clothing choices, David had gone with the old Levi's, the Doc Martens he'd bought with his first pay from the hotel and the green-and-black-checked shirt he hoped was more urban-trendy than loutish-slacker Westie. He fussed with the shirt, tucking it in, untucking, tucking, untucking. With some difficulty and hoping it wouldn't show up on the shirt, he applied extra deodorant, in case he'd forgotten to do that. He smiled tensely at the mirror, evaluated his skin, smoothed his eyebrows, examined his okay profile and the worse one, turned and twisted to see if his bum looked all right. Did it? He had no idea. He'd have to start doing push-ups or something; he was mushy, lazy. His boxer shorts were infuriatingly bunched up and constraining. He forced a hand into his jeans to straighten them and then wiggled – he felt marginally less trapped and full of loathing for himself. He wanted so much to appeal to Heather and for the night to be a crossroads, for life to be finally happening to him more and better.

At the last minute, on his way to meet her, he remembered once having overheard some girls say that the forearms were the sexiest part of a guy. He quickly rolled up the sleeves of his shirt.

Oh bloody hell, there she was. He was embarrassed to look at her standing on the corner: black jeans, grey T-shirt, her gleaming hair in pinned-up plaits. He had to make his face severe to avoid grinning or laughing. He wondered if the rolled-up shirtsleeves were a mistake.

David hadn't had all that much practice with going to parties, or in general with being social. His mum didn't invite friends over to their place for meals or anything, and anyway, they wouldn't really have had the right sort of house or the spare money for that. Before her new relationship, during those long years when Jan was single, she'd talked to him a lot about the catastrophe of her marriage to his dad, as well as that of her other relationships. It was important to be mindful, he'd learned from her, that most relationships turned into catastrophes, even without the likely STDs. Jan tried to be as open with him as possible. He'd had the Peter Mayle books when he was little, and when he turned fifteen she'd bought him a box of condoms that was still unopened in his closet. There was also the music they'd listened to for as long as he could remember – the Leonard Cohen, the Joni Mitchell, the Van Morrison. The lyrics usually telling you that love was doomed, heartbreak inevitable.

That night, though, walking with Heather, David wasn't as nervous as he would have expected to be. Rather, he was nervous, but strangely the situation didn't feel all that awkward.

Neither of them said much, yet there was something about her fast, tall-person stride, her swerving talk and absorbed listening – even, it appeared, when they weren't speaking – that made space for him.

Robbie's place was small and weatherboard. They loitered on the footpath outside, voices audible within. Was Heather even shyer and more reclusive than David was? Had she invited him just so she wouldn't have to go alone?

As a distraction, he said, 'That screen door, maybe because it's white, freaks me out a bit. I saw a true-crime show on TV years ago, where they did a reconstruction of a murder. It was the husband who killed his kids and wife. One of the details that stayed in my head – besides the guy's striped pyjamas – was the screen door of their house, which was similar to that. They kept showing it. The white was like white under a strobe.'

'How spooky.'

She smiled, then knocked. The door opened and there was a video camera trained on them. Heather immediately stepped behind David and he liked her making a shield of him.

'Robbie, you know I hate that!'

'It's a joke. It's not even turned on. I didn't know it was going to be you. Oh, hi.'

Apparently, he hadn't necessarily expected to see her, and of course not with David.

'This is David – he went to my school.'

'I think I've seen you around.'

Robbie lowered the camera and gestured for them to enter. He was wearing a black T-shirt flecked with colourful paint and khaki work trousers. Wasn't it a bit of a wank to be advertising that he was an artist?

Justifying David's presence, Heather said, 'We ran into each other near the pool today. He speaks great Italian and I've invited him to the conversation classes.'

Slightly thrown or stoned, Robbie slowly responded, 'Oh, cool.'

They stood on the edge of a dope fug at the entrance to the lounge room and were considered with sleepy distrust by five guys and two girls sitting in a vague circle, passing around a bong and half watching a video of *Apocalypse Now*. One of the girls had a goth look and the kind of blanket acne that would make you so self-conscious it might ruin your self-esteem and chances of finding love and happiness forever; how arbitrary and unfair!

A guy nursing a guitar said in a come-hither way to Heather, 'Will you join us?'

In smoking, was one of the implications, and she quietly replied, 'No, thanks, I'm good.'

'You're cute,' the clear-skinned girl said and laughed knowingly, sarcastically.

Was this about Heather and David being out of place, not being into the bong, or the girl perhaps being possessive of Robbie? A hesitation followed, Robbie hovering near Heather, whom he clearly valued but didn't know how to combine with his other friends. David didn't particularly care if these people approved of him or not; he'd done his time with such school-flavoured nonsense, but he did want to ease Heather's tension and appear substantial to Robbie.

'Cool movie,' David said. 'Are you guys doing Conrad for English?'

Belatedly, he thought that if they weren't doing advanced courses this might be taken as swotty or arrogant, or make them mistakenly conclude that he was posh. He'd been teased at Katoomba High for this sort of misconception and once for some reason for talking like a foreigner, whatever that meant.

'No, man. I wish,' Robbie said lightly, not giving away his level of English.

'I loved that book,' Heather said. 'It totally hypnotised me.'

'Exactly,' David said. 'Me too.'

Maybe to give them a reprieve from the smokers, Robbie told them, 'You need drinks. Follow me.'

In the kitchen at the back of the house, a beat-box was playing Pink Floyd to a guy in a singlet with a Celtic tattoo who was serving himself from a box of wine. Otherwise, there were signs of an old-school older woman's influence: smiley photos of Robbie on the fridge, lace curtains gathered with bows, pots of African violets, a big brown teapot in a friendly stripy jumper of a cosy beside a pile of *Woman's Day* magazines. One of David's nanas read those, calling them her 'books'; when he stayed with his grandparents in Merrylands, he read them and whatever else he found, including the Mills and Boon and Virginia Andrews stashed in a cupboard. (He hadn't known his other nana to read. She lived in a halfway house, and when they were alone together she liked to tell him to listen for the sirens that sounded especially for her, summoning her with secret messages from Claude, her lover.)

'It's good you came,' Robbie told Heather.

'We'll just stay for a bit,' she replied. 'Where's your nan?'

'Next door.'

Their obvious closeness caused a swell of desperation in David.

The guy with the tattoo and forearms that would probably attract girls, big time, was inhibiting the conversation. He declared, 'Wine!'

After a short silence, Robbie offered to put the kettle on.

'*Tea?*' the other guy asked, smirking.

Robbie retorted good-naturedly, 'Fuck off. Not everyone has to have booze.'

'I'll have both, if that's okay,' David said. He felt a bit outside himself, struggling to grasp that he was at a party with Heather and the situation between Robbie and her.

From the front room someone loudly moaned, 'Robbie.'

'Go back – I'll make the tea,' Heather said. 'If you don't mind, we might sit out here, maybe in the yard. Is that all right?' She wasn't really looking at anyone. 'You know what I'm like. I just wanted to say hello.'

Robbie told her, 'If you want. Whatever you want.'

Surely he had the hots for her. He flicked a glance at David, smiled and left with the other guy.

They were on their own.

'Sorry for dragging you to this. I feel bad, but I can't socialise in groups. I usually don't even try.'

'You didn't drag me. Can I do the tea?'

Faintly, they heard choppers. Maybe Martin Sheen was having his post-traumatic meltdown.

'Thanks – the tea bags are in that. I'll get the milk.'

Making tea made him feel for a moment that he was in a parallel-universe version of his own house, weird but normal.

'Full-cream milk, nice. I miss this. Since my mum's been in a relationship, we're getting skim milk. We used to get milk delivered, in the glass bottles, with the cream at the top.'

'We get it like that – unless the bill's not paid. I hate it when they start underlining how much you owe in red pen on that envelope they leave for the money.'

David said, 'I *hate* having no milk. Tea in the morning with no milk.'

'Yeah, starting the day with a disappointment.'

For decades after that night, they would both feel uneasy if a household they were in ran out of – or even risked running out of – milk. At the same time, they would feel guilty for the uneasiness because they knew they hadn't really experienced deprivation, the unrelenting disappointment of genuine poverty.

They put the mugs between them on the back step, along with a plastic cup of the wine that David tried as soon as he sat down. It was very bad, acidic, scratchy, burny.

'Do you like your mum's boyfriend?' she asked.

'Girlfriend. Yeah, I do. She's nice. She takes the pressure off.' He might have been babbling. He quickly drank more awful wine. 'Jesus. I don't drink, either. Well, I've sort of started teaching myself to. Sometimes the manager of the hotel lets me and another guy who works there finish off a bottle while we're cleaning up. I could only do a few sips to start with.'

A train passed, sounding close: a sound he found somehow poignant. It was warm and humid in the yard, which contained a few spindly gums, a Hills Hoist on a concrete square, a shed with its door ajar and a dim, oddly coloured light that was spilling out of this.

'What's it like, being tipsy?'

'Sort of heavy in the head, like your head might start spinning and you might keel over.'

He didn't know how to say that alcohol made the space between his thoughts and words get a bit bigger or more mystifying, but if he spoke, the words came out more stuck together. It made walking back and forth over pub carpet clearing tables, rinsing plates for the dishwasher, folding spare serviettes ad infinitum, all balloon out into something connected to his hunger for adventure or need to distract himself from that. There was a feeling, sort of bleak and sort of relaxing, of pushing his mind out of some window.

She said, 'I think I'm doing one of those pendulum swings away from what my parents did. They used some drugs when we were living in the city. I hardly remember that – I don't remember my dad at all – but my mum talks about it sometimes. She didn't have a very good time. I do remember the smell of dope and people hanging around in a kind of depressing way. Mum says she'd be fine with me trying any drug and would help me do it safely, but it doesn't attract me. I don't do anything. And the thing with drugs around school people is – would you want to be out of it around them?'

'God, no.'

'And it can be worse for girls.'

Yes. He had an image of limp female bodies being coaxed, directed, and felt contaminated just for being able to see this easily, without entirely suppressing a flicker of a flesh response. Sometimes being a guy seemed criminal; he thought of that – was it Catholic? – idea of babies born sinful and having to get pure through repentance or self-flagellation or whatever. Were men born with seeds of badness in them?

'Wish You Were Here' was rolling gently through the door behind them.

She pointed at the shed. 'That's where Robbie paints.'

'Is his art really good?' he asked fearfully.

'Oh yeah. You could look, if you want. The door's open – he was probably showing people before.'

David was curious, in spite of himself. They went over to the shed. Though they had to walk slowly, carrying cups, he felt impetuous and their elbows accidentally touching once sent him into sensory overdrive, as if the whole surface of his skin was sparkling or becoming aware that everything else was.

In this state, the contents of the shed struck him as full-on: multicoloured fairy lights, big, intense paintings against the walls, the paint fumes slicing deep into the nose and brain as petrol did. David was drawn to and disturbed by the odour and the paintings, too. They were of maze-like underground tunnels and had a fantasy-gothic vibe, but high quality, subtle. A bit unnerving.

It'd have reassured him to be able to consider Robbie a druggy try-hard artist. It wasn't so. Having a solid reason to admire him was painful. He was good-looking *and* capable of this potent stuff; girls would fall hard and hopelessly for the combo.

David followed Heather back out into the yard, not knowing what to say. He'd noticed that just after you'd had an experience with art that had an impact (it could also be a book, movie or music), for a while it was like no other communication could quite do the trick. It took time for your mind to be released from the spell.

'Pretty impressive.' And then, seeing the light of Robbie reflected in her face and compelled to instantly get as much hurt as possible out of the way, 'You two seem to be good friends. You went to school together in Lithgow?'

'Yeah, we hated that school. I only went for about a year, while my mum was working out there.'

'What work does she do?'

'She teaches yoga.'

He said witlessly, 'Oh. My mum's a social worker. So, you and Robbie hung out together in Lithgow?'

'He was my one real friend there. The only thing I regretted when I left Lithgow was that Robbie had to stay there.'

'Right. So you kept in touch?'

She nodded. 'Sometimes he came and stayed here in Blackheath with his nan for a weekend, if things were bad with his parents.'

'And then he moved in with his nana?'

She paused, unsure about how much information to share. 'His dad went to jail.'

'Shit.'

She added in an undertone 'There were some restraining orders that he didn't respect. Anyway, now Robbie's mum's living in a caravan on the Central Coast with some guy. Robbie doesn't talk about them much.'

'God.'

'I know.' She appeared keen to change the subject. 'But his nan is nice.'

'And he's studying Italian?' He was being too interested in Robbie.

'Not at school. Just with me. I've been teaching him a few things.'

She and Robbie knew each other in a way that mattered and had some past to it. He pictured them on a train together, not one of the newer ones with the goldy-reflective windows that wouldn't open. One of the atmospheric old ones with the leather or vinyl or whatever the seats were made from and the earthy-wind-through-old-country-train smell, a valley gliding by their window and Heather offering: *notte*, *not-te*, night.

There was a muffled shout. A few seconds later, the guy who'd been holding the guitar came unsteadily out into the yard with something on fire.

'Aaahhh,' he cried subduedly, almost as if he was being ironic.

Robbie, behind him, suggested, 'Chuck it under the clothesline. I guess that's why they say you shouldn't hang stuff over lampshades.' He was unperturbed. 'I'll get the hose.'

The guy did as instructed; the burning thing was a piece of cloth, maybe a bandana. The flame was already wilting, though there was a thin stream of smoke.

'Are you okay? Did you burn yourself?' Heather asked.

'Not that much.'

Why was pain embarrassing?

The hose did the job almost immediately, and next Robbie directed it at the guy's singed hands. 'This is Daniel, by the way,' he introduced him to the others.

'Thanks, mate,' Daniel said. 'I'm legless. Might get out of here.'

'You don't have to.'

'Yeah, but I might head off.'

'Us too,' Heather said.

'You just got here,' Robbie argued.

'But it's going to rain soon, and, you know.'

'You like walking in the rain.'

'I do.' She softened her departure with, 'Don't forget the Italian-conversation thing on Thursday.'

'The lady really won't mind if I show?'

'No, she sounded pretty relaxed. We'll just be chatting.'

David finished the horrible wine and said, 'Your paintings are amazing.'

David and Robbie hadn't worked out how to look at each other.

'I showed him,' Heather explained. 'I love the new one.'

'Yeah? Cheers. I can use Nan's car on Thursday. I can drive us.'

Heather's endorsement had made Robbie lift his chin. When soon after he lunged forward to hug her, she lowered her forehead to his shoulder.

They got away into the moist night with Daniel, who was flirting to show he was over his mishap; he kept turning towards Heather, despite the fact that she wasn't turning towards him. She must have had to deal with a lot of such brain-dead-horny boys and men acting like her beauty had something to do with them, was something they were invited to partake in.

'When's it going to rain?' she asked, not seeming to expect an answer.

At the turn-off to his house, Daniel hesitated. 'We'll see each other around?'

And then he sidled up and put an arm around her shoulders. She flinched, but Daniel stayed put. *This is how it's done*, his smug face said. Heather had gone blank, rigid. David wondered if he could help somehow, but he didn't want to presume anything.

Finding her voice, she said, 'We have to go, don't we, David? It's raining.'

It was, in fact, starting to rain; fitful drops were multiplying, accelerating.

'Yeah, we should hurry.'

She had to tug firmly to pull away from Daniel, who was trying to make a game where there wasn't one. He laughed coldly.

'Bye,' they all said.

And Heather and David were rushing away down Govetts Leap Road. She appeared slightly shaken.

'Uncomfortable,' he commented. 'Bit of a prick?'

'He was off his face.'

'No excuse.'

'No, no excuse. I'm glad you were there. What do you reckon, will we make it without getting drenched?'

'I doubt it.'

They were half running. How many hours had they spent going up and down that road to the station over the years? He had the intuition, maybe because of the rain smudging his vision, that the road they knew so completely was an illusion out of which they'd soon pass into their adult lives.

'*Parliamo in italiano?*' he proposed, to distance them from Daniel's dirtying of the mood.

'*Assolutamente.*'

When they reached Parklands, the rain was beating, almost stinging.

'It's really coming down!'

'Shall we go in there till it eases up?'

'Yeah,' she said.

They entered the private property and the partial shelter of trees.

'I wonder how many people died in this hotel,' Heather mused as they approached the cavity of the swimming pool, having to speak loudly over the rain.

'Probably stacks.'

He was thinking that many of those people would have died naked, in the bath or on the toilet like poor Elvis. And how embarrassing – but what sense did that make? Should a dead body inspire such shame? He was nearly tempted to say something to Heather about this, about embarrassment feeling like a straitjacket. Normally, he never really wanted to confide in anyone, but suddenly he thought that possibly he did, that he'd been waiting to do so. This had to be one of the loveliest, most nerve-racking, inebriating suspicions possible: you were beginning to know someone you could maybe let yourself be known by.

She was headed for the arcade of tangled trees and shrubs where he liked to go himself. He'd been doing this more often since school ended. (The week before, for example, one afternoon when his mum got disgruntled because David unthinkingly used a new towel, surprisingly nice and fluffy, which turned out to have been specially purchased for Carole. He'd also recently helped himself to strawberries he hadn't expected to discover in the fridge, intended for Carole's breakfast muesli.) Sometimes, he brought books with him there and would even read aloud a bit, maybe some poems by Keats or Plath, because it was as if they got and appreciated his loneliness or he did theirs – it was almost the same loneliness, which made the melancholy into a sort of shared adventure.

They stooped, entering that denser, browner darkness, and slowly came to where they could stand.

Abruptly, in semi-blindness, Italian was an extra layer of semi-blindness. Yes, they were 'good students', but this was still a new language in which they'd had little occasion to weld together words and thoughts beyond the formulaic phrases they were most secure with. Heather might have noticed this, too, because she broke a short silence with English.

'Are you soaked?'

Earlier, the switch to Italian had refreshed things and now the reverse switch brought a change that he couldn't quite identify. He had the impression that in each language different parts of him were veiled and exposed.

He said, 'Sopping – we might catch our deaths.'

He'd meant it as a kind of joke, something a grandmother would say, but it sounded serious. He sensed more than saw her, his throat tightening, moving her top away from her skin.

'We might,' she said, deadpan. 'I'm still sort of spun out by the whole formal–informal *Lei–tu* business in Italian. Well, it's the same in French with *vous* and *tu*. Actually, it seems worse in French, more complicated.'

'How do you mean?'

'Maybe I've just seen more French movies. Haven't you noticed how in French movies two people who've recently met and are getting to know one another, even getting close, will sometimes keep using *vous* for much longer than you'd think? So they're pretty friendly, but not *that* friendly? And then suddenly, a signal gets passed and bang, they've crossed the line into *tu*. Now they can be familiar with each other. I find it ambiguous.'

'You listen well. Yeah, it's tricky, but at least this isn't complicated only for us. Given that a set phrase, "Shall we call each other *tu*?", exists in both languages. You wouldn't need a standard way to check that the changeover was acceptable unless it could be confusing.'

'Right. It's incredible to me that there's this crossover point that two people have to recognise or decide on, and after that their closeness is *built* into every pronoun and verb they'll use to refer to one another. The structure has been transformed, like there was a key change in the music.'

'I know, it's pretty wild – like the verbs are made of metal that goes molten and gets moulded differently.'

'Yeah!'

'I suppose that stuff like that happens in English. I mean, language gets less formal when people know each other better. You just don't see it so much in the grammar. It comes across more through vocab, tone, body language.'

As he said this the idea hurtled into him – terror, delight, terror – that what they were saying could have somehow been about *them*. Was Heather asking where she and David were along the spectrum of intimacy? If they were in the vicinity of an invisible line? On the other hand, she could have been remembering the unpleasant situation earlier with Daniel, who'd crossed a line he shouldn't have.

But now she was saying, 'I think the rain might be stopping. Make a run for it?'

He scrambled after her through the shifting dark. Outside the tunnel of branches, the rain was morphing into a thick mist and the high wild grass and clumps of gorse were soggy. Jogging across the sloping grounds of the defunct hotel, he thought again of the guests who'd died there and hoped that some of them had gone in a lover's arms or at least the sort of sleep that feels like a nest. Heather was moving fast: she was up on the footpath of Govetts Leap Road before he knew it.

Propelling himself desperately after her, he slipped. He broke the fall somewhat with his hands, but his left kneecap nonetheless came down hard onto cement. The pain made his mind see cracking, fissures.

Next, she was standing over him, although he didn't think he'd made a sound.

'Are you all right?'

He was on all fours. He laughed to push away the shock and mortification, and managed, 'I think so.'

'What can I do?' Heather squatted beside him. 'If I put my arm under yours, I can help you stand.'

They hesitated, he lifted one of his hands from the footpath and she came closer. The bone trauma was confused with her nearness, then, with her arm encircling his back. His skin was plastered with his sodden shirt that was also against her skin. In his heart, there was heat and upheaval.

'Sorry,' he said. 'Pathetic.'

'Don't apologise! I was the one stupidly running.'

'Don't you apologise either.'

As they rose he leaned on her as little as possible, discerning even so her strength and elasticity. He was concerned that he wouldn't be able to walk at all.

'I'll just have to start slowly.' He sucked in his breath and gingerly took a step. 'Wow. Okay. Do you think we could go at this speed, just to the corner?'

'Of course,' she said gently. 'I'll get you home.'

'That won't be necessary.'

'You have to get up the hill – how far?'

'Unfortunately, to the top.'

'I'll come right up. It's nothing.'

They were taking tiny steps, his injured knee thrumming with distress; he couldn't refuse her help. Her kindness touched and dizzied him. Where she should have turned left down Cleopatra Street, they crossed and started to ascend. He heard his own loud breathing. The street was looking slightly different from how it usually did, more unsightly. And it was like his leg wasn't integrated into him in the old way. How peculiar it was that humans were carried through the world by these flesh cylinders that normally moved so easily they were hardly noticeable; only when something went wrong with a part of you did you realise how perfectly you were used to it working, how pain-free and reliable it had been before. Hysterical barking shot from the yard of the redbrick house opposite his, and then the stroppy Airedales turned sullenly silent.

'It's here.'

Ashen light washing the living-room blinds: his mother and Carole watching telly. Maybe a movie on SBS. Jan might have been asleep with her bed-socked feet on her girlfriend's lap.

Heather squinted at her green Swatch. 'It's not very late.'

He couldn't get his head around what time it might be. Time had gone somehow edgeless, transparent; it was as if he'd spent half his life with Heather that day and it had been slow and quick. They were by the scruffy tin letterbox protruding from an unpruned hedge at the end of his driveway, Heather still supporting him.

He tried to playfully go back to what they'd been saying earlier. '*We* used *tu* the first time we spoke Italian, straightaway.'

'We're basically the same age and we went to school together.' She seemed to be scrutinising the mist.

Awkwardly, he said, 'I'll go in around the back. That's where my room is – it used to be the sewing room of the old lady who lived here before us. Thanks for taking me to the party and everything, for this – for getting me home.' He hated that he'd made himself so uncool.

'No worries.'

A panel van with creepy fake-wood siding cruised past and he imagined a dangerous man inside it. He thought of the backpackers they'd found murdered in Belanglo State Forest.

'Are you sure you'll be okay walking home?'

'Yeah, I walk by myself all the time.' Her arm, which had gone loose, firmed again. 'Should I help you get around the back?'

'Um, if you don't mind, maybe just to the gate?'

They had to squash together a little to pass Carole's powder-blue VW and David hoped that he smelled okay, even though he was sweating. They were almost at the wooden lattice of the gate.

'Think you'll need an X-ray?'

'Nah, soon it'll be fine.'

The situation would have been better if he'd lived alone, independently, like a man. It was so claustrophobic to have the mind and body of an adult, without the control over your life and the privacy and cash of an adult. Not that – had this been his bachelor pad – it would necessarily have been right for him to invite her in or anything, or that she'd have accepted.

'Bye,' she said, turning into him for what at their school was the conventional friend-to-friend hug for greeting and farewelling. But had her face rested fleetingly against his shoulder, as it had against Robbie's? He hugged her lightly, rain-damp warmth against his chest. At least blushing was invisible in the dark. And she moved away.

When she was halfway down the drive, she turned and whisper-shouted, 'Thursday, four o'clock?'

That was what he was most looking forward to in the world, but he only said gruffly, '*Certo.*'

'*Bene.*'

And they parted.

He manoeuvred himself around the back of the house almost without feeling his leg – dominated by her abrupt absence, so strong it was a kind of presence – and stood gazing into the yard. The wire fence on the left-hand side was lost in the misty night, dark bush seeming to bleed in, while the hedge on the other side suggested the outer wall of an unkempt labyrinth. He turned to the house and saw the place where he'd discovered their silver tabby stiff and dead, killed by a snake.

He took off his shoes in the tiny laundry, leaning on the ancient washing tubs that even had a crank. (As their washing machine was broken, they washed by hand in these or in the bathtub, stirring the load around with the cricket bat his mother had bought him in primary school so he could practise alone and, in theory, stop so very clearly being the worst batsman in his class.) In the kitchen – seeing Heather on her way home, maybe running – he listened, heard nothing and went to the pantry, reached for the tube of Nestlé's Coffee and Milk. Bringing it to his lips, he remembered the enchantment of Robbie's shed, the fairy lights, the mastery. He squeezed and was lost for a moment in sugary milkiness, a shudder of secret pleasure, an inward collapse.

4

SHIPLEY ROAD

The start of October, but the day nearly end-of-year hot. Robbie drove Heather and David in his nana's Honda Civic over the crunchy gravel of a long, curving driveway. Three pink-and-grey galahs swept over on a line so clean and purposeful the swing of a compass could have created it. There was no other car parked at the house.

Heather got out first and had knocked by the time they reached her. There was only one other house in view to the right, distant. The deep quiet made Robbie feel furtive and even more out of place than he already did for not being a proper Italian student and probably being on the verge of making a prize fool of himself. He really preferred that people see he could do things well. Heather did appear to think he was quick on the uptake with the Italian. Most days when they talked on the phone, she'd mention a new word or phrase she'd learned, and if they were killing time at a train station, she'd explain something that took a bit of explaining, like a verb or a tense. He found the sounds and concepts intriguing, liked listening to her interest and sharpness, liked them taking – as they always had – each other's intellect seriously. She said he had a nice pronunciation, but she would because she was a softie. Which worried him a bit sometimes. He hoped this David was all right.

She knocked again. The house was one-storey, maybe quite old, with a handsome verandah going around the outside. By the door there was a churchy wooden bench with a tidy line of shoes beside it, two pairs of short black gumboots and two more of fancy runners. No one was answering and they started to relax.

'Did I get the time wrong? Or the day?' Heather wondered aloud.

'*She* might have got it wrong. Not you,' Robbie said. A breeze brought a scent that gave him a hunch they weren't seeing the main event.

'Where are you going?' she asked.

'To have a look.'

He was quickly at the corner of the house, turning, striding its length, turning.

Yes, it was all happening here: the back was the true front. The fragrance got pure and he saw that it came from pots of dainty white flowers edging the verandah like miniature foamy clouds. A splashing drew his attention to a fountain, marbly stone, the flow from an urn balanced on the graceful shoulder of a young woman. Past that were neat shrubs and masses of mauve rhododendrons, crepe myrtles with flowers of surprisingly deep pinks and purples, and then a dense clump of cedars that seemed part of an old forest; a glint of shiny white through the trunks, down low. Further back still, the garden ran into bush. Three tall gums were so casually magnificent he felt a sort of envy, wanted to paint them, get inside them and hang out there. Of course you knew in theory that rich people had it good, but it was a shock to actually *see* how picturesquely good they could have it, be confronted with the plush setting of their lives. There was no way to compare all this to the short redbrick fence, the short, scratchy lawn, the short house in Lithgow with its chilling seventies-eyeshadow-blue walls.

He'd have liked to wander off a bit into that garden, follow the winding pathway of greyish pebbles to the screen of cedars and investigate behind it. However, he supposed that if the Italian woman wasn't showing, they should be off. Heather arrived, David behind her, watching her. Keen as mustard, poor bugger.

'Wow,' she said. 'What should we do? Give it another few minutes and split?'

There was something odd jutting up from the verandah's roof.

'Check this out,' Robbie said, realising as he approached that it was a rainwater tank attached to a broad shower head. 'Cool, a shower.'

'They stand out here in the nuddy?' Heather asked, eyeing the next house. 'I guess the neighbours would just see a blur?'

The smidgen of horror in her voice was the tip of the iceberg of her self-consciousness, and this along with his own sense of inadequacy at being in that lovely place where he didn't belong was provoking. Why should they feel these things? Robbie was suddenly giddy, restless and inclined to be outrageous.

'It's boiling. Let's have a go.'

'What?' Heather exclaimed. 'You're joking, right?'

He was unbuttoning his shirt. 'Just to try it. She'll never know.'

'No way!' Heather laughed nervously.

David was looking doubtful, as he had that night at Robbie's house. He clearly wasn't an outgoing type and he was unsure about Robbie. Robbie gave them a brazen wink and pulled down his jeans. He wasn't shy like that. Girls told him his body was more than fine and women on the street and in shops did too by checking him out. He wasn't all that muscly, but he was tall and there was no spare fat on him. It was good to be shedding his gear, like his skin had been suffocating.

In his boxers, he went to stand under the thing. He had to force the tap a bit, but he got it going, smelling some sort of herb that, getting splashed, released a clean, bitterish perfume. He didn't know about herbs. The water was only slightly sun-heated and reminded him of his blood's warmth. He closed his eyes, his thoughts tingling more calmly.

Then talk. Heather, David – and another unknown voice. Throaty. It was unclear for a few seconds if it was a man's or a woman's. Low-pitched but buoyant, rolling. Talking Italian.

He turned and saw, first through water, a smallish woman with exceptional skin that matched her malty voice. Younger and slinkier than he'd expected, in coffee-coloured pants and a short dark-red blouse. She appeared self-assured, upbeat. Her bemused smile showed him he was under her shower, uninvited, in wet underwear. It was energising to let the water run for a little longer. She was openly amused now. He turned off the tap hard.

She said something in Italian that escaped him and then, in English, 'You've finished? I'll get you a towel.'

'Sorry,' he mumbled, finally fully shamed. 'It was so hot.'

The air on his wet skin was fantastic and so were the dark-green herbal odour and the fine floral one.

'She didn't really mind, did she?' he asked Heather.

She was back with a soft, thick towel and her soft, thick accent.

'Here.'

'*Grazie.*' He hardly looked at her.

'I'm Ada,' she introduced herself.

He nodded and, after a moment, added, 'Robbie.'

She invited the others to sit by a table at the other end of the verandah; he understood that.

He was tugging his shirt over a clammy arm when she asked him, 'Do you want to come and get dressed inside?'

'Um … okay, thanks.' He scooped up the childish mess of his jeans, socks and shoes. 'Sorry,' he said again, following Ada into the house

Dark floorboards under his damp feet gleamed in a beam of light gliding through the shade of drawn blinds. They passed a perfectly bare wooden dining table and entered a long lounge room.

'I'm glad you tried it. It is *very* hot today.'

She smiled, still amused and maybe partly because he was so crap at her language that she had to speak English to him. She was being polite.

'It was really nice.'

There were two enormous white lounges at a right angle to each other. Against that white, her skin was chestnut and it was difficult not to wonder how she'd respond to a mouth on it. He half turned away because he was trailing his shirt and otherwise wearing wet boxers; he had to empty his mind of sex.

'I hope I'm not dripping.'

'Don't worry,' she said, her hand going briefly to his arm in an automatic gesture of reassurance. 'You can dress here? I will go to get something for us to drink.'

As he was doing up his fly, he caught sight of what was hanging above the lounge, right in front of him. He leaned forward, waiting for the illusion to unravel.

It didn't. But these couldn't be what they seemed to be.

He was so stunned that he half fell onto the lounge, then scrambled to his knees, a hand over his mouth. Originals, seriously? He made himself breathe and raised a trembling hand to the glass that was all that separated him from what *did* appear to *be* a Lloyd Rees drawing. Two Lloyd Rees drawings.

Love a duck.

He'd pored endlessly over a library book of reproductions of Lloyd Rees's later landscapes, the ones from when his eyesight was on the way out. It gave Robbie a kind of hope to think that when you were old, seeing less, you might actually see more surely, more deeply. There could be irrefutable radiance on the other side of literal sight and showing off. The drawing he was staring at now had a Moreton Bay fig in the foreground. It was a total ripper: as buxom and nearly touchable in its details as a nude, as real and glowing as one of Degas's bathers.

The second drawing showed a gentle hill across a bay, probably near Sydney Harbour. Something was going on with the perspective. The view was vaguely aerial, as if at the same time you were looking at the hill from above *and* from the opposite shore. God that man had been able to draw, to show what he saw.

Robbie went to kneel on the second lounge. He already knew what hung above it from a sidelong glance he'd shot there after identifying the Rees drawings, but his overwhelmed brain hadn't been able to take the two discoveries together. Revelations could be so huge they had to be postponed while you braced yourself for them.

A Brett Whiteley. A metre by a metre or so. Blue.

The blue that had made Robbie want to shriek when he'd discovered it at the Art Gallery of New South Wales. Whiteley was a king of blue. Was – had been – *was*. It was wrong to think of these artists as dead because they were still kicking so hard. Another harbour scene, mainly water, from dizzily high up above, from some hot-air balloon of the mind. Squiggles for boats, the Harbour Bridge. And Christ, that blue, that dream of ultramarine that beckoned you, whispering: Come to me, dive in.

'You like art?'

He was even more unprepared for her than the last time. She owned all this, lived with it, slid her dark-brown eyes over it whenever she felt like it. He stood up.

'Yeah, I do. I can't believe you have these.'

He wanted to ask her things, ask her to explain how and why she came to have these and just generally to explain herself. He realised that he had to do up the buttons of his shirt. He managed awkwardly.

'I'm lucky,' Ada said, sounding surprised. 'I got them at good prices.' She'd lost her expression of light amusement. She repeated, 'You like art.'

He'd probably been daggy, too emotional. He wished he could tell her he painted.

'And you, too?' What a twit he was, yet he was asking: Could we understand each other?

She nodded. 'Oh yes. In fact, now I'm trying to write about it a bit. Trying – you can only try.'

'Write about it how?'

'Some reviews, a little criticism …'

'Right, right.'

She was by far the most glamorous person he'd ever met. He didn't know what he was doing in her company, but how thrilling, scary and predestined it felt to be there.

She considered the jug in her hands. 'I should take this out.'

Sitting with the others on the verandah, drinking lemony water, he absorbed almost nothing of the lesson. Which didn't really seem to be a lesson – more a laid-back, chatty improvisation. It was all in Italian and he could tell Ada was making an effort to speak slowly, but that didn't help him much and he passed the time half dopey and half petrified she'd ask him to participate actively. She left him alone, though, obviously judging that he couldn't have handled it.

At one point, she leaned back in her chair and crossed her legs. The fawn slip-on sandal on her top foot dangled, then fell. And there was her bare foot: slender, long-toed, toenails painted a bluish white in violent contrast with the nutty brown of her skin. He could only keep it in his peripheral vision, but he almost gave himself a headache with wanting to focus on it. He appeared to be the only one aware of the spectacle.

Until Ada noticed him noticing and stopped talking. There was a gap in the normal progression of time, and he had the chance to confirm that her eyes were, indeed, vastly brown. His heart thought that something grave was taking place, but how could he be sure?

Afterwards, she uncrossed her legs, slipped her foot back into the shoe and said decisively, '*Il congiuntivo.*'

Heather, enjoying the idea that languages could have *moods*, had recently mentioned this to him, the subjunctive. But Ada didn't go on because a man disrupted them.

Medium height and build, dark hair, olive skin. The tastefully simple jeans and beige shirt that plenty of money would buy. He arrived on the verandah as if returning home.

Ada smiled comfortably – of course, he was the bloke who'd have to exist in her life.

'Hi,' he said in English.

'You can speak Italian,' Ada told him. 'They do.'

'Okay, naturally, it's a conversation class,' he replied, his Italian flowing less like an unstoppable river than hers.

'Filippo,' she introduced him. '*Mio marito.*'

Filippo directed a couple of incomprehensible questions at Heather and she answered. Then he asked Robbie what his favourite subject was.

'Art.'

Heather added, 'Robbie *is* an artist. A painter.'

Bless you, Heather.

Ada looked at him and Filippo went on a bit, before changing to English when he saw that Robbie wasn't following. He said, 'You should show Ada your paintings.'

Heather had paid for another four lessons, one a week leading up to the exams, and she encouraged Robbie to come to them.

'It doesn't matter at all if you just want to listen,' she reassured him. 'She knows you're a beginner.'

But although he wanted to, very much wanted to go back to the unbelievable house with that art and that garden and Ada, he simply couldn't show up for another lesson. Couldn't risk speaking like a beginner, so much worse than the brainy Heather and David. He couldn't be the one who didn't get it and have Ada not admire him.

Heather had told Robbie that Italians seemed to be pretty concerned with making a good impression – and avoiding the opposite, *fare brutta figura* or *una figuraccia*. Robbie totally related to this fear, and it would occur to him decades later that he had spent a lot of time running from the possibility of making *una figuraccia*, people taking him for a thick hick. Back then, he asked Heather if she had any Italian textbooks she'd finished with and she gave him one, *Sempre Avanti!* (*Always Forward!*), and a little dictionary with a green plastic cover that he was soon attached to. He studied them at night, when his nan was in bed watching her shows. He puzzled over grammar and sounded out words, copying the prettiest or oddest ones into his art diary. Shadow was *ombra*, and to say it was to shiver as he had done following Ada into her house, a stray shaft of light making the cool wooden floor lustrous like a lake under a full moon.

5

STATION STREET

The funny boy who'd boldly used her shower and appeared so affected by her art had not returned to the house.

At the end of the third conversation hour with the other kids, she'd asked Heather if he'd found the first one boring and the girl had said, 'No, but I think he felt he wasn't at the right level. Which is a shame.'

Ada had agreed, remembering his closed face as she'd blathered on. Once or twice she'd thought she noticed a faint glimmer in him, then he'd appeared to catch himself and almost cringe, like an animal about to be enticed recalling past mistreatment.

'You really should see his paintings,' Heather told her. 'They're phenomenal and it would mean a lot to him. He lives near the station.'

'Oh.'

And she was given his number, feeling passive, not passive enough, carried along. She put off calling for a week.

Then, all at once, she called.

His 'hello' sounded very close, as if they were in the same room and had been sitting in a silence that he was just breaking. She'd forgotten that his voice was so deep and his accent so Australian in a way she wasn't used to. Not that she'd heard him talk much before this. She explained that Heather had suggested she get in touch to arrange to see his art, and she heard herself sounding pompous and foreign; her English had regressed into a mockery of itself. He might have sounded close, but the distances between them, in language, culture and age were of course huge. He was a bit baffled, she thought, yet he said she could come to his house the next afternoon. She noted the address and hung up too quickly, feeling that they hadn't properly said goodbye.

She parked in front of the house, a cottage. She'd expected something larger, less flimsy-looking, but she'd had no reason to expect anything. She again had the impression that she was being carried, half against her will, her rational, conscious will.

She knocked at his door exactly on time, maybe ridiculously so.

An elderly woman opened it and said brightly, 'Hello, I'm Marjorie, Robbie's aunt, his great-aunt, but he calls me Nana.'

'Pleased to meet you – Ada.'

She held out her hand as if for a business meeting and saw the other woman's puzzlement and readiness to be warmly disposed. Marjorie's short, curled hair was a pure white around a ruddy, frankly sympathetic face. I'm glad, Ada found herself thinking, that he has someone like this. But naturally, she didn't know what either of them was truly like, or what might be good for him. All she'd seen of him: his impudent shower on her verandah in his underwear; the apologetic manner in which he'd carried his clothes through her home; his height and pallor and eyes seduced by art and perhaps fame; his refusal to take part in the lesson; the oblique but deliberate glance at her foot and, just after this, forthrightly and for a longer interlude, more of those eyes. Her sense of him was somehow disproportionately larger than the fragments of experience that had created it.

He was waiting in a tiny kitchen at the back of the house in a paint-splattered black T-shirt, jeans and sheepskin slippers with their backs entirely trodden down. The three of them stood uncertainly in warm afternoon light and a scent of cheesy toast. The family resemblance was only clear in their hands, similarly strong and long. Ada was flustered, had been all morning, almost as if she'd been about to do an exam at university; she'd been particularly aware of this when she was choosing what to wear (sober grey pants, a long-sleeved cream shirt and bland moccasins). The discomfort had taken her back to a long-ago day, somewhere before but close to adolescence, when she'd maybe for one of the first times felt tensely visible as a female. She was at home in the living room with her parents, sitting opposite a cigar-smoking guest who was languidly saying something erudite as he studied her body with a sort of scholarly interest; her jaw had grown tired from what had seemed to be the compulsory smile.

Marjorie offered tea and Ada declined. She was touched, sometimes, by how Australians leaned on the crutch of their kettle.

Sensitive to Ada's restlessness and proud of Robbie, Marjorie said to him, 'Love, why don't you take her out to see your paintings? They're that good, it's beyond belief.'

After the close air of the house, it was refreshing to be in the yard that was filled by a clothesline hung with pinkish floral-patterned sheets smelling of laundry detergent. On the other side of this was a shed that he opened, standing back for her to enter.

A dim, windowless space drowning in the odour of paint.

'Hang on,' he said.

Lights came on, little coloured lights attached at different heights around the walls. She saw that he also had something like a desk lamp that he must have used while painting, but he didn't turn it on; he wanted her to view his work like this.

Four large oils, two against each of the longer walls. Of about a metre across by two high. An easel at the end of the room, a table cluttered with jars full of brushes. His face in the queer light was sincere and humble. Feeling the pressure of his need to impress her, she stepped quickly across the tarpaulin-covered cement towards a painting.

'That's still wet,' he said.

A lagoon at dusk or dawn. On its surface, the shimmering reflection of a cluster of buildings, a dome, a spire. (The influence of Whistler?) Above the water, there were stormy swirls of cloud in which she thought she distinguished purple and gold threads like glinting seams of precious mineral in stone.

The other three were more detailed, depicting winding underground tunnels in cross-section. Silver objects – one was a teapot and another could have been a bird cage – were lodged in the walls of these, camouflaged and suddenly flashing to her attention as she moved her head. She only wondered about possible models once more (Remedios Varo?). The works felt both playful and serious, poised, still. In that multicoloured gloom, they were private and unearthly.

She stepped back, relieved that he was undeniably talented, lifted by that, but also dismayed. She even noted in herself the panic and the light sting of held-back tears. Later that evening, unable to sleep, it would occur to her that she'd had an uncanny sense of recognition, of rediscovering some of her own half-formed perceptions or forgotten dreams.

In his shed, she remembered she had to comment, turned and saw she was alone. Groggy from the paint and the emotion, she fumbled with the door before getting it open. Light. A scraggly gum tree in the corner of the yard. No Robbie.

Then she spotted him and was alarmed. He was sitting cross-legged against the side of the shed, smoking moodily.

He said, 'Don't worry if it's not your kind of thing.'

She went to stand near him, conscious of being in that afternoon – not just rushing through it, but being inside a precise time and place, as she rarely seemed to be.

'It *is* my kind of thing. It's wonderful.'

She was determined not to say anything he'd take as empty flattery. Just how talented was he? She thought very, though being entranced made it difficult to judge. She didn't have the right words for him and certainly not in her gauche Italian-English.

'You have to say that, don't you? What else can you say? Would you be brave enough to tell me you didn't like it? Heather lent me a magazine with one of your articles in it. I got the feeling you didn't really like the guy's stuff, but you were trying not to be mean about it.'

This was true. She laughed, hurt. 'So *you* didn't like *my* work.'

Wasn't he going to stand up? Was his great-aunt watching from a window?

'No, no, I did like it. I liked it a lot, actually. You know how to say interesting things that are hard to say, and you make them sound simple.' He bit the side of his middle finger savagely. 'You're nice, though.'

'Don't do that. It will bleed.'

'My hands always bleed.'

She saw now – how had she missed it before? – that his fingernails and the skin around them were a wreck. She sank into a squat, still wondering if they were being observed.

'Is it a good idea to smoke?' She surprised herself by taking his cigarette and dragging on it. She'd only smoked socially and sporadically, God decades ago, practically, neither really enjoying it nor not enjoying it. And maybe it was this ambiguity that had appealed, the toying with a dubious version of herself, one less careful to be *nice*, more dimly lit. 'It's been so long since I've done this!'

'What?'

She handed back the cigarette without meeting his eyes. He took it and then brushed the side of her hand, which was shaking, with his thumb. She stood quickly, woozy.

He stood too, tall and beautiful. She moved towards the house. However, she couldn't go in and see that kind woman again.

'Could you say goodbye to her for me? I have to leave, I have another appointment. Thanks so much for showing me those. They really are very good. I know someone in Sydney who has a gallery. I'll tell him about you. Sorry for rushing off. *Ciao*.'

She focused, not on his thumb having skimmed the edge of her hand and the rippling effects of this touch, but on the narrow cement path between the house and a hedge. A segment of cement lurid with moss.

Robbie was behind her, asking, 'Could we talk sometime?'

She collided with the hedge, had to yank her shirt free. The house also was abrasive against her hand.

She changed to Italian: 'Talk about art? Why not, in the next conversation class – it would be good practice for you.'

She gave a sort of dim-witted, regal wave before getting into her car and she was revving the engine before the door was quite closed. Gripping the steering wheel, she saw chalky paint residue the colour of pistachio ice cream on her knuckles.

He came up to the window and she had to wind it down.

Point-blank, he said, 'I'm almost nineteen – I repeated a year of school … I never tell anyone.'

She looked at him and it was a mistake. 'Try to quit smoking.'

'What about you?'

'I never started. Bye.'

The rear-view mirror showed him in the middle of the street and the distance growing between them only seemed to clarify this: he was the most wakeful man she'd met and the one most familiar to her, though he obviously couldn't be that in any real way. She craved being close to him a shocking amount; she had almost immediately, out of nowhere and despite everything – the absurdity, the badness, the impossibility. She hadn't touched alcohol for ages, and now, as well as tearful, she felt tipsy and in the wild mood for wine.

At home, she decided to calm herself with a bath – but not in the tub in the garden, which was for the night-time and when she felt peaceful. She sat on the side of the bath while running it, then put her feet in and quickly pulled them out; they were bright red. She added more cold water and climbed in. It was still too hot. There was an *Artforum* by the bath that she tried unsuccessfully to get into, her mind slipping and sliding.

After a while, realising she was rather faint, she got out, stood staring down at her body and, when the floor had become extremely wet, wrapped herself in a towel. She went for a glass of water, but on her way to the kitchen sat on an armchair, instead.

Something slight and unusual happened. A gush of water. She opened her legs and saw that the fabric of the chair was darkened. A wet blot that wasn't bathwater.

A seal she'd half forgotten had broken, an inner sea was emptying itself, a small one; it was only a few weeks beyond when her period should have come. The pain started slowly.

She went to find tampons, remembered she should use pads and wondered if there'd be enough left over from the last time. She would bleed for a while. When she was rifling through the cupboard under the bathroom sink, the cramping began. She hadn't gone to the doctor, or even told Filippo, knowing that this might have happened again. She had resisted building any kind of story around a possibly temporary condition. Though it had contributed to her sense of oddness and instability, her uncertainties. It had technically been too early for morning sickness, but she'd been vaguely queasy while driving and her breasts had been premenstrual-tender and, she fancied, fuller, as if trying to overflow themselves. The main sensations had been an intermittent heavy weariness, some extra pressure on her bladder and an impression of being always full, as if she'd just eaten. Full but not necessarily satiated.

Pain proper. Stronger than the most intense period cramps she'd ever experienced. She wouldn't take any aspirin; she tried to sit again.

It got extreme, so that Ada had to stand for it, pain a visitor who had to be greeted ceremoniously. She found that it was better to be moving, gently walking back and forth or rocking. The spasms would pass, they would pass. Sometimes she was more or less comfortable on her hands and knees.

If there was sadness, it wasn't straightforward. This was the simpler outcome, after all, the more controllable and private. The repercussions of this belonged to her. The pain brought her low only in flashes. Yes, there was the idea that a thing wouldn't happen, might now never happen, a thing considered by many normal and natural and therefore good. A cycle was being interrupted, as one day all her cycles would end, cycles of fertility that would have been just a sort of quiet monologue, her vital cycles.

She couldn't think much about the impact of this on her marriage. She hadn't been certain of how much Filippo had wanted children. And what was wanting a child *about*, anyway? Belief in a biological or moral or emotional destiny? Prolonged survival through the continuance of your genetic material, memories of you? An unthinking: I can, so I do? More generous impulses? Wanting to give of yourself to another? Be transformed by another? The search for meaning, for greater significance than that which you could supply yourself? And was that fair, to ask a child for such meaning? Would a child have desired existence? Found it pleasant, overall, and preferable to not existing? She had waited so long to try because she hadn't been sure how to answer these questions, and she still wasn't.

She would go back on the pill. Could this loss somehow free her of Robbie, too?

6

CLEOPATRA STREET

It was Heather's study vacation, unreal days, rushed and lethargic, of hanging around the house looking over exam questions from previous years, variations on the same stale stuff, note-making with an increasingly tight hand, highlighting swathes of text in fluorescent orange and pink, saturation, emptiness, little leaps of stress and hope. She tried to rouse, steady and distract herself with caffeine. Nescafé instant. Bushells tea. And when she'd overdone those, Celestial Seasonings' Sleepytime, because she was always tired but also overstimulated and hardly ever tired at the right time in the right way. She was close to an end, an edge. And thinking of David.

The afternoon before her English exam, her *last* school exam, she was burning sandalwood incense (a gift from Marianne) to keep her spirits up. It was especially important not to let herself get down as the electricity had just been cut off and it would be an evening without hot water or light. She had a flashback to other disconnection nights that seemed to join together in her mind like interlinked caves lit by candles, torches, kerosene lamps and the effort to feel cosy and adventurous. Sometimes it was indeed that, or interesting, at least. And of course, it was important to remember that lots of people lived without electricity entirely, their nocturnal lives always pitch-black. Still, there was a grotty, doomed feeling to unpaid bills. She detested, when their rent was late, having to skulk past the estate agent's office. For the rest of her life, she would be able to nauseously recall the fake-wood interior of that place, as she also would a dog she and Marianne had owned for a while; Heather had overheard their neighbours saying the dog was a bit feral and underfed.

Marianne, who before she read the notification had been preparing to cast the I Ching, said, 'Bummer. Oh well, when we want baths, we'll boil up water on the camp stove for the bucket and I'll find those candles we had. I'll give you one of my sea sponges.'

Heather would have preferred not to wash by candlelight with a bucket and a sea sponge.

The phone rang. It was Ada, asking when Heather's final exam was, saying she'd like to throw a party to celebrate it being over. Just a little dinner. Filippo was an excellent cook. So, the next evening? In fact, could she pick up Heather in the afternoon after her exam? And wouldn't she stay overnight? David would be very welcome to come to the dinner. Heather embarrassedly said it would be lovely and mentioned that Robbie had already finished his exams. There was a pause. Had it been inappropriate to suggest that her other friend be invited? But then Ada quickly said that Robbie could come too – if he wanted to. Perhaps Heather could let the boys know?

Heather had always been shyly awkward and avoidant when it came to parties, and even more so if the parties were for her. She'd had two birthday parties, at ages nine and twelve, and been tense, drained by the attention focused on her, by her social strangeness, not recognising herself in the group setting and worrying that the few invited kids weren't having fun. She'd never been to a dinner party. The prospect was scary but exciting: a bonus visit to Ada's beautiful house with Robbie as a comfort blanket, delicious Italian, maybe David. Knowing it would all take place in Italian appeared to help her past the usual inhibitions and give the thing an aura of lightness and fun, of the fairy tale. Instead of just being nervous about the exam, she was now happy-nervous, idiotically jovial.

After hanging up, she called Robbie right away. They talked most days, easily, Heather sitting on the dusty, ratty old carpet with her back to the wall, wrapping and unwrapping the curly phone cord from around her hand, straightening and letting it curl again; chatting like this, she often found herself imagining they were on one of their big walks along the train line. She explained the dinner party.

'Would you be up for that?'

'Yeah, why not?'

He sounded pleased, really pleased, and her pleasure expanded. She wouldn't necessarily have predicted his reaction, given how withdrawn he'd been – after the shower stunt – during the only conversation class he'd attended. They were probably both more emotional than usual because of school finishing; he'd told her he felt funny after handing in his final painting, like there was suddenly no gravity anymore, he was one of those helium balloons a kid had let go of.

'That's nice of her,' he went on. 'Do you think she'd mind if I brought my camera and filmed her art collection?'

She could hear how admiringly unsettled he was by Ada and her artistic house. 'I doubt it. I can ask.'

He was attached to the old Camcorder his nan had got him from Vinnies one birthday. She suspected he sometimes used it as a protection of sorts, in social situations where he might have felt more exposed than usual.

Phoning David was much more complicated. They'd only spoken on the phone a couple of times, once to confirm an Italian class and once, the week before, to arrange a joint swim at the pool that had just been reopened.

Her hand was on the receiver when the phone rang again.

And it was him.

Her nerves jumped to an even higher pitch. It seemed almost mystical that each had thought of the other at precisely the same time.

'Hi, what a coincidence. I was just going to call *you*,' she said, thinking, I'm such a dork.

'Were you studying? I hope I didn't interrupt?'

'No, not at all. Ada just called me to invite us, me, you and Robbie, to dinner at her place tomorrow night. Would you want to come? Do you have to work?'

'No, I could come.'

'Great.' And she added, 'Our electricity got cut off,' because nothing else came into her head.

'Oh no – shit timing.'

'I know. But you can't study much on the last day, can you? And I have a big torch!' She laughed. 'How are you?'

'Pretty good. Actually, I don't suppose you've got time for a swim?'

She didn't really or she didn't know what she had time for. Everything was rather out of control. However, the idea of jumping into pretend-blue water in David's company was enticing.

Shortly after, they were swimming in neighbouring lanes and she had to not quite see him underwater because seeing him was a reminder that he could also see her; her brain kept escaping from this fact. But she liked his closeness. There were moments of dread and elation, and, for a couple of laps during which she attempted to train herself to breathe bilaterally, she nearly achieved something like rest.

Later, when they were approaching the Cleopatra Street corner, where they had to separate, he commented in Italian, 'My mum said you could stay at our place tonight. I told her about the electricity issue. I hope that was okay. You'd have light for studying. Just an idea, though.'

She would never be able to accept the offer – she was much, much too shy for that. And yet she was curious about his house, his domestic world. David appeared to like her a lot, but she couldn't tell if he liked her *that* way. (And what would that way even mean?) Maybe from his point of view they were simply becoming good friends, like she and Robbie were. Was it possible they were kindred spirits of a non-romantic type? And this proposal came from his mum, didn't it? His tone as he made it had been noncommittal. Anyway, if she stayed at his house she'd be so nervous she wouldn't be able to sleep at all and that would be stupid before a Higher School Certificate exam.

Astoundingly, she responded, 'Oh thanks. I'll check with my mum.'

Was it the Italian again? Who was she in that language? Though she was still certain she wouldn't take him up on the offer.

At home she called, 'Hi,' and her mother's response sounded a little flat and mopey.

The house smelled of their lentil curry from the night before. There was an open CD box on the coffee table. Going to close it, Heather saw that it was *Tracy Chapman* but it had *Watermark* inside it. She spent a while searching for the *Watermark* box, which turned out to have *Graceland* inside it. She put *Watermark* away after blowing what looked like carpet fluff off the back of it (maybe that was why it had been having trouble starting), then briefly tried to find the *Graceland* box. It wasn't where it should have been on the rack; she seemed to remember having stood on it and cracked it badly, but couldn't remember what had happened after that. And *Tracy Chapman* could have been anywhere.

Giving up, she went to the bathroom to change into her trackies and a sloppy joe, and to hang her cozzie and towel over the shower rod to dry. She was shivery and in the mirror her skin was chalk-white, goosebumpy, a bit alien. God, what would David think of her body? Because she hadn't entirely stopped considering his invitation, she knew she wouldn't be able to concentrate on study.

She made for her room, where she quickly slotted the *Temple of Low Men* cassette into her Walkman and lay down on her bed, wondering if she was a freak. For sure, people at school thought she was on account of how little experience she'd had with drugs and boys. She knew some of the students in her class, as well as Robbie, had had sex for the first time at fourteen or fifteen; at Lithgow High, a Year Seven girl had even got pregnant. Heather had been frightened quite a lot in Year Seven. She had briefly 'gone with' a boy, because he had made it known that he wanted that and she'd sort of felt obliged, though she hardly knew him. It had only involved some clammy hand-holding and the passing of messages on torn-out pages of exercise books across lines of school desks. There hadn't been much to the messages and they'd barely spoken to each other, either. While this lasted, she had been nervous that they might have to pash, but luckily she had quickly come up with a vague reason for them to break up well before the social at the end of the year.

The night before the dance, Heather had stayed over at the house of a classmate who had lent her an appropriate outfit, similar to ones shown in *Dolly* magazine: a black bubble skirt with white polka dots and a stonewash denim jacket. Because Heather didn't really know what to do, the generous girl had taught her to apply mascara, coral-pink lipstick and matching nail polish, and had even crimped her hair. Heather could still bring back those strangely sweet and sharp odours of cooking hair, nail varnish and hairspray.

As they were leaving for the dance, her friend's grandfather, more enthusiastic now they were all 'dolled up', as he put it, said to Heather, 'You look like a slick chick, like Kylie Minogue. You could be sixteen.'

She'd started to turn visible like that every so often. For example, when for a group PE session she had to wear a leotard as high-cut as a *Solid Gold* dancer's. It was like she was giving out a signal, on and off, without being fully in charge of it. Being seen in the new way made her even shyer than she normally was.

There had been an unnerving looseness to the assembly hall without chairs and uniforms in it. Disco lights crisscrossed darkness and an immense screen showed video clips of the Top-40 songs that were playing. Heather felt quietly important and less of a dork than usual with her trendy look that was attracting attention, yet bogus, too, split from herself. It was hard not to giggle at the romantic songs that she couldn't take seriously or completely avoid wanting to take seriously. Older boys asked her to dance and she accepted, this being the goal. Their body language was both approving and guarded, a bit stubborn; they liked to wedge a knee between hers during the slow dances. It was all intriguingly grown-up if not exactly fun. There was a definite tugging inside her chest, some kind of hunger to confess random things and be thoughtfully, fondly understood. To nuzzle into someone with her body and mind – but those boys weren't the ones to do it with.

Her first kiss happened at her next school. All she really remembered of it was how self-conscious and afraid she was, hoping the boy found her acceptable; she did what she thought she was supposed to do, too distracted to wonder if she enjoyed it.

And that was pretty much it, as far as her experience, if you could call it that, went. But in her head she was no innocent. She'd grown up helping herself to Marianne's books (even erotic ones by Anaïs Nin and Henry Miller) and watching movies for adults. At a cinema in the city, Marianne had insisted that she and her eight-year-old daughter be allowed in to see *Purple Rain*, despite its R-rating, if the rating was just to do with sex. Particular sex scenes in movies and books warmed and softened her, seeming to make an extra heart beat between her legs. Waiting to fall asleep at night, she imagined things, made up rich, romantic scenarios, working in tender and passionate details from movies like *Room with a View* and fascinatingly sensual foreign ones she'd seen on SBS, as well as from novels by Brontë and Austen, and French and Russian ones, anything gripping she was reading. Since Robbie's party, a lot of this had involved David. In fact, it had been more and more challenging to think about anything that did not in some way involve or circle him. It made her ask herself if she could be in love or falling in love – if that ever really happened or could be trusted even remotely.

Marianne didn't trust it, which was why she had decided to go totally anti-men and become a celibate yogi. Her mother's run of disappointing, hurtful relationships (many of which Heather had witnessed from up close and/or heard about at length) had made her consider romantic love as not much more than an invention to be exploited by religion and capitalism. She reckoned that the chances of encountering a version of it that was kind, interesting and rewarding were close to nil. Marianne also claimed that sex wasn't a big enough deal to justify all the bother. Traditional relationships and families (a lot of Heather's classmates were from 'split' ones) had basically had their day. The sixties and seventies had led them to this realisation. Her mother's generation had experimented with 'wild' behaviour and questioned everything, coming out the other side of it all pretty damn cynical. Relationships were complicated and complicated tended to mean an awful mess.

But while Heather was mulling these things over, she was also remembering her swim with David earlier, the feeling of him being nearby in the water, the two of them swimming in parallel. And then the cool, fresh air after they pulled themselves out and were standing by the pool in wet costumes. Droplets of water streaming from their skin and the comforting smell of poolside chlorine mixing with that of pine resin and rhododendron flowers coming into their heaviest sweetness.

Unbelievably, only an hour or so later, she was packing her sports bag. The first things that went in were her favourite pencil case containing some new lucky black felt-tip pens and *Heart of Darkness*, which she probably wouldn't read that night but was necessary as a talisman. Then she quickly assembled her outfit for Ada's dinner. She was trying not to notice what she was doing, trying to hold on to the stretchy Italian thinking.

She hugged her surprised mother goodbye, entering Marianne's gloom more deeply for those few seconds of bodily contact and feeling both betrayed and unfaithful. 'You'll be all right? You won't even be able to watch telly.'

'I've got my radio, and I'll meditate. It'll be like a meditation retreat.'

'Well, good luck,' Heather encouraged her, though she was the one with the exam the following day.

David's house was nestled behind a straggle of cedars and pines. It was as small as hers but older and had dark wooden cladding and a short, discoloured cement deck. There was a sort of pause after he opened the door, during which they didn't hug.

'Dinner will be latish, so there's time for you to study.'

'Cool, thank you so much.'

They walked through a lounge room, old-fashioned wallpaper, a dark-blue seventies sofa, a bricked-up fireplace with an oil heater in front of it, an undersized primitive TV similar to the one at her house. Their stuff was as modest and op-shoppy as Heather's and Marianne's but maybe in slightly better shape and tidier. There was the disconcerting odour of someone else's house and she felt stiff-jawed with repressed panic and the urge to leave. She'd been to very few sleepovers (never to one at a boy's house) and had gone to them out of an obscure sense of obligation, always getting the impression that everyone could smell her discomfort and weirdness, as dogs smell fear.

Next, she was meeting Jan and Carole. Jan was a tad wan but benevolent. Carole, without being especially tall, had excellent posture and in general there appeared to be something rather staunch about her. It was reassuring to notice the bookshelf they were standing in front of, a *Herald* on top of it, along with a Margaret Atwood that Marianne and Heather had read in turn a while back.

Jan said, 'We're just having pasta, nothing special. Are you okay with garlic?'

'I love it. And pasta. I could eat pasta every night.'

'We can make up a bed for you later on the lounge, or we have a folding bed that we can put in David's room. Whatever you prefer.'

She wished she wasn't being given the choice. Was his mother asking her to spell out if this was some kind of date? Heather thought it might have been simpler to have dealings with more conservative parents who'd spare you such sexually tinged uneasiness. It had been dumb of her to come.

'Whatever is easier,' she said, observing the well-trodden russet carpet.

'We can figure that out later. She has to study now,' David said.

His room had a different vibe to the rest of the place, satisfyingly David-esque. There were full bookshelves and a basic stereo. A desk with nothing on it but a blue metal lamp. The blinds were raised on the window, and through an old wooden screen warmish air smelling of cedars wafted in. Outside, it was getting dark.

'Um,' he said, 'I guess I should leave you to it.'

She hoped he had somewhere okay to hang out while he was allowing her to be alone. When he'd gone, she tried to be calm while staying vigilant and didn't dare look around much, especially not at his bed, which was covered by a vintage patchwork quilt made from jumpers. What did he think about in that bed? Did he touch himself in it? Quickly, she scoped his books and was moved to see that he'd kept some from when he was a kid. She still had a few of these herself: *The Wind in the Willows*, *Where the Wild Things Are* and *In the Night Kitchen*, *Charlotte's Web*, *Winnie-the-Pooh*, *Tales of Snugglepot and Cuddlepie*. He didn't have any of the *Anne* books, but he did have some Adrian Mole and Jules Verne. He had school stuff and extensions of it. He had more poetry and Shakespeare than she did, different Russians, more Sartre and less de Beauvoir, exactly the same Jane Austen volumes; he had a few crime novels she didn't recognise and old-school ones like Conan Doyle and G.K. Chesterton.

She forced herself through the motions of going over her notes, the woodsy night-breeze touching her face every so often. After a completely unmeasurable interval, just as she was starting to feel more composed, David knocked again and fresh adrenaline spurted into her system.

'Yes? Come in,' she called from his own bedroom.

Dinner wasn't too bad because David and Carole kept the chatting afloat, she and Jan mostly mute and trying to occasionally smile at each other without staring. Heather saw how Carole might create a mood-lightening, focus-softening effect. It must have been a real relief for David to have her around. At first, the meal had the subtly eerie taste of other people's home cooking, but then Heather started to enjoy it. The sauce was homemade pesto and the flavours of the basil and garlic were nicely pungent. She was also comforted by the Bürgen bread, which was the one they sometimes got at her house. For afters, there was a bowl of Ferrero Rocher to share and half a mango each, cut so that cubes stood up from the concave skin.

'Good work, David,' Carole said pleasantly, apparently referring to the mangoes.

He looked away and Heather realised they were a treat he'd prepared for her.

When she went to help with the gathering of dishes, Carole told her, 'No, you're a guest. Just feel at home, watch the TV, read, do what you'd normally do. Your exam's being held at Katoomba High? I can drive you tomorrow, if you want. It's on my way to work.'

'Gosh, thanks, that'd be great.'

'The green towel in the bathroom is for you,' Jan said, folding her arms across her chest. 'Whenever you want a shower.'

'Oh. Thanks, thanks so much for everything.'

She weed as quietly as possible against the side of the toilet bowl and only flushed once the shower was running. Thank God she didn't have her period. There were prettily old blue tiles beneath a little louvred window on one of the bathroom walls, and, staring at them through the transparent shower curtain while she was under the water, she half forgot herself – until suddenly worrying that she'd taken too long and used up too much hot water. She hurried out and through the rest of her preparations, getting into almost-new full-length pyjamas that had been a gift from her grandparents (she normally slept in a T-shirt and underpants). In the quadrant of the mirror that hadn't fogged up, she saw the violent pink of her cheeks. She made sure all her gear was back in her bag, particularly her underwear, then removed the scrunchie from her hair and wondered about the slight curl it had left; she indecisively combed this out with her hands, leaving it, if anything, fluffier. She used a square of toilet paper to clean fingerprints that might have been hers from the mirror, determined to erase all traces of her presence; seeing no bin, she put that paper into her bag, so she wouldn't have to flush the toilet again. Her stomach was still knotted with the desire to disappear.

She came hot-cheeked out of the bathroom, but luckily the lights were off and there was only a remote television glow from the lounge room and lamplight emanating from David's half-open bedroom door.

She waited a moment, her scalp tingling, and crossed the threshold.

She said, 'It's me.'

A CD was playing – contemplative and intense – and he was sitting with a book on a camp bed that had been set up at one end of his, against the wall.

'What are you reading?'

'*Heart of Darkness*. I haven't read it since last year. It's bloody good.'

'I know. I hope the questions I get will be all right.'

'They will be. Don't worry. And you'll be amazing.'

'Don't say that.'

He closed the book and her eyes went to her own copy on his desk. She belatedly identified the music: *Astral Weeks*, 'Madame George'.

'I love this album. It's sad.'

She didn't know how to say that the sadness it made her feel was mixed up with memories of listening to it when she was little and associating it with Marianne's younger years and heartbreaks.

He seemed slightly disoriented. 'Yeah, isn't it? You can have my bed, I changed the sheets, and I'll sleep here, if that's okay. It's just that Mum and Carole watch TV out there.'

'The folding bed will be good for me.'

'No, I honestly like sleeping on this. I'll have my shower now.'

When he was gone, she sat on the side of his bed, feeling the roughish-soft texture of a maroon portion of the quilt, and then went and sank down onto her knees in front of his music collection. She'd have been so embarrassed if he'd looked at her music before she'd had time to hide a few things – the old Madonna and Bananarama, et cetera. He had more Van Morrison and Pink Floyd than she did and quite a bit of jazz, which she knew nothing about, and hardly any classical (only *In the Hall of the Mountain King* and *Glassworks*, topics of school assignments). Heather had a fair amount of the latter, most of which Marianne had given her. Her mother had been made to take many oppressive years of piano lessons as a girl and so she almost never wanted to listen to classical music anymore. Yet on the odd moody Sunday, after the video clips on *Rage* had finished, she wanted to listen to something by Chopin, Debussy or Satie that she'd once laboured over. Sunday afternoons could be like trapdoors they fell through slowly. The music made the falling sensation sadder (*elegiac*, she could have written in an essay in the next day's exam), but at the same time beautiful.

She was in David's house. And it was all somehow magical. They hadn't been friends very long – six weeks and a couple of days. How could she keep suspecting she felt closer to him than she ever had to anyone? Was she kidding herself badly, coming under a stupid 'love' spell? She was so used to hiding from people, but with him she was tempted to do that much less. It was confusing and frightening.

Wandering the room, she picked up his *Heart of Darkness* and, flicking through it, studied the fragments of his handwriting in the margins: fluid, sloping, some jerkier angles. He underlined bits he liked, occasionally putting an exclamation or question mark after them. Heather loved that he loved to read; it made her hope they could make sense to each other.

She heard the bathroom door and David calling out a good night.

'Good night,' Carole's and Jan's voices called back in unison.

And there he was in black tracksuit bottoms and a white T-shirt, hair wet-dark and something, more mature or direct, newly revealed in his face.

She put down his book, shaking.

'Do you want to study more, or, I mean, are you tired? Do you want to sleep?'

'I probably shouldn't think about the exam anymore now. I could try to fall asleep,' she said uncertainly.

He cleared his throat. 'We could get into bed – our beds – and listen to music for a while? Something relaxing?'

'That'd be good.'

'Maybe some jazz, laid-back? If you like jazz?'

'Whatever you like.'

'But would *you* like that, really?'

'I haven't heard that much jazz, but I would. Really.'

They hadn't made eye contact since the showers. While he was choosing the music, she got into his bed very quickly; her pyjama legs rode up, one of them twisting exasperatingly. She pulled the quilt made of jumpers up high, though she wasn't cold at all and didn't want the prickle of heat.

'Shall I turn the light off?'

'Yes, please – that'll help me get sleepy.'

She smelled the Pears soap and the Head and Shoulders shampoo she'd seen in the bathroom. She turned on her side and saw the red numbers of his clock radio.

The springs on his bed squeaked long and comically as he got into it, and he laughed.

'Sorry. This was my granddad's camping bed. I'll try not to toss and turn.'

'I feel bad for making you sleep on that. You're sure it's comfortable?'

'Absolutely.'

The idea of her impending exam abruptly became more concrete and ominous.

'Can you distract me from tomorrow? Tell me something, anything?'

She tried to pay attention to the low-volumed music. A trumpet, as if gently musing.

'Yes, I'll tell you … give me a minute … about …'

'When you were a kid?'

'My first memories? Is that boring?'

'No way.'

No one had suggested such a conversation topic to her before. She rolled onto her back and considered the fuzzy grey-black ceiling. The TV ebbed and flowed through the wall, seeming both human and artificial, soporific and then alarming.

'Now that I think about it, I guess they are pretty death-related.'

'Oh? Interesting. Go on.'

'Yeah, well, there are also some hazy ones of an island off the coast of Tasmania, where we stayed for about six months. We were living with a guy my mum was seeing and they were both on the dole. For Christmas, they spent all their money on presents and decorations from Chinatown in Hobart, so there was bugger all left for food.'

It was a relief that they could talk to each other about having no money, knowing that the other knew what this was like, understood.

'Our Christmas dinner was turnips, turnip chips, and we all got the runs. I don't remember that, or even really the guy. His beard, maybe. I remember some blackberry bushes that grew near the side of our hut. And – but I've heard stories about it, so maybe I just think I remember – my pet rabbit's funeral. There was a piece of wire poking into his cage like a blade of grass and he tried to eat it. That was the theory, anyway. He choked. Apparently, I insisted on having a funeral and I made up a song for it.'

'Do you remember the lyrics?'

'Why did I mention the song?'

'How did it go?'

'Do I have to tell you?'

'No, of course you don't.'

He sighed. 'It went: *Don't you worry, little bunny.* Something like that.'

She smiled sadly, unseen in the dark. 'You didn't want him to be scared of being dead.'

'Bloody hell, I can't *believe* I told you that.'

'I'm glad you did.'

He raced on, 'I remember not liking having to have naps in the afternoon. Afterwards, I was confused, like someone had stolen time from me or let time continue without me. There was one day I was in bed with the blanket over my head, trying to imagine being dead. I remember that very sharply – wondering if it would just be like seeing in the dark.'

'I vaguely remember thinking stuff like that.'

'You do?'

'Yeah.' They were silent for a moment. She began again: 'When I was very young, Marianne would sometimes put "Puff the Magic Dragon" on the record player for me to go to sleep to. And it was so mournful. Autumn mists and dragons living forever but not little boys, and that sort of thing.' The words and their tone had carried over into the feeling of waking alone in the afternoon in a curtained room.

'Tragic.'

'I'll say.'

'And what about your first memories? Clear ones.'

'Oh … I see a sticker with a duck on it above the hook I was supposed to hang my bag on at preschool. There's a photo of me crying and holding the front gate of that place, like I wish I could escape or not be left there. I don't remember that … I remember sitting by myself in a yard looking at the bark peeling off a tree. It was my birthday. I tend to get melancholy on birthdays.'

'I'm a bit like that.'

'Yeah?'

'Yeah, I cried when I turned ten because my age was going to be in double digits from then on. It seemed like the end of childhood, you know, like the end of *Winnie-the-Pooh* or something.' He chuckled. 'Now I try to just let my birthdays slide past.'

'That's smart. I never want anyone to know when mine is. I hate the idea that people would feel obligated to celebrate me, to make a fuss. It makes me too self-conscious.'

'I get that. I'm not a party person, either.'

Confiding in him came almost too easily: it was strange how he unlocked something, made her chatty, and she had to work to stay distant and cautious enough. She didn't want to overshare, the way her mother did. But David was sharing, too, and what he told her was so intelligible and welcome to her.

She said, 'Carole's friendly.'

'Yeah, she is. It's kind of bizarre but good to have her around. Mum was off relationships for so long. Which was better of course than her being in horrible ones. But her moods have been way better since Carole. She's stopping therapy. I mean, she'll keep being a counsellor – she just won't get counselling herself, anymore. Apart from the clinical supervision sessions she has.'

'My mum's been in therapy for ages, as long as I can remember. Are any adults not in therapy and/or therapists? As far as men go, she reckons she'll never be interested in them again.'

'I don't think mine will be, either.'

They laughed.

'It's bad when they're depressed.'

'Yeah, isn't it.'

It was relaxing to be able to say those things. Heather wondered how her mother was getting along at home in the dark. She tried to picture Marianne with a new bloke or a woman, a version of Carole who'd defuse some of her tension, make the whole household lighter, perhaps render Heather's role less central; she couldn't really see it.

David asked, 'How many days do you guys have till payday?'

'Four.'

'I was thinking that I could give you some money – or lend you or whatever. I'm good for cash, with the pub. I could even cover your electricity bill. If your mum would be cool with that. Or just give you some cash to keep to yourself.'

She was moved. 'That is such a nice idea, thanks, but I couldn't take your money. We'll be fine and, anyway, tomorrow is the dinner at Ada's and I'm staying over at her place. I'm getting a lot of hospitality.' She laughed awkwardly.

Caution again, a soft fear. A 'move' wasn't going to be made, was it? She was so inexperienced, having only kissed two boys in her whole life (including for the school play). Now, lying in David's bed, she'd have been shatteringly terrified by anything physically confronting, and somehow she imagined he knew this. (Not that she hadn't pictured how a kiss or cuddle might begin.) The TV came more loudly through the wall, then went almost inaudible, subliminal.

He said, 'I should let you sleep. Do you think you'll be able to?'

'I don't know. Usually before exams or anything I'm nervous about, I think: I hope I fall asleep. And then I don't.'

'Me too. So is not hoping the answer?'

'I guess. Hope for nothing.' Hope for nothing.

'Sometimes it works for me if I start counting backwards from one hundred in my head. We could try that.'

'Okay, let's do that.' She was sceptical but liked that they'd be attempting it together.

'Should I turn off the music?'

'No, it's really nice. Leave it on. And let's not say good night.'

'Okay. We won't.'

The next morning Heather marvelled: the counting backwards had worked. She'd managed to be calm enough in David's bed, with David just a step or two away, to sleep. It was miraculous, proof of his specialness.

She was about to get into Carole's VDub when David, who'd come outside to see her off, stepped forward quickly and hugged her, saying, 'I won't say good luck.'

'No, don't. Thanks for everything. I'll see you tonight.'

The hug was quick but tight and warm, and she leaned into him a little, wanting to lean in more. After they separated, he secretively put something into her hand and she realised, when she was already in the car and it was too late to return it, that he'd given her a neatly folded fifty-dollar note. It was shockingly generous and sweet and she had to be stern with herself to repress tears. How was it that he could do both things so much, stir and comfort her? He remained on the cement deck to watch them go, as solemn as if he was seeing off a loved one (a loved one!) on a long sea voyage in some grim past. The parting did feel significant. She smiled a thank-you. Leaving him behind, the wait for the evening to bring them together again and clarify their affection for one another was already a tautness and a fizz inside her. A wonderful dewy, leafy smell entered through her window as the car pulled out of the driveway. It was hard to get her head around the fact that school was ending and depositing her in an unexplored realm; her exam nerves jostled against this vague shimmer.

A last glance at David – still on the deck – and she remembered an elderly woman she'd once sat next to on a train, who had said, 'Be sure to enjoy every minute of your life.' There had appeared to be regret in this, more than a hint of: I wish I had done that more. And of: It sounds easier than it is. Heather thought now, Yes, I must always pay attention, particularly to joy as it comes and not just in wistful retrospect. I mustn't let worry stop me from enjoying, must let myself soften and open enough to be happy. Let me not look around me, when I am nearing death, with grieving eyes.

7

SHIPLEY ROAD

Few people were sitting for three-unit English and the hall was still and curiously serene. Heather wasn't oppressed by the state-high-school atmosphere that she used to find daunting. She was only conscious of a low throb of adrenaline as she filled the lines in a green booklet with her felt-tip pen that seemed, almost independently of her, to know its stuff enough to be doggedly tunnelling her out of the enclosure of school. She finished early and checked her answers, already more interested in what lay beyond. Returning to herself, she felt the warmth of David's money, its preciousness radiating through her jeans pocket into her thigh. She wasn't going to spend it.

The sky was clear and the air smelled of a Blue Mountains town surrounded by bush and valleys, of the wide world, as she walked towards Ada at the school gate. She was a vision of freedom. The authority in her petite frame was always a slight surprise. She wore cool retro-sixties sunglasses, a black T-shirt, pale jeans, and in the strong light her lavishly pigmented skin and jet-black hair were dramatic, as if belonging to an actress or a model in an outrageously unaffordable European *Vogue*. Heather felt a burst of fondness; each time she'd been in the woman's company she'd relaxed a little more, admired and enjoyed more wholeheartedly that mobile, thoughtful face.

They double-kissed as usual and then Ada embraced Heather for the first time, enfolding her in a glamorously woody, musky perfume bubble such as you might pass through outside a theatre. It gave Heather a victorious rush. She felt the threat of tears for the second time that day.

Ada said, 'You must be starving.'

And yes, indeed. She liked the Italian phrase, the idea that she was as hungry as a wolf.

Ada drove them to the Paragon, where she instructed, 'Order whatever you want. It's on me.'

'You don't have to do that.'

'Of course I don't, but let me.'

They sat at one of the stylish old wooden booths beside a wood-panelled wall out of which sculpted white classical figures emerged. Studying the menu, Heather carefully chose a toasted sandwich – not a full hot meal or anything.

'That's all?'

She nodded, but after the sandwich vanished, Ada insisted, 'We *have* to share one of those ice-cream things.'

Heather smiled, wanting to behave gratefully but appropriately. Sometimes she got the sense that people thought she was thanking them or apologising too much.

The sundae was full-on. (She might have preferred simple Streets vanilla ice cream with normal, fake-tasting chocolate topping out of a bottle and no crushed peanuts.) Yet sharing the dessert with Ada was a fun indulgence, like takeaway meals splurged on right after payday, only without any worry haunting it. Ada ate next to nothing and ruminatively off the end of her spoon, endorsing the festivity much more than the food itself. They spoke Italian and speaking the language felt easier than it ever had. Some doubt, some severity in Heather was being released. Haphazardly, in answer to Ada's questions, she described what she thought she'd written about *Heart of Darkness* and *Wuthering Heights*. She had a wobble or two, once had to correct a mistaken gender, but mainly she savoured a delightful, casual recklessness. It was like walking on steppingstones with trampolines inside them that bounced her ever onwards, like trying to fly without being overly concerned about falling, just going with it.

Ada kept nodding kindly and after a while she leaned forward and placed a small, streamlined object – indigo, a matte finish – on the table between them.

'I thought a present was necessary.'

Heather blushed, giddy from all the extravagance, the foreign language, memories of David and the anticipation of David. She picked it up, happily embarrassed and already treasuring whatever it was.

It clicked open: a compact mirror, which came with its own lipstick, a dark, glistening crimson.

Ada said, 'I got us both one.'

Heather adored that the Italian word for lipstick started with 'red'.

'Thank you, thank you so much. You shouldn't have.'

'Of course I should have. Pretty, no? Bordeaux? Try it now! Shall I, too?'

Nonchalantly, Ada applied a daring Bordeaux coating and was almost indecently stunning. Heather cleaned her mouth and did her best to emulate those gestures without giggling at the caressing sensation.

When she said, '*Mamma mia*,' her lips were someone else's. Those of an adult, frolicsome and sexy.

As they arrived at the house, Ada told Heather that Filippo hadn't been working for the last few months. He used to do something legal for a bank in the city; it was taking him a while to find another job.

Inside, there was an appetising aroma of simmering tomatoes, meat and herbs, and everything appeared as harmonious and refined as ever.

Filippo, in an olive-green apron, announced, 'I'm making my *ragù*. Very *slowly* is the only way.'

The women followed him to the kitchen door, their conversation suspended.

'What can I do?' Ada asked.

'Absolutely nothing,' he replied.

Heather tried to hold herself straight, not too rigidly, and to make her face look natural. 'Can *I* help?'

'No. You are the celebrated one.'

'I'll show her the guest room,' Ada said and, once they were out of earshot, 'Are you all right?'

She was observant. In addition to her usual gawkiness, Heather had just realised that the outfit she'd brought for later wouldn't do. Her favourite top was lugubrious, after all: Marianne was right. Heather had fallen for it and saved up for ages, but she suddenly understood that it was really only a bizarre T-shirt, its swirling black and grey probably all wrong for a dinner with Italians.

'I forgot to bring a top.'

'I'll lend you one. Do you want to call your mother? Tell her about your exam? Then relax, have a shower, as you like. Give me your bag. I'll leave it in your room, which is that door – see?'

The chat with her mother was a pure classic.

'Hi, it's me. I'm at Ada's. How are you?'

'God, what a day. Well, I didn't sleep well last night, I hardly slept at all …' Dark laughter, then the flow into anecdotes of frustration and bad luck.

'Oh no, you poor thing, how awful,' et cetera. The labour to suggest more positive perspectives. Heather's responses and tones were those of listener and soother.

Belatedly: 'But how was your *exam*?'

'It was okay, I think.'

Eventually, her mother concluded, 'Anyway, I'll leave you to it, but we should have talked more about you. No more school, hey? I must be getting old.'

Heather felt unsettled in the stomach and somehow murky in familiar ways, but after hanging up she went and pushed open the door to the guest bedroom. Calm late-afternoon sunshine. Through wooden venetian blinds, a stout companionable pine. In a glass bowl on a little antique desk, the heads of three white roses floated, and bending over them was like inhaling sweet tea with lemon in it, the beginning of summer. The telephone call slowly began to recede.

Showering, she thought of David.

Ada had left some clothes for her on the bed. A sky-blue nightie of a kind she'd never owned and four tops to choose from. Heather had just put on the plainest of these, a dressy black singlet top, with her black Lee's, when Ada knocked and asked if she could come in.

She tried to push down her shyness.

'How pretty … but why don't you bring *that* one' – Ada indicated a whitish silk blouse – 'and follow me.'

She hadn't been able to see herself in the white top at all. It was too luxurious and pristine, so well ironed or even dry-cleaned that she'd have been constantly nervous about it getting crushed or stained. And she generally avoided light colours, considering them too visible, too attention-attracting.

Ada and Filippo's bedroom was on the other side of the house. At first glance the space was minimalist and airy, occupied only by a bed on a low frame. But as Ada slid across the door of a built-in wardrobe, Heather turned and saw a corner that was utterly replete: a dull-gold chaise longue draped in an apricot-embroidered black silk kimono, a standing lamp, a table holding books (Isabel Allende, Milan Kundera, Italo Calvino) and another bowl of floating rose heads. Almost tripping on emerald-green leather slippers, she steadied herself on a dressing table lush with perfume bottles, hairbrushes and tangled necklaces.

'So much perfume!'

'Mea culpa. Shalimar is my favourite. We'll use it later.' She tossed the bottle onto the bed. 'Okay, we need some shoes for you, and you can help me decide what to wear. But first try on the blouse – just to see.'

So Ada didn't consider the Blundstones Heather had on and wore everywhere rather proudly (her only presentable footwear) as good enough? She wasn't hurt, feeling pleasantly malleable under Ada's influence. This was a new kind of feminine intimacy. Ada was unbuttoning her shirt; her body and manner of inhabiting it were so different from Heather's mother's. Marianne was long-limbed, broad-shouldered, heavy-breasted and stretch-marked on the tummy and thighs. When Heather first met her grandparents, going to stay with them in Adelaide while her mother was on a meditation retreat, she was surprised and then not to find her grandmother so elfin – the woman's tiny, frail presence was the backdrop for Marianne's view of herself as a chunky 'Big Girl', her propensity to stoop and make a slight cave of her chest. Several times a day, Marianne sharply pulled her shoulders back and tucked in her tailbone, as if she were one of her own yoga students just upbraided for sloppiness. She was attractive (Heather thought so, a lot of people had thought so) and yet she was drawn, more often since her celibacy, to jabbing at herself with critical comments on her appearance and especially weight.

Ada, in a diaphanous black bra, seemed to enjoy her alluring body. Heather glimpsed her marvellous skin, neat little breasts with dusky nipples, compact strength, the sheer muscular wall of an elegant stomach.

She turned childishly away to squirm out of the black top, and muffled, asked, 'Do you do a lot of exercise?'

'I go to the gym. I'm vain. What do you think?'

She'd put on a semi-transparent navy blouse with fine white polka dots; she was so lithe in it.

'Beautiful!'

Hating being exposed in an old Kmart bra, Heather hurried on the white blouse.

'When you're ready,' Ada said gently, 'come over here.'

Heather and Marianne had bare Ikea rods for their clothes hangers and milk crates for underwear, jumpers and jeans. Her Adelaide grandmother, whom Heather thought of as being reasonably well-off, didn't have anywhere near as many clothes as Ada did, and hers were huddled in a dark sepulchral wardrobe; Ada's was enormous and fresh, with an abundance of compartments. Her tall stack of T-shirts had a sort of uplifting importance, as if each would express and encourage a precise, self-confident mood. Everything she owned, including those T-shirts that Heather timidly stroked while the other woman squatted to ponder at least thirty pairs of shoes for unimaginable nuances of purpose, had a texture that would make you feel rich, discerning, comforted, excited.

'These? What's your European shoe size?'

'I don't know.'

Heels. A tracery of baby-soft black leather looking like it had never been out in any weather. She got into them, her ankles firmly encircled. The length was fine and they were barely tight across the toes. She laughed a bit madly, with an impression of being a spy, of slipping out through a crack in her identity into another that was more sophisticated and padded.

'Stockings will help. Take these.'

The classy packaging was unopened and through the viewing window she could see they were some subtle variation on fishnet, so adult. This was way too much; she shook her head.

'Really, I have lots of others – look.'

It was true: a drawer contained five identical packets.

Ada went on, 'The best stockings in the world, at least in my opinion, Austrian. Made not so far from Trieste, my city. Please keep them.'

Heather accepted, reluctant and thrilled, and said she'd finish getting dressed in the guest room. She couldn't put on stockings in front of Ada.

'But promise you'll wear that blouse? It suits you to perfection!' Alongside the tender bossiness, a kind of gaiety shone out of Ada, intensifying every so often. '*You* are perfect, so lovely,' she said radiantly.

No one had ever quite said this to her before, clearly, freely, good-naturedly. Heather bowed her head, one hand over her face, and turned to go, but Ada pursued her and sprayed her wrists and neck with perfume that was like their delectable shared secret.

Smiling faintly, Filippo considered Heather.

'Nice blouse. I believe I know it. Prosecco.'

He handed her a glass and she sipped, lofty and novel to herself in heels, silk and the crisp flavour and effervescence of the alcohol.

Ada made a move to help with the cooking and he suavely waved her off, yet a moment later as she reached past him for the bottle of Prosecco, he kissed her cheekbone.

'You're drinking?' he asked.

Ada half smiled and said, 'One must drink to the end of school. Cheers! And some music, don't you think?'

He pushed a dish of large pale-green olives towards Heather, who was already hungry again. 'What do we want to hear?'

'Something happy?' Ada suggested.

Filippo said, 'I'll take care of it,' leaving the room, and returning as the music began.

The volume was loud and the electronic equipment so good that the sound was like a fine syrup enriching the air and passing into Heather's bones.

'Wow, what is this?'

'*Lakmé*. "The Flower Duet".'

Heather repeated *Lakmé* under her breath. The voices and the melodies they sang were a sorrowful tease, impossibly exquisite. The olives were lightly brined.

'You call this happy?' Ada asked.

'Oh?' he said. 'I don't know. It was the most beautiful thing I could think of. You want something different?'

'No, no, it was the right choice. It's *too* beautiful.'

Behind the house, Ada had decorated with paper lanterns that were dreamy after sundown. Green and yellow on the verandah, blue on the edge of the fountain, red in a cedar, purple visible in gaps between trees. The borrowed silk blouse Heather wore billowed and subsided in a breeze that also stirred Ada's potent perfume and the scent from the pots of Star Jasmine. Of course, this was the Blue Mountains – at its borders the garden shaded into bush and she recognised and knew the clean open sky – but she also understood she was in a new place and shivered, anticipating epiphanies.

'Tired?' Ada asked, linking their arms and leading her along the pathway, dawdling to guard their refilled glasses from spilling.

She was, deeply, drunkenly, though with school suddenly erasing itself like magic ink, the fatigue was benign and zingy with excitement. In the grip of the wavering shoes and the nearly imperceptible encasement of the stockings she could see through their lattice, Heather trod warily on the pebbles.

'No. This garden is so extraordinary.'

'You think? It was my fantasy of a garden, I suppose.'

Her tone was analytic and slightly distant, as if they were discussing an enigmatic film they'd seen. Heather tightened her grasp on Ada's arm and, during an interval of blankness or drifting, gazed at the crimson she was leaving on the rim of her glass.

'Have you seen the bathtub?'

Ada tugged them past the cedars, where they seemed to be rushing into deep night, and then there was a discontinuity, a clearing, a romantic haven. White rosebushes – that odour again, stronger, of tea-scented citrusy-sweet summer – and a porcelain bathtub appearing almost phosphorescent in the dusk; it was sunken in the earth, with large, flat stones at either end.

'Does it work?' Heather asked, enchanted.

'Yes! You must have a bath here later – wait, I think that was a car. David and Robbie?' From the way she pronounced their names, Heather could tell Ada respected her friends. 'We'll have champagne now.'

Ada laughed, the sound joyful and nerve-racking. Heather was struck by the uncanniness of having spoken Italian for hours, her mind buzzing and continually rearranging itself, surrendering more and more to something low in her – intuition? She was breathless from the possible nearness of David and shocked to note how unbound she felt. She had a flickering cold intimation of the danger of this. And of what it would be like to find out that he only wanted her as a friend. Her ankles teetered in the fancy foreign shoes.

8

'A toast,' Ada said huskily, her glass high. 'To you all, to the end of school, to the past and to the future.'

To the younger people, those Italian words were intoxicating: singsong, plump, sprung. Listening, they felt an expansion, something within them becoming more elastic, elongating. The occasion was a sort of initiation ritual, Ada and Filippo ushering them into their language and culture, into adulthood. They had never before sat down to such a table, made of solid, glossy wood, so extravagant with candles, food and wine and laid with a level of ceremony that would have befitted a religious rite.

David had been particularly impressed by the tiramisu – simple and yet so perfect and delicately delicious – and had lingered over his final coffee-soaked cakey spoonful as if it was teaching him something. They were sipping from dainty glasses of mightily sweet and lemony *limoncello* when Robbie picked up his video camera and began to film. To David in his increasingly inebriated condition, it appeared that Robbie had some new depth to him, perhaps because he had been unusually still and quiet until then. In the candlelight, he had the concentrated, expectant look of a person following a bright trail through the dark.

Heather didn't quite seem like herself, either. The snazzy white blouse and the lipstick she was wearing were probably Ada's, and the alcohol had loosened her face somehow. Her beauty was almost unbearable. She had hardly glanced at him all night and now she was staring at her empty bowl.

Ada said, 'Please don't film us, Robbie. Heather doesn't like it.'

'Oh sorry. Sorry Heather, I didn't think.' He obeyed immediately, getting up and going to leave his camera on a bookshelf near the sofas.

In that moment, a half-full wine bottle was knocked over. Ada shrieked, covering her mouth with her hand. There was a shocking dark slash across the centre of the white tablecloth.

Heather said, 'Oh my God, I'm so sorry!' Her alarm and embarrassment had made her retreat into English.

'No, it's nothing. Nothing. It just scared me.' Ada had stood and was moving candleholders, plates and bottles to the top of a sideboard. 'I don't know why it scared me.'

Filippo remained composed. 'Kids, come with me.' His tone was playfully authoritarian. 'I think we should introduce the boys to "The Flower Duet". What do you say, Heather?'

'Oh no, please let me help with the table.' She was fussing hopelessly with the tablecloth.

'No, really, enough! I order you to go and sit down.' Ada bunched and gathered the stained fabric into her arms.

Robbie said, 'I'll help.'

'That's not necessary.'

But he stayed beside her.

In the lounge room, lamps with orange tasselled shades cast pools of light into the surrounding half-light and made the floorboards appear lacquered.

Filippo, attending to the CD player, commanded them, 'Sit.'

Heather sat down on one of the two long, pale sofas, and David next to her.

'Before I press *play*,' Filippo said, 'we need more *limoncello*. I'll be right back.'

'I'm so clumsy!' Heather whispered. 'How mortifying.'

'You're not clumsy.' David smiled, profoundly affected by being closer to her all of a sudden, by her jerky eyes and low, private voice.

Filippo was back with a silver tray. 'This is the best *limoncello* you can get, in Australia, at least. It's from Sorrento, near Naples. The lemons there are special.' He handed Heather a fresh glass.

Before taking it, she said, 'Sure you want to trust me with this, after that disaster?'

'Ah, but of course we trust you.'

Accepting his own glass, it occurred to David that this one could be the turning point into true drunkenness; he was on the edge of that already. He'd have to be very careful of what he said and did from here on in. He'd promised himself he'd make his confession to Heather that night.

'Now we must *listen*.' Filippo, jokey and imperious, might have been tipsy himself. 'Prepare yourselves. Be comfortable.'

He sat alone on the other sofa with his liqueur, pointing the remote at the stereo and then half reclining and seeming to close his eyes. Only then did David notice the painting on the wall behind him, the nearly nocturnal dark blue of it and the floaty quality ringing some kind of bell.

And then came the music. They all went motionless. The sound system was totally amazing, the best David had ever heard. And God, the song: it entered him, played in his skull, chest and groin. Clarity, sweetness, purity so angelic he felt like he was being pulled along by a current or a spell, hallucinating, maybe losing his mind in a dazzling, gorgeous way.

After a while, Filippo got up and left the room, and David recognised this as the chance he couldn't miss. He turned to Heather. She was much less guarded than usual, wine-tousled, her long, sumptuous hair hanging around her face. Catching his eye, she restlessly combed back her hair with her fingers. He'd have loved to do that himself, plunge his hands into her hair, hold her head.

'What incredible voices,' she said, with one of her attention-paying-yet-remote expressions.

He nodded and, smelling warm spiciness, asked, 'You're wearing perfume?'

'Yes, Ada's.'

Now she smiled more openly, pushed up one of her sleeves a little and raised her bare wrist towards him. He found the gesture tender. It was, wasn't it? But then again, maybe she was only being friendly. David quickly finished his *limoncello*, feeling the heat it planted inside him.

'It's Shalimar,' she elaborated.

And they both said, 'Like in the Van Morrison song.'

He laughed, lost and high on sugared Sorrento lemons and persuasive women's voices and especially her. He hesitated, as if on the cusp of a fall, and then began bending and lowering his face towards her wrist.

Ada felt Robbie's unrelenting eyes dredging her as if she were a lake containing evidence of a crime. That was about right – she was evidence of a crime. And when his eyes weren't on her she felt rejected and empty. She couldn't have cared less about the wine on the tablecloth, and yet the cry that had escaped her had needed voicing. She wished she'd reassured poor Heather better.

'Really, Robbie, I'll take care of this,' she'd tried to convince him when he made efforts to 'help', but she was nevertheless leading him to the kitchen.

How could she have stopped him without speaking strangely? This was happening because she couldn't organise her mind properly; and he wasn't helping. She stiffly lowered the stained fabric into the sink. She should have gone to fetch some laundry detergent, but she couldn't focus on that. He was behind her, silent. She vacantly considered the label on the dishwashing liquid: the symbol of a lemon. She was doing the wrong thing, with the tablecloth and the boy. *Boy!* Yes, he was within reach of childhood and she was not. Sadness welled in her, the realisation that she was beyond childhood but still wanted to play. She put in the plug, squirted soap and began to fill the sink. The water was hot and she made it cooler, then swirled around the tablecloth that was too bulky for the sink and almost made it overflow. One of her sleeves was getting wet.

'Can't I do something?' he asked in his shaky, adorable Italian.

'No! Absolutely not. There's nothing to do here. Go back with the others.' She kneaded the tablecloth crossly.

'Let me help you.' He came closer.

One of those disconcerting shivers you sometimes get in the heat ran through her and she laughed a little.

'No. Please go back.' And she said it again in his language in case that made it more real to him; yet her English as it often did came out sounding approximate, experimental.

Water was slopping out of the sink onto the bench that she and Filippo had chosen when they were renovating the house, fashioning their perfect home in which to live their ideal life. Her blouse was also wet over her belly button, the filmy fabric coolly adhering. She had a sense of vertigo, of his nearness like the lip of a drop. For no reason, she turned on the tap again and water ricocheting off the tablecloth spurted her face.

Robbie turned off the tap and felt for the droplets on her face with the back of his hand. This was a kind of story that, having begun to tell itself, would continue. He'd come so near that she only had to relax marginally to lean into him.

That had already happened. She'd done it, relaxed her weight into his long, firm warmth, his too-young, too-lovely body that unnaturally or completely naturally was asking for hers. A good person wouldn't do this. Even an imperfect person or a downright bad one with any common sense wouldn't let this occur. But logic wasn't guiding her now, not the part of her that was starving for play, for him. She was so frightened, and there was the guilty fear and then the shameful but luscious fear, her stomach nervily expecting joy.

She rested her head against his shoulder. Not having to pretend anymore that this wasn't what it was. Having his arms around her was an explosion of relief, though it also made her ache. Again, he wiped water from her cheek, his breath against her temple. Beautiful. She would look back on this night as the moment of her life in which she'd felt the strongest pleasure, glee in the flesh fully meshed with fantasy.

'We can't,' she whispered.

Wondering what was keeping his wife, Filippo got up from the sofa and headed for the kitchen. Approaching the doorway, he backtracked a step and stopped.

Embracing.

Ada and the boy. They – he was holding her from behind, snug between his body and the sink.

The angle of her abandoned head. Oh their lust.

On the hall table, where mail and keys got tossed, there was a small knife; he must have left it there when he'd gone aproned to greet the women. It jarred, so he picked it up and pocketed it before going back to the lounge room. He sat on the sofa once more to listen to the sublime end of 'The Flower Duet'.

It made sense. In fact, he'd seen it. However, there was seeing and then there was recognising what you were seeing for a hole in your reality. A widening hole in that naïve, pathetically trusting fucking stupid dream of being endlessly safely loved and cherished, desired, adored, soothed, accompanied, blah blah, every old and forever-recurring hurt salved, all the holes filled, that thinnest lying myth.

He knew Ada. Knew or was at least used to watching her, and he'd noticed her patterns changing, her transparency misting over. Her absent-haunted look, the fidgeting, the tossing and turning in bed, the getting up at around four. Such broken sleep could veil a person and strip her of cheerfulness (it did his mother), but Ada had been smiley and sprightlier than usual.

Causing him once or twice to ask, 'What's the joke?'

'Huh? Nothing.'

He'd also noticed her laughing a lot at something he said, something she hadn't seemed to follow. He'd thought the miscarriage was to blame for her general distraction and her lack of sexual interest. Her wounding, crushing reluctance to make love to him – even, perhaps especially, to kiss him. He'd felt her wince at his approach, felt it something severe. She never craved him anymore. If ages had gone by and he was desperately horny, he virtually had to corner her, stop her from staring past his intention, leave her no resort but open rejection. And she was too kind for that. Kind or trained to please. Was there a difference? When sex was finally happening, it was that: sex happening, Ada unaroused and as if quietly waiting somewhere distant for him to finish with her body before she took up residence there again. One atypical time he'd found her instantly, implausibly wetter than he could remember her being.

When he commented on this, she said, 'Oh? I guess I'm ovulating. Come here.'

But she wasn't engaged, didn't come; she no longer ever wanted any fore- or afterplay.

'No, no,' she might say. 'I'm just really tired, but that was lovely.'

A stupefied silence followed the music and into it came Ada and Robbie, returning from the kitchen at a languid, entitled pace. They were flushed from the vivid realm of experience they'd just had to leave. And unsuccessfully trying to hide it. She was ravishing and, *porca miseria*, so was he.

'I can drive the boys back,' Filippo said.

'Now?' Ada asked, a little shocked – as they all were – by this brusque end to their festive evening. 'Oh, are you sure?'

'Of course,' he told her in English, because he wanted the hardness and chill of an English expression. 'I'm stone-cold sober.'

In the car, he was dully amazed at how functional and affable he was being. He dropped off David, who was visibly taken aback and saddened because he'd had to say goodbye to the girl, Heather, earlier than planned; still, he did what he could to smile and say '*Grazie*' as he got out.

Finding the way to Robbie's house was more robotic. Filippo's vision cleared somewhat, once he'd pulled up out the front of the poor, boxy place. She got a buzz from his humble background, did she? Filippo had been beneath her also (and he was even more now, he supposed, that he was out of work), but not so much. He had come from a tacky immigrant lowish middle class of orange brick and the try-hard grandiosity of white columns and plaster of Paris swans, the claustrophobia of family photos seedy with age, foreignness and foreign intimacies. However, this was different, frugal. Plus, the kid was a bloody artist. It had been predestined: art was her fantasy, her bliss, and of course sooner or later some guy had always been going to *be* that shimmering chimera. And here he was. Obscenely young and pretty to boot.

'Thanks a lot for the lift.'

How cool he was playing it!

'Wait,' Filippo stopped him.

The boy took his hand off the door handle.

'Hey, why don't you come back to our place and stay over? Heather's in the guest room, but you could sleep on a sofa.'

The proposal came from an urge like the one that on occasion caused him to bite a small lesion inside his cheek: a curiosity about the pain, the depth and extent of it. Filippo hadn't made a scene when he'd seen them in the kitchen and he couldn't now. But the idea of somehow forcing them to reveal what they were so badly hiding was tempting

He had a cloudy inspiration. 'I could take you and Heather on a walk tomorrow morning. If you wanted. We could go to Hargraves Lookout for the view of the Megalong, or to Mount Blackheath. Have you seen the hang-gliders launching there? It might be cool to film them.'

Robbie didn't understand what was occurring, but who did? Perhaps it crossed the kid's mind that Filippo suspected something, that he could be trying to test or trap him.

'Um, well, my nan's expecting me.'

'The lights are off – so she'll be asleep, won't she?' He'd spoken so smoothly, he might have had a plan.

'Probably. But if she doesn't see me in the morning, she'll worry.'

'Leave her a note.'

Robbie hesitated. Slightly spooked, finally? It was difficult to tell in the night hardly touched by a far-off streetlight. He either didn't know how to gracefully decline or couldn't say no to the chance to go back to Ada.

'Okay. Can you wait for a minute?'

Leaving his camera on the passenger seat, the boy got out of the car and went inside the house. Filippo's heart speeded, seemed to stall and shudder, then speeded again. The boy returned.

It was distorted, the usual sense of space expanding as Blackheath's main drag was left behind – peace now shoved inside out into hollowness. And too soon, the crunch of the gravel driveway under the wheels and Ada's half-shadowed face in the kitchen window gazing down into the sink, gravely beatific, like a Madonna at the holy infant in a painting. She was so absorbed in thought that she hadn't heard the car, or she was listening to music. Though he had caused this, Filippo suffered acute distress because Robbie and Ada were about to see one another again. He had to delay it.

'Did you see what Ada did with the lanterns in the garden? Come on, I'll show you. They'd look great on film, I bet.' He was leading the way around the house, Robbie obliged to follow.

Indeed, the paper lanterns would have struck a child as mythical. Yellow and green on the verandah, azure at the rim of the fountain, crimson nestled among the branches of a cedar, and violet, which you saw from certain angles, gleaming mysteriously on the other side of the little copse. Whatever was on Robbie's mind, he began to film.

There was a thin sound of running water that confused Filippo because it wasn't coming from the fountain. Then he deduced that Heather must have been in the bathtub beyond the trees; Ada would have suggested it. If anything, his turmoil was intensifying in the dreamlike garden he'd always found so calming. All he could think of was escaping into the bush.

'Might take myself for a walk,' he said. 'Why don't you go and say hello to Heather.'

'Heather?'

'Yes, see that purple light past the trees? That's where she is. She's your age, isn't she?' he added. 'I'll see you later.'

He moved so fast and carelessly then that tea tree stung his face; he was on his private track. He wished he never had to go back, wished to go bush for good.

9

Robbie was rapt with Ada's lantern-lit garden. What an eye she had, what vision. He imagined her lingering here at different times of the day and in different moods, in whatever she wore to bed, her feet bare, her hair down and unkempt or up and exposing her neck. He thought of her now in the kitchen by the sink, where they'd embraced. Jesus, had he really done that? Had she really responded as he'd thought she had? He was off his head. He wondered what he was doing here and for how long Filippo would be gone. Hanging around outside a house reminded him of his interminable attempts to get away from the shortness of air in the short bloody house in Lithgow. How he was lured out into the neighbouring streets, as if by a call or a coaxing tune, some ice-cream-van music that only he could hear. And he went after the promise of it, but couldn't go far enough. It was like struggling to make a run for it in a nightmare. Smoke from coal fires, currawong song, the verges of near-empty streets, the listening to what he had to believe wasn't only inside him, and watching and waiting for the night that would come, for the Southern Cross to appear or anything else that would help him shuck off all the low things, rise up over that town, be lifted away.

He realised he was biting the sides of his fingers and running his tongue over the grooves in his teeth in that old way, and he forced himself to stop. He must confide in Heather immediately. A confession was about to erupt out of him and he needed her to hear it and tell him if he was crazy. He haphazardly filmed the dark garden, the colours Ada had chosen to electrify it, a purple twinkle brightening as he neared the black cedars.

They had a bathtub out here. What didn't they have? Heather was in it. He'd never seen her like that before, shadowy skin purpled by the lantern light. Quickly, he looked away.

'Hi. It's me.'

'Robbie! God, you scared me. Didn't Filippo take you home?'

'We took David home. Filippo said I could come back here and stay over. I wasn't sure if I should. But he wants to take us for a bushwalk tomorrow – he seemed keen on the idea … Hey, can we have a deep and meaningful?'

'Of course, but can you sit with your back to me or something?'

'Oh okay, sorry, yeah. This good?'

'Yeah. I'm drunk.'

He heard the fountain; it was impressively loud at night and somehow intimate, like a timid voice finally speaking up. 'This is … I have to tell you. I think, I mean, I know I am in love with Ada.'

'Oh?'

He liked that she didn't sound shocked. Or amused.

'Yeah.'

'I was starting to get that idea.'

'You were?' Talking about it was superb. Sweet as. 'I know it's complicated. But I don't just have the hots for her. At first I thought it was that.'

'Which would be understandable.'

'Right! Because she's *gorgeous* and *so* smart and … incredible.' He heard in his voice the elation and semi-suffering that had been crisscrossing him for weeks. 'But I've had crushes before and they weren't like this, at all. I can't explain it properly. I'm just in love with her, so in love with her, it's …'

'It's what?'

He could find no words that didn't diminish the reach, momentum and shifting shades of it. 'Strong … happy. I'm smiling all the time like a fucking dickhead. I'm so wired I think about her for most of the night.' He would lie there with an impression of something tenderly wound around his heart, not caring if he fell asleep. 'I'm getting up early, and even though I'm getting bugger-all sleep, I have the most energy. I'm doing heaps of painting, heaps of drawing, filming with the Camcorder. I've been running home from the station. Which is not far, right? But you know I usually hate running – I get stitches and feel like I'm dying. Now I'm getting into it. I sprint.'

He didn't add that he'd been dancing in his bedroom to songs he suddenly found heart-rendingly romantic or that otherwise reflected his sense of being violently alive, like 'Linger', 'Nothing Compares 2 U', 'Throw Your Arms Around

Me', 'With or Without You', 'Wish You Were Here', 'Beds Are Burning'. Even crappy and silly songs could make him a bit high. He was having more fun when he hung out with his nan, too, whom he was seeing more than ever for the blessing that she was. Thank Christ she had helped him escape Lithgow and turned out in general to be such good value, mellow and sturdy – really not an unpredictable temper-loser at all. Her intentions appeared to be simple and kind and they were matched by her actions. He was touched by so much innocence, her neatly arranged TV guide, elastic-waisted trousers in pastel colours, knickknacks on doilies, and the fact that since she'd taken him in, she'd switched with no fuss from the brands she bought before to No Name jam and bread and everything. She told him it was normal for teenagers to have hollow legs, encouraging him to dig into her tin of cheap chocolate biscuits, which in his opinion were at least as good as Mint Slices. These days, if they were watching one of her shows while they were having their tea, *Magnum P.I.*, *Columbo*, *Murder, She Wrote* or something like that, he laughed a lot at anything even a bit funny or unexpected. She kept saying, 'Someone's in a good mood.' And he beamed, grateful for all his luck, warm with wonderfulness, trying to imagine what Ada was doing and what being alive was feeling like to her in that moment.

'I get that. It's intense. And Ada *is* amazing.'

'Isn't she!'

'So you've felt this for a while?'

'Since the beginning, really, since we met her. I tried, but I couldn't let go of it. But I couldn't go to any more conversation classes because my Italian sucks. Then last week, she called me and she came to Nan's to see my paintings. I had the worst butterflies. I was shaking. But I didn't want her to leave. I need to be around her … Sometimes when I'm by myself, it's like she's possessing me. Does that sound mad?'

Heather said, 'No, it doesn't.'

She didn't say, *Mate, you're insane.* She didn't comment on the age difference (which he couldn't have cared less about). You could explain things to Heather, because she wanted the explanation and she felt her way inside it, like a person carefully entering a dark house. Which made you feel that your thoughts and feelings might have been worth understanding. She had been the first person to whom he could say stuff like, *I really love, when it's hot, that sort of haze that hangs over a road after it's rained.* And she would say, *Me too. And the smell of it!* Or, Robbie: *Can you believe how soft that light is, how slanted?* Heather: *It* is *unbelievable, isn't it? Really beautiful. And a bit sad.* Robbie: *Yeah, exactly.* Before meeting her, if he'd ever let himself make comments like these, people tended to look at him as if he were at best pretty fucking strange or at worst a total nutcase.

He'd even been able to mention a bit about his parents, just to her and just the bare outlines, which couldn't be filled in. She'd kept to his non-dramatic tone, nodding, and he'd seen in her face that she was getting it, gauging and recognising the weight of what stayed to one side of words. And she was ready for the words he had. He'd tried to convey that what comforts there had been had maybe made things harder, because he couldn't entirely reject and separate himself from it all. For example, sometimes a brave effort had been made and on payday the takeaway from the milk bar had brought merry feeling into the house: oily butcher paper spread open on the table, Tip Top bread thickly coated with margarine and the butties mouthwatering, pacifying dumb fun on the telly. With Heather, he didn't have to worry about appearing tough or cool. If it was just him and her, his stomach didn't have to be contracting with embarrassment or self-disgust. Somehow, simply, her attitude told him he was okay – not tainted, not insane. Reasonable, in fact. Apparently, it didn't cross her mind that his attachment to art was daydreamy and faggy in a bad way. Not only that, but she understood it was a calling. She did. She knew it was the path for him, sacred. Heather was precious.

Now she asked, 'She doesn't know, does she?'

'Well … we hugged in the kitchen before. Or I hugged her.'

'Hugged! Tonight!'

'I know. It was before Filippo said he'd take David and me home.'

'With us all in the next room?'

'Wild, hey? I couldn't stop myself.'

'What did she do? Did she hug you back?'

His exaltation was woven into the trippy mauve light against which the cedars were so black.

'I think so. Sort of. It seemed to go for a while.'

'Then what happened?'

'She said we couldn't … I mean, I guess it's possible that she didn't want to hurt my feelings …'

'Or she could feel the same.'

'Oh God, I don't know! What if she thinks I'm stupid and sex-crazy? I have to talk to her.'

'But you can't talk to her tonight because Filippo's here.'

'He was weird before. I didn't know if I should agree to the walking thing.'

'Italians can be pretty social, right?'

'I guess. And he could be pissed, despite what he said. After we got here, it was like he didn't want to go inside. He said he'd show me the lanterns in the garden, then he went off for a walk. I've been trying not to think about him. Thinking about him makes me feel sick.'

How could there be such a defect in something so transcendent?

'I could try to talk to her quickly before he comes back. And then leave as soon as I can tomorrow, right after the walk or whatever.'

'Be careful.'

He turned to look at her, only at her face. She smiled floppily. Sweet, cheap-drunk Heather, who valued him. Who would have thought he'd find this friend at the Year Seven Social, of all places, and during 'Time of My Life'? He could still see her vigilant eyes framed by crimped hair. Their meeting had been like accidentally wandering from the choked wood of Lithgow High into a sunlit glade.

'I'm so bloody nervous!' he said. 'If she tells me to get lost, I'll walk all the way home tonight.'

There was a bereft undulation in his chest and, before he could stand up to go, he had to put his hand over it and see Heather smile at him again.

*

In later years, Robbie would often remember Heather in the bathtub, smiling at him. He would also remember – but not until a significant portion of their lives had slipped by – David's demeanour as he'd said goodbye and climbed out of Filippo's car that night.

It would be an email exchange with David that provoked this memory and encouraged Robbie, at last, to fully like or perhaps trust him. David's tone in those messages would be timid and tentative, sad. The first one would mention finding Robbie's email address on his webpage and being impressed by the art shown there; the second that David's marriage had ended, that he was writing a book and moving back to Australia. Only in the third would he finally ask, confiding that he had wanted to do so for far too long, if Robbie had any news of Heather. If he knew what had happened to her; if he knew if she was well.

David's demeanour that night, or how Robbie recalled it after reading those emails: like he was still with them, but scarcely. Like a vital light in him was being extinguished.

10

CROWN STREET

Filippo, walking the bush path, felt the knife in his pocket. It was a good knife; he got a subtle satisfaction from slicing tomatoes with it. His mother had been an expert slicer of everything and he saw himself as a teenager in the doorway of her room, its closed salmon-pink curtains and sepia corners, her laid-out stillness during those depressions so corpse-like that her alert voice always took him aback. The inertia had seemed a sort of abandonment, faithlessness, a slight vulgarity, but now he felt something close to admiration for her, for getting through such periods, for not entirely succumbing to whatever low forces had been dragging at her.

He half slid down a decline and, at the same time, his memory slithered to the day in 1980 when his happiness with Ada had begun. It was inevitable.

A November afternoon, the weather getting muggier, clothing scantier, the city's sex drive ramping up just as the tensions of study were tightening in the lead-up to final exams and the year's end. In the air, there was the frenzied feeling of almost glimpsing time itself. His housemate, Genna, another disenchanted law student taking too long to finish her degree, had gone to work a shift at the Chauvel Cinema, leaving Filippo home alone, stressed and drained. Shortly after moving into their shared terrace in Surry Hills, he'd started suffering from insomnia. Funnily, this hadn't happened to him when he lived with his parents, as if then the role of insomniac had belonged indisputably to his mother. The traffic noise on Crown Street could be bad and his bedroom was at the front of the house. Garbage trucks woke him in the early hours as he was sinking into shallow unconsciousness. Nearly delirious from exhaustion, Filippo sensed a cruel pleasure taken in causing the brusque, brutal rain of glass bottles that left him painfully awake for hours. Sometimes he finally managed to doze again, his busy thinking continuing on a nearby track that he stepped back onto as soon as he was woken once more by the testy voices of drunks.

A reliable solace had ceased to be that: sleep had turned sinister. It was a surprising loss of control; it was learning to see and therefore fear a fundamental fragility he'd been oblivious to.

That warm afternoon, he was trying to memorise notes for a Torts exam and he had an ear infection coming on. He perceived a strange swollenness, his pulse vibrating in his skull and a kind of distant soughing. The study wasn't absorbing him; he was really only seeing the shapes of words, the sizes of margins and paragraphs, blue ballpoint ink on blue-lined white pages. Before he knew it, an unproductive day would have slipped through his fingers and another night of doubtful sleep would be upon him. This prospect filled him with dread. The only thing he could think of doing that might have improved his mental state – although his ear made it unadvisable – was to go for a jog.

The light in Centennial Park was peachy and drugging, the green of the treetops dusty-deep, and the smell of warm grass made him want to curl up in it and sleep endlessly. Running, he got sweaty fast, but eventually he forgot his ear being odd and found a kind of rhythm that lifted him at least briefly out of the ruts of his mind.

Back at home, he showered with the bathroom door open, which he liked doing when Genna was out. He never had in his childhood home, where his mother or one of his brothers was always around or about to unpredictably return. It gave him a sense of looseness, of vacationing inside a less inhibited person than himself. The bathroom grew steamy as he stood under the water (long showers, frowned upon by his parents, were now one of his few pleasures) and considered masturbating. He tried touching himself a little but couldn't suspend disbelief enough to engage with any fantasy, possibly on account of his ear that he was becoming conscious of again. He felt sexless and penned in.

He was rinsing away Genna's Wella Balsam when he heard movement in the house, maybe the sticky door being pushed open and steps coming down the creaky hallway. Genna wasn't due back for hours. Could it be Ada? She was the only other person with a key. Ada had been Genna's pen pal for years – part of Genna's Italian-learning project that hadn't really taken off, as indeed was Filippo – and now that she was visiting Australia, she stayed with them on and off around her travels to other parts of the country. Already back from Melbourne, was she? Annoyed to have his privacy disrupted right when he needed as much peace as possible for studying and attempting to sleep, he turned off the water and reached for his towel.

Hearing a bag tossed down and a tap running in the kitchen, which was adjacent to the bathroom, he quickly dried off behind the open door. He didn't have any clothes with him; he'd stripped out of his soiled running outfit in the kitchen.

'Genna?' he called, once he'd secured as best he could the smallish towel around his waist.

'*Sono Ada*,' she identified herself with her assertively tidy northern cadence.

'Oh,' he responded.

'The Great Ocean Road is breathtaking!' she said as if she were performing in a tourist advert, when he came out of the bathroom.

'So I hear.'

He wondered as he always did if she was finding his Italian less middle class than hers and coarsely Roman in ways he didn't know how to conceal. He smiled spasmodically, snatched his damp shorts and T-shirt from the chair where he'd draped them and hurried past her to the stairs; he was holding the edges of his towel together at his hip with one hand.

'I was just out running. Genna's at work. I'll go and get dressed.'

'I surprised you.'

She didn't sound apologetic. This was intriguing: Ada appeared incapable of finding her own presence awkward, of feeling guilty about it. In the blue skirt and white top in which she'd come back from Melbourne, she was a wisp of a thing but dignified. The dark hair that brushed her shoulders was satiny and her skin had been tanned into a more sombre shade than usual.

He wasn't at all drawn to socialising with her and definitely wasn't at that moment in a social mood. Yet it would have been rude to stay up in his bedroom after flashing by her half naked, so when he'd put on fresh shorts and T-shirt, he returned downstairs. The floor, he noticed grouchily, was gritty under his feet; it had been Genna's turn to do the floors. During the several weeks Ada had stayed with them, she hadn't done or offered to do any domestic chore and nor had she removed her long hairs from the bath plug. She had the relaxed, forgetful air of someone who'd lived with her doting family as if at a pleasant hotel.

She'd raised the blinds on the window that looked onto the poky concreted backyard (he preferred them down for the shade and cool) and made coffee in his *moka* pot. She probably wouldn't even empty and rinse that, though admittedly she'd filled one of the ritzy espresso cups she'd given Genna for him. Sugared, unfortunately. Her sandals were strewn on the floor in front of the sink and she was sitting on the sofa with her legs crossed under her in a carefree little-girl fashion.

She was one of those Italians with a capacity for ceaseless talk, seeming to think in the form of a rolling monologue, one word, one anecdote inexorably spawning the next. He was resentful listening to her delighted evocation of fancy-free adventuring and landscapes; it was too distant from his own unslept, bogged-down boredom and anxiety, his grey and fettered life. Ada had recently graduated from a degree in Art History, and as a gift her parents had funded her leisurely Australian voyage of discoveries.

He made minimal contributions, but listening and witnessing her enthusiasm somehow became, quite unexpectedly, a diversion. A respite. It was actually better to be borne for a while on the swell of her self-propagating Italian than to wearily converse with himself in his head. Italian was familiar, and unfamiliar, disassociated from his parents and their Leichhardt world. She asked him if he travelled much and he replied, 'Hardly at all.' She might have been surprised by how few words he offered, because she tried different conversation topics, movies, Malcolm Fraser; her evident sense of personal involvement in art and politics showed Filippo how detached he felt from almost everything. He was aware of her, the proper Italian, trying to get the measure of his abnormality. Italians liked to get a grip on your character, to be able to define and narrate you. Filippo's mother described him as *introverso*. Was that how Ada would think of him, too?

It slowly occurred to him that if she wasn't exactly or consciously flirting, there was nonetheless – in her seeking points of connection or argument, a way to unlock him – an exploratory patience. The impulse driving her might have been impersonal, a hunger for Italian-language companionship, a traveller's loneliness, but still or even because of that, he abruptly found the situation erotic. He noted how amazed he was at the idea that the striking Ada might be attracted to him. Outside of a couple of high-school non-events and a brief relationship with a fellow student in his second year of university that had left him feeling humiliated (suspecting, when she chucked him, that he'd been judged an inexperienced, disappointing lover, no Don Giovanni), he'd seldom felt that women were interested in him.

'I don't want to leave. I think I'd like to try staying here, living in Australia.'

'Would you?'

Music started up next door, behind the wall the sofa leaned against, and as if this was his cue, Filippo made a move. Subtly enough, to start with, that it could have been easily brushed aside and he might have pretended it had been a misunderstanding. He touched Ada's knee. Three fingertips on the knee beneath the thin skirt. He had an impression of lowering to the floor a heavy weight he'd been carrying.

She gave him an entertained half-smile, which he took to mean: How accustomed I am to male attention and how long this has taken you. Are you even really Italian? She leaned back like she was preparing to better observe the spectacle of him and his next actions that would finally explain him.

Encouraged and piqued, he shifted his fingers to the skirt's hem, went under it back to that thin knee and, hand flexed as if to smooth out creases in fabric, slowly up along her remarkably soft thigh.

They considered one another in the late light coursing in where she'd raised the blinds and he felt stunned, felt a little pressure in his ear but not unpleasantly – it was simply a facet of his receptiveness, his deep concentration. He tilted his head and the whispery whooshing sound was like a seashell against his ear and so was she, an arcane melody. He went on lifting her skirt till he saw darkness beneath white cotton. He was breathing unevenly, but she appeared to be agreeing to whatever gratification he could provide.

'Here?' she asked.

'Yes, here.'

'Do you have a condom?'

'I'll get one in a minute.'

Genna's box was in the cupboard under the bathroom sink.

She unfolded her legs and lifted her hips so he could take off her underpants. Her serenity and hedonism truly astounded him.

He left her alone. He even took the time to carry their cups with residual sugar in the bottoms of them to the kitchen and, passing the window, to lower the blinds with a violent clatter. He found a condom quickly, thankfully. The expiry date was still far off; those futuristic numbers seemed an undecipherable message.

He returned to her.

'You don't like sun?' she asked.

'Not when it's hot. Not in my face.'

'What kind of Australian are you? Or Italian, for that matter?'

'Good questions. Maybe I'm neither. I'm nothing.'

In the restored dimness, her skin made him think of leatherwood honey. His heart was hurtling hysterically, but it was as if the frontier between them was suddenly porous, her naturalness passing across it into his movements, which grew as smooth as those of someone else. Gripping her fine ankle, he had a vision of the fragile bones of a spatchcock and the half-appalled intuition that bits of her would snap easily. He tried to breathe before he kissed the inside of her thigh with closed lips, establishing contact, and then opening his mouth.

The taste of her was fascinating, lightly flavoursome, sweet and savoury. He hadn't gone down much on the girl who'd left him, largely out of nervousness; doing so he'd felt very unsure that he was doing what she wanted, how she wanted, and a little like he was ticking a box in order to move on to more straightforwardly pleasurable business. Now he wasn't rushing or particularly self-judging and his arousal was mixed with his interest in her mysterious enjoyment. Like her confidence, her pleasure somehow flowed into his. Even the expression *going down* was making a nice kind of sense: he'd sunk way below the level of ordinary communication and he wasn't lonely because he could gauge his influence over Ada's contracting muscles, heart rate and thinking. The honesty of it and his power to please were such rare things, the excitement they gave him richer than any he'd felt sexually.

She wasn't vocal. Her thighs started shuddering – he couldn't have said after how long – and she locked them around him, saying, 'Stop. Come up here.'

She kissed him for the first time when he was lying over her and faintly wondering if they'd roll off the sofa and if he was crushing her. It was all extreme and enfolding. He fancied he felt her streamlined mind from the inside, her clear, clean self-regard; he'd never before had the impression of blurring into another person and her superior manner of being. Her breathing turned frantic before she came, triggering the jolt of his own end, which felt so longed for and shatteringly conclusive.

The neighbour's music stopped. He had recognised the last song without remembering its name, something about the heart and the wind. The trucks changing gears on Cleveland Street had become a murmur. Anything beyond Filippo and Ada together was of a laughably lesser order, barely existing. She chuckled. He did too, almost alarmed by the sounds he'd made that weren't really distinguishable from sounds of suffering. Suffering muffled and slowed.

11

SHIPLEY ROAD

He returned to the house via the road, taking in the absence of the car. He felt no better. If anything, more disconsolate for having let himself recall the beginning of his best years. What did the car being gone mean? Ada had to be driving the boy home.

He walked through the house. Empty, yes. That she hadn't wanted Robbie to stay over, not with Filippo around, was an extra if unnecessary confirmation of guilt. There was a perfume bottle on their bed; uncapping and bringing it to his nose, he discovered the scent she'd been wearing every day. He couldn't endure this. His face was moist.

They were tears and he got them under control, but he couldn't wait in the faux tranquillity of the house, picturing her and the boy in the car. They were talking, or perhaps they weren't.

Filippo stood on the verandah in the coloured lantern light. The blue one by the fountain had burned itself out; he could still intermittently make out a violet luminescence beyond the cedars, near the spot he'd considered with idiotic sentimentality as the garden's heart.

Stepping down from the verandah, he went over a little on his ankle, reeling like a drunkard, regaining his balance and then drifting towards that place. A long time ago, when he arrived home from work on certain summer evenings, Ada would be bathing there. He might have been feeling tired, somewhat dispirited and city-grimy, yet he was also proud to be returning to her from a day of earning well, from a dull world he abandoned by amusingly telling her about it. He liked to strip off immediately and get in at the tap end to wash off the superficiality and let her regard him for a few minutes in her aristocratic way before he undid such haughtiness. Back when her skin was his freely given treat.

It wasn't Ada in the bath now.

'Heather?'

She sat up jerkily, sploshing water out of the tub and covering her chest with her arms.

In that funny light the girl was an uncommon thing, a night-blooming flower of youth. He felt soreness or instability in his ankle and the stingy itch of a nick he must have inflicted on his thumb.

'Sorry to scare you.' He chose Italian because he'd been speaking that language to Ada in his head.

'That's okay.' She attempted to recover her equilibrium. 'It's your garden.'

He smirked with a sort of crooked hilarity. 'Yes.'

'Ada said I could use this. What a bath.'

'Do you like it? The others are out – Ada must be driving Robbie home.'

'Oh, right.'

Would she know what was happening between his wife and her friend? He sat down on one of the smooth stones by the bath.

'Do you mind if I stay here for a bit? I'll look … that way …' He stared at the scrubby extremity of the garden, which was fully black, making him feel blind.

'No, that's fine,' she said uncertainly.

He heard water moving.

'You know, your Italian is excellent.'

'I make mistakes, and my vocabulary is pretty limited.'

His comment had given her an embarrassed pleasure.

'I'm not hearing any mistakes. Don't think about those, anyway. If you do, you're paralysed. Why do we need to be perfect?'

He saw from the corner of his eye that her arms remained folded across her chest.

'*This* is perfect, your garden. Absolutely. Paradise.'

'Well, thank you. I thought so. When we first moved up here, I'd get off the train after a day in town and hardly be able to believe how clean the air was – like air from the start of time. I especially loved the mist. I wanted to eat it.' Dejection was making him queasy and killing his capacity for rational conversation, rational anything. Befuddled, he continued, 'You love things that you want badly. You can't resist believing in their purity.' He rubbed his hands together, an odd gesture in the warm air. 'Do you want more hot water?'

'No, I'm fine. Thanks.'

Oh, when would Ada be back? She seemed to have been gone forever.

'You're a fabulous cook,' the girl said, clearly battling to make conversation.

He'd worked diligently on the meal and didn't want to be reminded of it. 'Really, listen to you – you must have been Italian in a past life!'

He genuinely wasn't used to encountering Anglos with a crush on his first language matched by any real fluidity, ear or sensitivity to the balancing acts of grammar. She was more of a natural than the boys. Or more of a scholar, or both. When she made a sound suggesting discomfort with compliments, he turned to look at her openly.

'And you're beautiful. Sorry.'

Why apologise? The apology unsettled him, and her also – she'd brought her knees to her chest.

'I won't sleep tonight,' he went on quickly.

'Oh. No?'

She was maintaining her politeness, her good-guest role. It was rather tragic how vulnerable trying to be nice made you.

'I should probably go inside,' she said.

'Why don't I turn around, you can get out, get dressed, and we'll just keep each other company for a bit?'

'Actually, I might go to bed.' Her voice was slightly mechanical now, fitting his mood.

'That's what you want?' She was gazing down into the tub. 'You don't like me at all? You don't have a boyfriend, do you? Obviously, lots of boys … David … Don't tell me you're in love?'

His muddle silenced her for a moment, but then she said, clearly, 'Could you please turn around?'

He stood. 'Why don't I help you dry off? I don't think Ada would even mind. I mean, she does what she wants, doesn't she? Have you noticed that Ada and Robbie are the same type of person? For them life is so … light.'

'Oh? I don't think life is light to Robbie. I'd have said the opposite.'

She was getting worried. She was an anxious person, in any case, folded and tied up in herself; he recognised this. He himself, before Ada, had been awfully constrained by – fear of what exactly? What judgements? Rejections, harshness? Was it really all down to the babyish fear of not being loved? Enough, in the right ways, deeply, truly?

Stepping out of the bath, she reached for a towel behind which she sought to hide.

'As it happens, I was very timid at your age. Naturally …' But where had he been going with that?

He approached her and brushed his knuckles from her dry shoulder and, beneath the towel, down her ribs to her wet, warm flank.

A sharp, barely audible noise in the back of her throat. The towel trailed on the ground. 'Don't …'

Something like a tussle, a tackle, a tumble, with a hint of Ada's perfume. It was a relief to think less. You could do the unthinkable with so little thinking: you were just doing it.

The linguist had ceased speaking. Her inconceivable skin was water-plumped, her breathing frayed. She was suffocating on silence like a fish on air; he too was breathing hard. It was necessary to go far inside her, as far as it was possible to go outside of himself.

But nothing eased his way. It frustrated him to fumble and push, realising she was probably a virgin. Holding her tightly, he managed to turn her over. She remained rigid, yet it appeared to him at this point that she had somehow vacated herself. She had gone so quiet that he was hardly sure she was breathing; she was a deserted white road. He tried a caress that couldn't be completed. An unbearable fact he'd always suspected was being verified.

He became angrier and more controlled. He spat into his hand, smelling his own sweat, the reek of a victim or a perpetrator. Of one animal, an utterly discrete unit, overriding another. He was aware of pain, drawn to it, addicted. There was no give and no sense of occupation. There was a savage simplification, reduction, narrowing. It went fast, without a giddy expansion of feeling towards fullness and release. An ending crashed backwards into him, down on him, his whimper the reaction to a short-circuiting. It was the same as with the rest of life: the pleasure already over before you understood that you hadn't fully felt it.

Some time later, the girl was rising onto her hands and knees. Slowly standing. He was in a crouch, a distance back from her, trying not to notice the hair spilling from a lopsided topknot, the pale nakedness he'd used.

She found her clothes, dressed, fled.

He stood, woozily thinking he might pass out, might prefer to. Strange rough sensations certainly seemed to suggest he was sick, as did the recurrent vision of Ada in the arms of a perfect boy. He was dripping down his thigh towards the jeans only just lowered, perhaps bloodied. He pulled off his clothes, picked up the knife that had fallen from his pocket and took it with him like a companion into the bath. He supposed the water was cold; it was soothing or intolerable, hard to tell, as if water were new to him, a new language. He submerged himself to his chin, fondling the slick knife.

This was not his garden. The light was on in the guest room of what had been their house.

Cedars, a fading purple lantern, coarse bush, night air dense with cicada droning. He thought of those jettisoned exoskeletons that had astonished him as a child. The plain evidence of transformation, so filmy and crushable.

12

It wasn't entirely unexpected. Very young, Heather had detected the possibility of it. At the sour threshold of pubs, in stagnant or restless city and suburban streets and parks, slack time at railway stations and on trains, in tunnels, anywhere almost empty without an easy, immediate exit. The looks and stances of certain men alone and in groups suggested it or didn't rule it out.

But the night she bathed under the stars in Ada's idyllic garden, this had slipped her mind. There was a sense (was this what you felt the day your death came into clear view?) of: Oh, now I see how it will go. Not that there was any accepting or recognising herself in the knowledge. Only a letting go of recognition.

When she understood that fending him off was wasted energy, he was pure downward pressure, she withdrew from room to room, turning off lights. Leaving him on the dark, abandoned edge, where sometimes pain was a crushed ribcage, a twisted wrist, a forcing, jabs; and sometimes it was duller, an angry heat.

She thought, Let no one ever find out. As if the abasement and shame were hers. As if all she'd ever want after this would be silent control, the most complete solitude.

She'd collided with thorns and petals, a rosebush. She tried to focus on the nauseating scent that should have been beautiful, holding on to what she could, asking herself how long and was it nearly over and wasn't it already over. Like a kid would keep asking if she was there yet when obviously she wasn't, the question just to give a beat to anxiety, hypnotise herself into not noticing that time was so nonsensical.

*

Time would remain confusing, after that night. There would be jump cuts, rewinding, suspension, spiralling, sleeplessness undoing days. And many years in which she would not speak Italian, refusing to fall back into that Heather, too terribly undefended.

But there would be rituals that would help her to redesign time and make it, if only transiently, her own: reading, study, jobs, French, more study, big walks, all of those laps she swam; the friendship with Robbie that, following an interruption, she sought out again.

Skyping with him one morning, Heather would shock herself by beginning to speak of it.

Beforehand, they discussed his painting and her graduation. He asked, 'So how do you feel?'

A shrug. 'I can't believe it took me so long to finish.'

Behind him, an open window, Adriatic light.

'Now was evidently the right time.'

'I guess … All that light in your room!'

'Yeah', he said, 'I'm addicted to it – that's why I can't stop coming here.'

'I know.'

His hand passed across his forehead. She smiled at him.

And, after beginning to speak of it, she saw – across time zones and a video stream that froze for a couple of seconds or seemed to – that he was taking it in. He was wanting her to understand she was precious to him.

She almost said something in Italian, then.

13

GOVETTS LEAP

Having left tipsy Heather in her bath, Robbie made his way back to the house, pulsating with trepidation. He didn't know how to approach Ada and he prayed that Filippo wouldn't come home too soon; this was all so unbelievable and fragile and it had probably been a mistake to accept the invitation to return. He decided to enter the house by the front door, so as not to startle Ada.

But then he saw her – sitting on the bench by the door. She started.

'I thought … Filippo didn't take you home?'

She'd spoken in English, as she had when she came to see his paintings. Her accent, like the scent of flowers in her garden, went from light to thick.

'No. He said I should come back here and stay over.'

He was seeing a lot of fear in her, he thought, and he wanted that to disappear. She *did* like him, didn't she?

Physically, at least, yes. In the kitchen, her body had turned soft and attentive.

Her voice dropping, 'And where is he?'

'Gone for a walk.'

'You can't stay here. You shouldn't be here, don't you understand? What happened …'

'I know, I know,' he said, relieved that they were acknowledging what was going on.

She stood. 'I'm married and you're a boy.'

'I'm not – I told you I'm almost nineteen.'

'I could still be your mother.'

'No, you couldn't.'

'I could.'

'Well, so what? You're not.'

She avoided looking at him, her hands on her hips. Then she said, 'I'll drive you home.'

'Ada …' he began but didn't know how to continue. He was terrified even to have spoken her name, which sounded like an admission.

'Don't say anything. Come on, let's go.'

'What will you tell him?'

'I'll say you changed your mind, you wanted to go home. Wait, I'll get my keys.'

She went into the house and seemed to spring back out of it almost at once. She opened the driver's door but paused.

'I drank quite a lot of wine,' she said. 'I don't normally.'

'I can drive.'

'*Can* you drive?'

'I've had my licence for two years. I drive my nan's car, remember?'

She was hesitating. 'You drank too.'

'Not that much.'

She appeared to accept his offer because she saw no alternative to it. 'Okay.'

His seatbelt had already clicked on when it occurred to him to mention, 'I can get us to my place, no worries, but then you still have to get yourself back here after, don't you?'

'I'm crazy,' she said, clearly not having thought of that. 'Oh, I'll manage.'

'You're sure?'

'Yes, please just go.'

It was a Volvo, for Christ's sake. The car moved with great smoothness and smelled intoxicatingly of leather and her perfume. While he was driving, though every so often he was aware of the shaky beat of his heart, something in him slowed down. He adored being with her in the car; it was like slipping into a life of shared intimate spaces. As they waited at the railway crossing, the gate blocking access to the tracks was piercingly white. Everything was in sharp focus, barrelling into his eyes, into all his senses.

Later, when he should have turned right, he didn't. Neither of them commented on this as he continued on and eventually glided down into the dip of Govetts Leap Road. Muted light pulsed in an occasional late-night-TV house. Pine-rich air was coming off Parklands and through his open window.

With a delay of minutes, she asked mildly, 'Robbie, but what are you doing? *Ma che fai?*' His language and then hers.

'I thought we could go to Govetts Leap?'

Sitting very straight, she didn't answer.

He parked not far from the lookout, by a clump of trees, and she got out before he did, slamming the door. He caught up with her in front of the view, masses and shades of darkness in the night fresh with eucalypt vapour. There was that brimming quiet of the bush, a sense of the usual tight frame having been taken away to leave room for spreading dense whorls, for changing the way you see.

Excruciatingly shy all of a sudden, he said, 'It seems so spongy – like if you walked over the treetops they'd feel like carpet.'

'You shouldn't have come back to the house,' she said. 'This is dangerous.'

'I know and I'm really sorry about Filippo. I really don't want to make life hard for you.' He swallowed, sobered, revolted by the possibility of causing her pain, of her ever feeling any pain. 'Not at all. I'll do whatever you want me to do. But I have to tell you that I think about you *all* the time! I want to be *with* you. I worship you.' He was bewildered. 'Tell me what to do.'

Was he talking like a child? He was devastated, because if she told him to stay away from her, he'd obey. He'd try to; he'd have to.

After a while, she said, 'I think about you, too.'

The whiplash of euphoria. He wouldn't be able to bear not touching her for much longer. However, her body language remained defensive and he was as stupidly nervous as if he'd never even kissed a girl before and he might stuff it up, be ridiculous or repellent and get his heart broken.

He'd been with quite a few girls. He knew how many, more or less. But the details of most of those encounters were pretty fuzzy (partly, perhaps, because of the drugs involved). And most of the ones he recalled best had been awkward, a bit of a letdown or depressing. Only a couple had been fun or appeared that way in retrospect, lending themselves to being reworked in fantasies of a fairly automatic kind. Not one of those girls had remotely affected him as Ada did, and he and Ada had hardly touched. He had wondered how many men *she* had been with. More out of an interest in her mind than jealousy. He hoped she hadn't had any nasty experiences with bastards or experiences (don't picture them) that had made her unhappy. He cared for her so much that he wanted her to have had a nice time in bed with other men! Yet it wasn't easy for him to think of her lovers as significant and cherished, the sex slow, deep-eyed, hand-holdy, confidential, adventurous. Don't see any of that. Don't. And one of her lovers had obviously been – obviously *was* – her husband.

She glanced sideways at him. They were looking at each other grimly. Then she turned back to the view.

Attempting to focus, he said, 'I get the feeling you're like me, at least in some ways.'

He didn't know what exactly he meant by this. He also thought that underneath her posh social polish, she'd been waiting – mainly without satisfaction – to be moved.

She made a sound suggesting ambivalence, and maybe tears.

'Please don't cry.'

'You watch people.'

'Not that well. I get distracted, I can't do portraits … But you, yes. How could anyone not watch you?'

'Usually, people watch enough to judge. They see I'm a bit strange, foreign. Some notice me sexually. And that's all. I don't think anyone's ever watched me like you do.'

He inched towards her a little with a feeling of having to choose gestures that wouldn't be erasable. And the fear that a misstep would make everything dissolve. He'd taken the initiative in the kitchen, and if something else was going to happen, he wanted it to be her doing and only if it was going to make her happy. He wondered absurdly if his painful erection was visible. How much better it would be to have your craving tucked tidily away like a woman's, or at least be able to black it out with willpower.

Here was the signal: she rested her hand on his forearm and suddenly seemed to be saying, Come to me.

He moved his thumb over her palm and, when they turned towards one another, put her hand over his heart so she could feel the knocking. Did she understand this? Hyperalert, he smelled her classy perfume and even shampoo. He was realising that until then he'd been rather glazed with girls; his so-called experience had been thin and bloodless.

She kissed him softly, the curtain going up on her desire. Difficult as it was, he tried to barely respond – to better observe her coming at him. Spellbinding. She paused and it appeared that tension was leaking out of her or changing. He breathed in, awash with emotion, and then the kissing turned deep, rapturous.

Somehow, they got back to the car. God, this was *happening* and not just in his head. Was this place too public? Would the trees he had parked against screen them, if someone came along? But he couldn't trouble himself with these matters, because she had unbuttoned her shirt. And she was lowering the zipper at the side of her pants and bending at the waist, as she did so, to peel them down. She was opulent.

'I must seem old to you.'

He laughed: her age couldn't have been further from his mind. 'You're the most beautiful woman I've ever seen. In every way.'

Now she laughed.

'Oh no,' he said. 'I don't have anything on me – do you?'

'Huh?'

'Ah … a condom.'

'I take the pill.'

'Oh. Good.'

Her hands under his shirt, her lips on his throat, her skin, any control leaving. He lifted her; she was small but muscular. When he lowered her onto the bonnet, he was surprised by the strength in her tensed thighs. He felt like crying.

She was lusciously slippery. He'd never had sex without a condom before and there was such an ease to it, a cradled closeness. He could scarcely believe that pleasure so deluxe, fine-grained, overflowing, existed outside of art, existed at all. Please let her be feeling this, he thought. At least some of this wild joy, and please let me last for a while. Let me give her pleasure. Amazingly, he wasn't charging into blind inwardness as he might have expected; he wasn't losing a vivid sense of Ada. His hands were full of her touchingly tiny wrists and shoulders, her thrillingly strong buttocks and thighs. He was half lost in the dizzy angles of her face, the sweet blur of their kisses. In the radiant dark, he saw with the realest part of himself.

They shouldn't and couldn't have prevented it, because their hearts and bodies were supposed to join. The only pale comparison to this was certain rare paintings or songs that, once you'd seen or heard them, you couldn't imagine not being in the world as they were so complete, themselves and right. Before they were in the world, they were just waiting off-stage, and to experience them was to recognise them and to have sheer beauty make the wire of you turn forgiving, liquefy. Being with Ada was like that: time-smudging, time-stretching. He wanted it to last forever and it was already a kind of forever because there was nothing now that he wanted more than being alive next to her, no other place that he wanted to be. He felt so much, surely as much as it was possible to feel, which softened all the dark thoughts. What had come before this or would follow, any awfulness or sleaze shrank back towards the vanishing point, leaving him and Ada in the foreground. In this blissful clarity and softness. This love. Art, love.

II

THE INNER WEST

1962–1993

14

VICTORIA PARK

1993

Jan said to the therapist, 'Often in November, around the eleventh, I think about that day, that year. Not only in November. I dream of it, too, sometimes. Not like before, not often. But it does keep coming back.'

'And what do you feel when you wake up from those dreams?'

'Oh God. Doom …' She laughed. 'Sadness, some kind of regret, I think. Well, everything came apart after that. I mean, obviously it was all very fragile before that. But in a way that was the start of the real chaos.'

Instead of looking at the therapist, who seemed to be paying discreet attention, Jan stared out of the large window beside her armchair. The upper segment was leadlight diamonds of dark blue and green, and through the lower transparent one she made out a closely pruned hedge.

She went on, 'But it's funny, because even so, I find myself missing Glebe. The Glebe of back then. I wake up nostalgic.'

'You mentioned regret. Do you think you could have somehow acted differently?'

'Maybe.'

'How so?'

'I don't know exactly – but in the dreams, I feel too passive. Of course, dreams can be like that, can't they? Something carrying you that you can't control.'

'Do you want to talk about that day? Or what you feel nostalgic about?'

'Gosh, where would I start?'

'Anywhere.'

The therapist was trying not to spook her, leaving things as open as possible, trying to gain her confidence. The office smelled of some herbal essential oil; Jan wasn't sure what kind. Outside in the early evening, the hedge was turning into its silhouette.

'You could start with the first thing you remember, for example. Or the first thing you remember from the dreams.'

'Oh … Glen slamming the door.'

'He was angry?'

'Probably. But listen, I don't feel like talking about him.'

Jan had never been a stroppy person; on the contrary, her manner was generally unobtrusive, even submissive. Yet for some reason, she quite enjoyed the novelty of being petulant with the therapist.

'What *would*' – the word was lightly emphasised – 'you like to talk about?'

'Alicia and Lorna. I've been thinking about Lorna much more than I used to, trying to imagine how things were for her.'

'Why do you think that might be?'

'I don't know if it's because I'm getting close to the age she was then. Or if I was just too scared before – of imagining what she went through. I feel guilty for that.'

'Guilty? You've used that word before.'

Jan smiled. There was a pause.

'And you've been remembering Alicia a lot, too?'

'Yes, but I always have.'

'You miss her?'

'Yes.'

'Would you like to tell me about how you and she met?'

'It was at the end of our first year of uni.'

*

1974

They have been sitting in Malouf's final English lecture, to either side of a boy of whom Jan will not later recall much beyond his apparent boredom.

When they pack away their notebooks and stand up from their desks, he becomes livelier and asks, 'Where do you live?'

Jan is surprised by the question and even more by the fact that he has picked her to flirt with, instead of the black-haired girl in a forest-green shirt to his left.

'Glebe.'

'Oh? And where did you go to school?'

She supposes he is the kind of person who orients himself with stuff like that. 'Outside of Sydney.'

She would prefer to leave it there, but unfortunately he wants more information. The other girl is listening. Jan has noticed her before in lectures and once at Fisher Library. She carts around a folky string bag with books protruding from it that looks to be a burden for her long, slight body. Her nose is forceful, a little hooked, and her mouth large. Jan has the impression that her gaze is meticulous, maybe unforgiving. The ultra-black hair, always plaited, nearly reaches her waist. None of this, yet something about her – her seriousness, a certain air of drama? – reminds Jan of her favourite English teacher from high school, Mrs Forsythe.

'Boarding school?' the boy insists.

Quickly, she replies, 'Merrylands High School.'

He has to fumble with the rarely used pages of an internal atlas. The Western Suburbs, surely not.

'What on earth were you doing in Merrylands? That's poor.'

And he's from – Mosman? Woollahra? Later, she will be almost positive he really added, *That's poor.* But absolutely sure this is what he meant. Since the beginning of university, she has been aware of being among private-school, North Shore types. She knows she is smart enough to be where she is, that her marks got her there and keep her there, but she has to remind herself of this. The boy's reaction shouldn't be any shock. Well, she isn't the one to deny that Merrylands isn't a posh area. But he'd assumed he'd never chat up someone from such a hole and this fact is humiliating.

Just then, the girl that reminds her of Mrs Forsythe asks, 'Come for a drink to the Lansdowne?'

The boy's exclusion from the invitation is clear.

Jan nods.

'Good, let's go.' She offers her a paper bag. 'Chocolate frog?'

Jan takes one and eats it as they amble through the Anglophile peace of the Main Quad, where the jacaranda is in luminous bloom, the ground beneath it mauvish blue with fallen blossoms. Out of the corner of her eye, the tree appears to hang above its reflection in a still lake. The sudden beauty and the childish sweetness filling her mouth give her an urge to laugh.

In the green wedge of Victoria Park, a dishevelled Ibis stands on a garbage bin, ransacking.

'Janet, what are you studying, besides English?'

'Social work. You?'

'Psychology.'

They pass the swimming pool, where Jan does her laps three or four times a week and the chlorine on the air makes her half close her eyes for a moment and breathe more deeply. Seeing herself diving in, sliding through the bright, trembling surface into cool fake blue, shedding her weight.

'I swim there,' she says timidly.

'Oh? I'm not much of a swimmer, but I can walk forever. We should go for a big walk together, one day. I'm Alicia, by the way.'

'How big is a big walk?'

'For example, we could bus it to Leichhardt, have a coffee at Bar Italia, go from there, head down Norton Street, then all the way along Parramatta Road and on into the city. Something like that?'

'That'd be nice.'

Jan is thinking, She knew my name. Since she was small, almost everyone has called her Jan, which is blunt, ugly and Westie. The way Alicia says it is pretty and respectful.

Alicia goes on, 'Imagine what it was like when these roads were Aboriginal walking trails, and around those there were just trees, rainforest.'

No one has talked to Jan quite like this before. She grew up among people who casually said 'Abo'. Her father tells a story about walking unknowingly down a street near Redfern Station and suddenly realising that for the first time in his life he was surrounded by Aboriginal people and therefore in a scrape, when to his great good luck some policemen arrived just in time. There with Alicia, Jan has a dizzying sense of expansion, of something within her becoming more elastic, elongating. How extraordinary are the vast, old Moreton Bay figs they walk under, their spreading crowns, rhinoceros-hide trunks and scent of warm leaves and shed fruit. Even the smog from cars and buses hurrying or halting along the edges of the park is inebriating. Jan gets a version of the old tingle from when she was little on the train and hearing the announcement: *Next stop: Central.* The nervous joy of arriving in Sydney, at long last.

15

CALLAN PARK
10 November 1975

Lorna has taken her medication with a cup of not-great tea, hoping it's for the last time on both counts. You've got to get them thinking you're harmless, that you've pretty much carked it. So she potters around in her nightie all sleepy, or sits on the side of her bed, trying to keep her feet in whatever sunshine sneaks in through the barred window. She is picturing the river that isn't far away. Greenish brown, like Claude's eyes. It reassures and taunts her to know it's there, flowing water the colour of his eyes. Imagine being on a ferry gliding away down that river, bound for the sea.

She loses track of her handbag and gets scared, because you really can't trust any of that lot – but there it is on her bedside table. Phew. Good. You're okay. She is attached to her handbag, her one bit of turf in this place. It's leatherette, a pale green she is fond of, and inside it are her smokes, her cards, her wallet containing her Communist Party of Australia Member's Card and a photo of tanned baby Glen in a sailor's suit. In those days, the little bloke's legs were that fat they used to stop her in the street to ask, 'What der yer feed 'im?' And she was so smitten with his very flesh, showing it off as proof that she could have a hand in perfection.

She takes out her deck to settle herself down, shuffling properly, like she's showing her opponents at an RSL-club poker match her style. But for now, just a hand or two of Patience. She realises she is rocking back and forth, like she might think, I'm singing that bloody song again. Forcing herself to stop, she pushes her teeth back in and stands up to get ready for lunch. Something important is coming and she is damn well going to dress for it.

She wishes she still had that blue suit she wore to go away in, and the matching hat with the veil, which made her feel so Grace Kelly when they got to Lightning Ridge, but of course you lose things over the years. Anyhow, slacks are probably a better choice now than a skirt. It's always a shame not to be showing her excellent legs, but there'll be time for that, won't there? She'll have to content herself with a nice-enough blouse that won't draw too much attention. She tucks a cardigan through the strap of her handbag and, right when she is about to leave the room, his message arrives.

The sirens.

Distant, but coming closer, closer. Then receding, but leaving a bright trail.

Pleasure breaks over her like a thumping wave: knocks and rolls through her and goes on fizzing. She walks to the dining room as tall as a person who knows she is in love with someone who is in love with her.

A tin of smoked mussels on toast would have gone down a real treat. She'd have been tickled with that. Or with her corned beef and white sauce and silver beet, or her roast chook stuffed with breadcrumbs. She'd have started with the parson's nose, the lovely, juicy fat around that dinky bone. With a beer on the side. Or a shandy, say.

Instead, what they get is those curried sausages with the sultanas that wedge themselves in her dentures. She'll eat what she's given, will polish off the lot, but she doesn't see the point of having the sweet and savoury together, not if you're going to do both things badly. And you wouldn't call that rice hot. Mean little portion, too, like for a kid with no appetite to speak of. She hates these plastic trays that the kiddie servings are lined up on – inmates' trays. It's not that she isn't familiar with not having enough or good enough to eat. Well, there was Hammondville, wasn't there? Where you were bloody grateful to get bread and dripping, and actually there was nothing wrong with that. Pop on a bit of salt and pepper and it was delicious. She'd got picked out, with a few of the other kids living on the estate, for looking malnourished. That's what the church people reckoned and they organised a holiday, to feed them up. The problem with a holiday like that is the holiday part – the not lasting – and afterwards, well you know what they meant by malnourished, don't you? And you've seen that houses don't always have floors made of dirt. It's possible to live in airy, shiny, clean places where there is plenty to go around and people are nice to each other, even if it's sort of pretend. What she has to do is take herself on a holiday that will never bloody end.

She goes into the TV room and – surprise, surprise – nothing decent on. The telly is like the window of a bus, with dead-boring scenery drifting past. This is usually the situation when you really fancy a bit of quality – some ballerinas dancing 'Swan Lake' or one of Bill Collins's best choices for *The Golden Years of Hollywood*, like *Gone with the Wind*, *Casablanca*, *Rear Window*, something with Fred Astaire. In place of the good stuff, what you get is American soap operas, don't you? All of them talking a lot of rot and romance you couldn't be bothered believing in. Now everyone in here is asleep or nearly. She herself almost drops off, because she's tired enough. But at the same time, there's energy in her that's got nothing to do with being tired or not. A kind of power.

She mutters, for her own benefit, 'I'm off for a smoke. Where are me fags?' And she heads out into the corridor.

At the end of it, there is a sight she hadn't expected. Or had she? Something funny on the lino, like some poor thing pissed herself – but the stain is glowing. Because it's light, really, not a stain at all. It's an open door and she has, in fact, dressed for that.

16

THE LANSDOWNE

'You were telling me that you and Alicia went for a drink together, the day you met?'

The therapist was a compact, strong-looking woman, probably slightly older than Jan, but not by much.

'Right.'

'So that was the start of your friendship?'

'Yes, it was. Alicia just sort of took for granted that we'd become friends. I thought she must have been very outgoing.'

'More than you?'

'Much more.'

'Did you make any other close friends at university?'

She shook her head.

'And why not, do you think?'

'Oh, who can say? I was married. And there was the class thing, the coming from the Western Suburbs and often being broke. And just chance? I should say that even before uni, I wasn't much of a social type. I did have a couple of girlfriends, but outside of school we didn't spend all that much time together. They liked going to the beach and I occasionally went with them, but I wasn't a sunbaker like they were. The ocean scared me a bit. I was comfortable with swimming laps in pools. Plus, I got burned easily and I didn't like being watched by the boys. Another thing that embarrassed me was that I did better at school than they did. When we were younger, I could tell they thought I was a bit abnormal, but it didn't seem to matter so much. I used to let them copy my homework sometimes, or my answers in exams. But around the middle of high school, the difference in the marks we got started to be more obvious, and I felt more abnormal and somehow guilty, and often I tried not to answer questions during lessons and not to seem like a know-it-all. Anyway, after Glen and I got together, those friendships more or less ended.

'Thinking about it, I suppose my parents were also pretty far from being socially outgoing. Not that I mean to blame them …'

She turned from the dusk through the window to the therapist and smiled vaguely. The therapist smiled vaguely back.

She continued, 'But they hardly had any friends, almost none beyond family. And I remember that often when relatives would "call around", as they said, uninvited, my mother would hear the car pulling into our driveway and give me this look of dread. She'd say, "Oh no! I wish I could pretend I wasn't here." I should say that some of our relatives would sort of colonise your house for hours. You'd offer them tea or coffee, and then more, and be worried that they'd want to be asked to stay on for a meal and you might not have enough to go around. Anyway, I learned that dread of my mother's, I think. Learned that it was more restful to be alone.'

'And with Alicia, could you relax with her?'

'I wouldn't say that.'

Not even in the present moment was it easy for her to let herself go against the headrest of the armchair that had the faintly animal texture of felt.

*

Alicia has been trying to push through Jan's silence. But talking is a difficult task, Jan's face tight, her jaw frozen from how much she wants the other girl to like her. She hasn't been in pubs much and before this it was almost always in a ladies' lounge. She can only stare at the carpet beneath her chair, as if waiting for her focus to adjust and allow her to make sense of its patterns. Smells of beer, damp closed rooms and age; the air in here is both languid and disquieting.

Eventually, Alicia asks, 'Have you read *The Second Sex*?'

Jan looks up. Mrs Forsythe lent it to her. The experience of reading it was one of the significant things to have happened to her. At least, she suspects it will have been, once some of the lines that she copied into a notebook – bracingly precise and sometimes beautiful; full of the potential for justice, strength, freedom, half-envisioned possibilities – have infused in her brain enough for her whole self to drink them in. She isn't quite sure how to express this or if it would sound stupid. So she only says, but without lowering her eyes, 'Yes, I have.'

Alicia smiles. 'And what are you reading now?'

'*Voss*, of course.' They have to read this for their exam. 'And *Pride and Prejudice* and *Orlando*.'

Alicia nods approvingly. 'I love Austen and Woolf. And White, of course. I'm juggling *One Hundred Years of Solitude* and *Hopscotch*.'

This is the first Jan has heard of these novels. She will seek them out and read them soon after.

'To the books we can't, or don't want to, live without.'

They raise their glasses. Jan has been essentially teetotal until then, like her parents. The wine intense in her throat and nose, she exults, thinking: I'm a university student sipping wine in a Sydney pub with an intellectual. We're like Parisian existentialists!

Someone has put Roberta Flack on the jukebox, which seems to prompt Alicia to ask, 'And what are you listening to?'

'Mainly *Blue* – Joni.'

She's said this like she knows the woman personally. The embarrassment! Blushing, Jan looks down again.

Alicia reassures her, 'That's one of my favourite albums. I've been listening to a lot of Leonard. You go to the movies much?'

She nods, holding a mouthful of wine for as long as she can before it seeps into her. Her face hot, she swallows. 'I go to the Union quite often. I went to all the French New Wave movies. I also like the Academy Twin.'

'Let's go to something together sometime.'

Beginning a second glass of wine, Alicia tells Jan that she too lives in Glebe, in one of the Housing Commission terraces on Westmoreland Street, where she recently 'moved in with a poet'.

Has she mentioned the Housing Commission to help put Jan at ease, show she doesn't mind being associated with poverty or something like that? Jan is pretty sure Alicia can't be from that kind of background, not with her confidence, her slinky, silky shirt and her posh-school way of talking (SCEGGS, one of those places?).

Alicia goes on to describe her boyfriend as 'a little older'. His mother died when he was young and he was raised by his grandmother in a flat in Petersham, an eccentric annex on a subdivided villa overrun by cats. He did English at Sydney Uni, lived in a commune for a while and started writing poetry, which he'd published in *Honi Soit*, *Southerly* and other journals. Now he is the editor of a poetry magazine he founded himself, *The Source*. He is interested 'in jazz, prog rock and maybe in experimenting with alternatives to monogamy'.

Alicia's laughter makes it hard to know how to take this last bit of information. Then she points to Jan's wedding ring, the gesture turning into a sort of disillusioned question as her hand rolls and her palm turns up. 'Oh no, you're not really *married*?'

Jan feels horribly straight. 'Afraid so.'

'Your parents put a lot of pressure on you?'

*

'Do you remember how you answered?' the therapist asked, pen poised.

Checking her watch, Jan saw that the session would end in five minutes. She had noticed, with her own clients, that it was often close to the end of a session that something difficult was raised. Something that had been brewing; something that the client would rather not say, and yet, when it was almost too late, finally blurted out. The tone of this could be passive-aggressive: *Will you be able to dismiss me, after hearing this?* But Jan was a therapist herself and reserved. Still shy, if that was the word. Shy or cagey? Was there a difference?

'Vaguely, no doubt ... *Don't all parents put pressure on their children?*'

'And how would you answer now?'

This therapist wasn't bad, actually. She knew how to go from placid – almost letting Jan feel she was alone – to alert. She knew how to offer questions like inevitable pathways through Jan's own thoughts.

'Now I might say that I got married quickly because my mother thought I was a whore.'

17

BALMAIN ROAD
10 November 1975

And there it is, almost too easy. She can hardly credit it, but still she makes herself walk towards the yellowy-white blaze, as if she was just taking herself for a bit of a stroll. Steady, my girl, steady. You wear yourself out and drive yourself round the bend hoping for a door like that, open to the outside.

Christ Almighty, getting away from the sick-sad reek of watery pea-and-ham soup, piss and disinfectant into lovely, unsoiled air. Going out into the open air of your own free will, escaping because you bloody well choose to! All the bastards who take this for granted.

And the open gate isn't even a surprise at the point she is at. It is hers. Sometimes, rarely, events lay themselves out along a line as clean and purposeful as the flight of a bird. She is out and away into the live park, not hurrying too much, a little wobble in the pins. Who'll notice she's done a runner and how long will it take them? Luckily, people tend to be less on the ball than they reckon they are. It's hot. The kind of earthy, leafy heat that makes you suspect you could be dreaming. The cicadas are very loud and close, like the heart pounding in the ears, like the rhythmic hissing of snakes, and she must get away fast.

She knows where the bus stop is, and when she has crossed the road to it she sits down on the bench to wait, all innocent. She is zingy and jaunty and she shouldn't laugh. Everything is riding on the bus coming soon. She is thinking of her secret five-buck note, which she has stashed in one of the inner compartments of her handbag. You've got to have a bit of cash for doing a bunk. She used to have a friend, a long way back, a clever Irish girl who insisted that you *always* had to have a wee bit of fuck-off-quick money. Because really, you never know what's coming. And was she ever right. The fiver won't get her too far, but it's only as far as Claude that she needs to go. A currawong sings, like he was tipping his hat to her and encouraging her to keep her nerve. For some reason, the bird makes her think of the river again. She'd prefer to be sitting by the water, waiting for a boat. A barge, a cruise ship, a dinghy, any bloody thing, she wouldn't be fussed. But for now, a bus will have to do. Oh come on, bus.

There you go. Isn't it? Yes. Yes, praise be, the 440. That'll get her right into the city. She could hop off at Hyde Park and maybe get a train to Circular Quay.

Over with her to the curb. The next test will be the driver, who has seen her and is preparing to stop. He's starting to look her over. He's young and a redhead like herself, which could be in her favour. It says so much about a person, maybe everything important you need to know, how they treat you when they've got you in their power. Whether they use the power or refuse it. What you have on your side in such a situation is that you are seeing them, aren't you? Who they are underneath.

So the redheads eye each other, and then she smiles and steps up carefully. He is taking stock. Does he know where – what – she's on her way from? Can he tell? She does her best to come across as oh so sane, you wouldn't believe how sane and normal. Like no one's running her life but herself. She remembers to show her pass, her bloody hands shaking.

He waves the pass away and smiles back. 'You're right, love. Have a seat.'

Did he wink? What a lovely chap, a real comrade. The luck.

As she is sitting down, towards the back of the bus where there is no one else, she hears the sirens. She could almost pass out from the excitement and happiness. The sirens saying: You bloody beauty, that's the way, that's my girl, good'un that you are, on you go. Come to me.

18

MERRYLANDS

1962

The first time her mother is displeased enough with Jan to create a lasting memory, she is seven years old.

The day has been a stinker and even as the light goes there is no sign of any merciful southerly buster. Nearby someone is hosing a yard, and through the window of her parents' bedroom comes a hint of the delicious smell of cement, asphalt and lawn finally getting the soaking they've been dying for. Covering Jan's face like a bridal veil, the scratchy lace curtain makes the view of the Evening in Paris bottle dissolve entirely into black. She is so completely on her own that she wonders if she wants to cry, but at the same time, the feeling is sort of like being excitingly invisible.

It is the deep, dark blue of the perfume bottle, which sits on a doily on the imitation-walnut dresser in her parents' bedroom, that Jan is drawn to. That and the idea of night-time in Paris. (How do you even begin to imagine that?) The blue is the colour of something very mysterious – slightly unnerving – that you might discover in an enchanted underground chamber, or of a fruit, possibly poisonous, that would grow on a tree in some kind of fable. The eau de cologne was an anniversary gift to Betty from her husband, so special that she hardly ever uses it.

Now Jan is on her knees in front of the dressing table, facing one and then the next of its three mirrors, the outer two of which she closes in around herself, creating an intimate room lined with her reflections. In those versions of her face she sees elation, something actressy and panicky. Because of the forbidden perfumed trickle down her chest. It's beautifully cool.

She has let this happen, has listened to temptation.

Betty asks, 'That's not my Evening in Paris I can smell, is it?'

Jan lies because it's clear from her mother's tone that she knows the answer and is disgusted by it. 'No, no.'

Betty doesn't go crook on her daughter openly, doesn't even say, 'Oh *Ja-an*' – her characteristic way of disapproving. She just lets there be an atmosphere of heavy disappointment. Later, Jan overhears her mother telling her father about the lie, with that same repulsed tone.

She creeps outside. Cicadas that she imagines clinging low to the walls of the house croak in time with the thumping of her heart. Mozzies come for her and she doesn't care. She is a liar and a thief. The sky is virtually the blue of Evening in Paris, and streetlights and living-room lights are being turned on, making the houses look like boxes leaking radiance. It is the time when, even if you'd prefer to hang around outdoors in the air that finally feels like being gently touched, you are supposed to be inside, setting the table. She smells a pepper tree and the perfume she hasn't been able to rub off, despite the red tracks she has made with her knuckles and the hurt in her chest bones. She doesn't know if she likes the strangeness of the scent, which seems to have changed a bit. Her headache is fading; maybe it's growing on her. She crosses the inhospitable lawn in her bare feet.

Unavoidably, a bindi-eye gets her and she freezes, muscles clenching, pain flaring and very slowly dulling, but like a splinter staying lodged in her.

*

'It might have been around that time,' Jan told the therapist, 'that I started occasionally having a dream in which I thought I'd committed a crime. The details changed – but a murder, usually. I wasn't sure I'd done it. But I had an inkling that it could have been me.'

'Go on.'

*

1971–1973

The one-storey lemon fibro-and-brick house is set among other similar houses, a few scattered gums, the odd pepper tree or willow, rectangles of battling lawn and concreted driveway, and the asphalted loop of Edna Avenue. Jan's father has done his best to beautify the front yard with red and pink geraniums, bird of paradise and the shrub Jan used to think of as the 'Jewel Tree' on account of its evocative name – *jade plant* – and intriguingly plump little leaves.

In later years, living in the far less ordered and hygienically irreproachable houses of her adulthood, she will sometimes remember her childhood home's mix of odours with nostalgia: Omo laundry detergent, starch spray and warm steam from the iron, Mr Sheen furniture polish, shoe polish, Imperial Leather soap, Dettol, calamine lotion, Oil of Ulan moisturiser, Bay Rum aftershave, something like simmering mince or tinned mushrooms being heated up to go on toast.

It's not a house of many books. There are a few Bibles, *The Fortunes of Richard Mahony* and a couple of other novels along those lines, *The Man from Snowy River and Other Verses*, Charlie Chaplin's autobiography. More plentiful are the piles of *Reader's Digest* and *New Idea*, *Woman's Day* and *The Women's Weekly*. There is usually a folded *Telegraph* or *Sun Herald* and a TV guide on the narrow tiled counter between the kitchen and the living room that they call the servery. Every day, for long periods, the house is cosy with the sound of the television. The *Looney Tunes* theme song will always remind Jan of sitting or lying on the carpet in front of that set in rosy early-morning light, while that of the *Twilight Zone* will conjure an armchair in the same room, the bewitching screen surrounded by darkness that is by turns homey and unknown.

Since Jan was sixteen or so, she and Betty have been talking less easily than they used to. Betty felt particularly let down by Jan's decision to stop attending church regularly, in favour of – this was her justification – taking up swimming at the new Merrylands Swimming Centre. (Her brother, Alex, was the first of them to resist church and Jan feels that her mother is more tolerant when it comes to him. Not that he hasn't been a source of disappointment, but he doesn't seem to concern himself anywhere near as much as Jan does with trying to be 'good'.) However, she and her mother do still yarn quite a bit in the kitchen, or more often, from sofa to armchair in front of the telly, maybe with their tea on their laps on bed trays. They muse about the behaviour of family members, actors and royals. Betty's interest in the latter is partly related to her 'people' hailing from Cornwall (the ones who weren't Irish), though that was a way back and Jan isn't sure exactly how far back or in what circumstances they left England. (Betty pronounces it '*En*gland', instead of '*In*gland', which Jan supposes to be the proper British way.)

Betty is kind and considerate and especially generous with food. They are all keen on their tucker and Betty makes the dishes she knows her family loves: cutlets with tinned potatoes, beans and peas (the soft, salty vegetables yummily topped with melting margarine), stovetop chicken, weekend lamb roasts to which they add Cornwell's Mint Sauce, tapioca, bread-and-butter custard … The servings can be a bit on the modest side, in Jan's and Alex's opinion. Jan vaguely understands that this has to do with Betty having lived through the Depression, when her father, an Anglican minister, had been out of work for years and years. Apparently, when their family was lucky enough to have a jar of jam, they had to share it – not just between the six children and two parents, but also with the friend and next-door neighbour they called Aunty Di. Jan has wondered how you'd share a jar of jam between two households, how you'd teach the little ones to suffocate their cravings so much. In light of the eked-out jam, Jan certainly understands the delight Betty takes in her favourite sweet treats, Darrell Lea's liquorice and Rocky Road (which she calls Rocky, like it was some cheeky friend), as well as the Quality Streets chocolates she savours on special occasions (putting on her glasses to study the descriptions of the different kinds, before solemnly choosing and then passing the box around).

*

'And your father?'

*

Morris is a man of great decency and conscientiousness, dependable and scrupulously polite. Jan once saw him clean the soles of his shoes on his handkerchief before entering a stranger's house. He brings Betty a cup of tea and a biscuit or two – a Ginger Nut, say, and a Scotch Finger or a Monte Carlo – in bed each morning, before he eats his Weet-Bix out of a bowl he has left out the night before on the kitchen table, upside down, with a spoon beside it. Every week he polishes the family's shoes, afterwards leaving them on sheets of newspaper outside the back door to dry. If Jan and Alex have ever gone anywhere by train, when they return to Merrylands Station, they always find a phone booth and call 6324049, the one number they will never for their whole lives forget. Once he comes on the line, they'll say, *It's me, I'm at the station.* He'll say, *Right*. Or: *Very good*, in his formal way they imagine he learned growing up on the fruit orchard in Young. *I'll be down there shortly. Have you had your tea? There's a plate here for you.*

Alongside all this, there is Bob Santamaria's *Point of View* that he watches on Channel 9 and the way he and Alex clash over the views expressed in it (on the Labor Party, American politics, communists, et cetera). Alex is also forthright in telling Morris not to agree with their relatives when they say that there are too many Yugoslavians, Greeks and Italians around and the foreigners drive badly; their father would usually only say the latter about men in hats and women in Volvos. Jan does what she can to give a wide berth to these conversations, though her instincts tell her that Alex is right. Here, too, she feels that she must be a good girl, must say things or not say things in order to make her parents happy.

Morris tries to protest, 'I've got nothing against the immigrants who make a go of themselves. Some of them are fine people, upstanding citizens.'

He cites his admiration for Mr Cincotta of the Cincotta Chemist shops, or his appreciation for the pleasant staff and the spring rolls, sweet-and-sour pork and chicken chow mein at the Shanghai Garden, where they have been a few times for gatherings with the better-off Central Coast relatives.

Things get tense between him and Alex, who puts up a Che Guevara poster on his bedroom wall, gets arrested along with one hundred and seventy-two others at an anti-Vietnam moratorium march (after which he even spends a night in a jail cell), starts going to gigs at the Hordern Pavilion (Jethro Tull first) with money saved from his paper round and lets his hair grow long (refusing to allow Betty to cut it with the clippers, as was their habit). Morris is so alarmed by the long hair that, at a certain point, though he has never been a physically aggressive or confrontational man, he goes after Alex with scissors.

Jan hears the kerfuffle and comes out of her bedroom in time to see Alex and her father to either side of the kitchen table, Morris holding Betty's good sewing scissors high in one hand, blades splayed, and Alex somewhere between incredulous and smirking.

Closing the scissors with a clean snipping sound, Morris swallows and says, 'I suppose you think it was a disadvantage to be born in Merrylands.'

And Alex replies, 'Oh yeah, I do. Definitely.'

He is thinking, as perhaps they all are, Well, how can you come from Merrylands and not be self-conscious about your lack of financial, social and cultural prestige? But Jan is used to this thought being unspoken and it is disorienting to hear it said out loud. There is a grim flicker in Morris's face, followed by a sort of shock, a loosening of the jaw that is upsetting to watch. Alex's face is troubled too, but also flushed with a boyish teenage triumph that Jan is both disturbed by and slightly envious of. She can see that he feels like iron filings pulled towards the magnet of the truth.

Not long after, he gets chucked out of school on account of the hair and takes off hitchhiking for several months, in something of the spirit, he later tells Jan, of *Easy Rider*. (He comes back skiting about having been jailed for vagrancy in the Northern Territory and returns to school, where by then most of the boys have hair as long as his.)

Yet, it's not true that Alex has always got away with doing what he's wanted to do. When he was little, he liked the idea of learning ballet and Morris insisted he take a martial arts class, instead. And in high school, Alex was set on studying art, for which he showed considerable flair, but he ended up giving in to his parents' preference for technical drawing.

*

'Do you think they were afraid he might be gay?' the therapist asked.

'Maybe. Or he might become so. Which is funny.'

'Funny why?'

'Oh, well he's always been hetero. But yes, it was the times and their backgrounds. I mean, I'm sure pretty much everyone they'd ever known was homophobic. I remember my mother would occasionally point out a couple of men walking together down a street and knowingly say, "There's a pair." When she found out about Rock Hudson being gay, she felt betrayed. And now by Raymond Burr, too! She adored him in *Perry Mason*.

'Anyway, I don't mean to give the impression that my father didn't respect the arts. That's really not true. It was just that, for the most part, the arts were distant from his life. He was suspicious of modern art. I remember him telling a sort of cautionary tale about some people who had been impressed by an experimental painting, declared it a brilliant work of genius, and then found out that it had actually been painted by a chimpanzee. So they'd been hoodwinked, shown up as fools. It seemed humiliating to him that you could fall for thinking something was good only to have it publicly revealed that you didn't know what you were talking about, you had no taste. But he did like some traditional art. He took us a couple of times, when we were kids, to the Art Gallery of New South Wales. I guess that was considered to be one of the things you did during an excursion to the city. It was free, also.

'Once, we stood for quite a long time in front of a painting he liked in the permanent collection. It was of a rural scene that might have reminded him of growing up in the country.'

'Anything else about the painting?'

'I think it might have been called *Spring something-or-other.* If I'm remembering correctly, there were some cows in a paddock, maybe being fed by a farmer? It might have been around dawn – the shadows of the fence posts were purply. At least, they are in my memory. Sorry, I can't describe art.'

'You can. I can see it. Is this a nice memory?'

'Yeah, it is.'

'Would you like to tell me more about what you said before?'

'Hmm?'

'About your mother thinking you were a whore.'

'Oh.'

*

1973

Betty is lying on her bed, as she often is in the afternoons, when she isn't at her job as a doctor's secretary.

'Sorry, did I wake you up?' Jan asks her now.

'No, love. You're good. I took some Mylanta and thought I'd get up for a bit. I was pooped. But I wasn't asleep, just resting my eyes. What's doing?'

Her skin appears flushed, as it frequently does; Jan has inherited this pink-tending skin.

'A boy from school asked me to the dance.' Jan has been wondering how to bring this up for weeks.

'Oh? Sit down for a minute.'

She sits on the side of her mother's bed, gazing at the dressing table. Where the Evening in Paris used to sit, there is a bottle of 4711 and a cut-glass ring holder that her mother doesn't use anymore because her arthritis won't let her take off her wedding and engagement rings. Jan sometimes sees her holding her hands in front of her, studying her swollen, bent fingers as if forcing herself to look pain and disfigurement in the eye.

'Is he a nice boy?'

'Yes, he's nice.'

'And are you ... going with each other?' She is being very careful to sound like an almost-amused observer, someone suspending judgement, only needing information.

'We've been talking a bit.'

'Have you? Is he bright? Does he get good marks?'

'Yes.'

'Look at me, love.'

Betty believes she has a touch of the sixth sense. In her first job, as a cashier at Winns department store, she caught out another employee who was stealing because she had 'had a feeling' about it. Some belief in clairvoyance runs in the family; a distant cousin reads tea leaves. Jan turns and Betty's stare, as if preparing to sink into her secret thoughts, makes her even more nervous.

'His people, they aren't Catholic?'

'No, no.'

Betty can exhale after this, with huge relief.

Foreseeing further questions to which it could be hard to respond, Jan is forced to say, 'Actually, I don't think they're church people.'

This is odd, worrying. 'You mean not at all? Not even his mother?'

Jan doesn't want to explain that his mother is a communist and in a psychiatric institution. 'No, I don't think so.'

'Do you know what his father does?'

'I gather that, at the moment, he's not working. He has a bad back.'

'Oh Ja-an.'

This is a different kind of worry. Betty is far from pleased, but a week later she does enquire after Glen's father's bad back. Adding, 'Poor thing.' Because of course, she has had her own experience of a father out of work, and she can be as compassionate as she can be disapproving.

Two months pass and, one airless afternoon, Jan is heading for her bedroom with a gliding step so she won't spill the cup of International Roast meant to help her concentrate on her Shakespeare study notes. In the kitchen, she dunked a Milk Arrowroot in this, most of which collapsed and disappeared below the surface.

She is noticing, irritated, a lump of biscuit floating in her coffee, when her mother asks, 'Could you come in here for a minute, please?'

It is the voice she would use with a rude stranger. In her bedroom doorway, in her loose pink chenille dressing gown and rollers and paler than usual, perhaps indisposed, Betty turns to enter the room.

Jan doesn't know why exactly, but she replies, 'Just a minute,' and sets her coffee on the small high table beside their black phone. 'Maybe I heard the car,' she calls, though it is too early for her father to be getting home.

She goes to spy on the street through the front door's fly screen, her face leaning against the mesh; she likes the cool feel of it and its softly metallic smell that recalls the inside of an old, hardly used garage. Then she retrieves her coffee and carries it into her mother's room.

There are two books on the dusky-rose quilted bedspread. They had been hidden in the drawer of Jan's bedside table, under the leatherette Bible she got for her twelfth birthday.

The Rapture of Lol V. Stein.

And Jan's diary.

Her toes curl into the black-and-white shag carpet. Oh Lord. The book was lent to her by Mrs Forsythe, the day she also lent her *The Second Sex*, *Claudine at School* and a collection of poetry entitled *Ariel.* It is somewhat weird. A novel that gets you imagining along slanted lines, fascinatingly foreign and sensual. Yet, reading it, she has sometimes felt she was rediscovering some of her own half-formed perceptions, like a language she had forgotten or not entirely realised she knew. An incantation entering her as music might and playing in her skull, chest and groin. To do with emotions and needs. A feeling of nearly dissolving. Sex.

Jan's diary has sex in it, too. In a recent entry, she wrote about losing her virginity to Glen in the shed smelling of greyhounds behind his house at Guildford. Not in much detail, thank God, but she did refer to a number of painful attempts and the impression that she was locked up and not meant to open. That there was a wall in her, which he couldn't push through, something trapped in her that he couldn't release. The concern that maybe she wasn't anatomically right.

In an earlier diary entry, she described Mrs Forsythe lending her the books one day when Jan had stayed back after class to discuss an essay with her. And the two of them also talking about how Gough Whitlam, in his first days in office, had abolished the luxury tax on contraceptives and included the pill in the Pharmaceutical Benefits Scheme, lowering its cost to one dollar per month.

Mrs Forsythe had said, 'A prime minister willing to stand behind feminism. It's like a dream.' Adding, 'You can call me Helen,' and offering to walk with Jan across the school grounds, so they could keep chatting about politics and books for a while longer.

As they were nearing the oval, Jan saw one of the edgy plovers noticing them, and a moment later they were being dive-bombed.

Jan explained to Helen that this happened often at that time of year and the birds were only trying to protect their babies, but the episode seemed to make her teacher anxious and she had stumbled a little, running in her platform shoes and thrillingly short skirt, before taking Jan's arm.

Now Jan wants to say to her mother, 'How could you read my diary?' But there are some kinds of outrage that feel too deep and dangerously final to put into words. She is contemplating the diagonal lines in the bedspread's stitching, to avoid focusing on the books, which seem to radiate grubby heat. Neither of them can meet the other's eye.

Betty doesn't say, 'Oh Ja-an.' She is trying to make a silent stand.

Jan's feet are getting clammy against the carpet and she is suddenly aware, sickeningly, of the sensation of her breasts against her blouse. She feels perverted and watched. Realising that her hands are trembling and she might spill her coffee, she gulps some that goes down the wrong way. Her coughing makes her drop the cup.

At that point, her mother does say, 'Oh Ja-an.' And: 'I just can't believe it.'

What exactly?

'I'll clean it up,' Jan manages.

Working with bucket and scrubbing brush, she babbles, 'Glen and I want to get married.' She knows this will not redeem her and she wonders if it could be true.

'Don't wet it too much. You'll only make it worse.'

With those words, her mother shuts down into the paralysis of mute sulking that will last for weeks. Their talk, when it starts again, will not be what it was. The carpet won't be either; if you know where to look, there will always be a dirty patch, something like a small shadow.

*

'I realise how *ordinary* this is,' Jan said. 'Compared to things I hear every day from my clients, God. Compared to the experiences of so many women, maybe most women. This minor example, without physical violence, is insignificant.'

'No, it's not,' the therapist assured her.

'Well, not to me. When a person who has had the ability to make you feel good about yourself as a child decides you are *impure* … No matter how much of a feminist you are or you become, no matter how much you try to make allowances … My mother was an unemployed minister's daughter from Canley Vale, whose family hadn't been able to afford for her to go further than primary school. And it occurs to me that she can't ever have felt very confident in her literacy. When she writes messages on Christmas cards, she shows them to my father to have him check them for mistakes. Not that she isn't intelligent. She *is*, which my father recognises too. He says she *could have done anything*, meaning if she'd had the chance to study, maybe if she hadn't been a woman or one of her class, she'd have been capable of taking on any profession she might have wanted … I'm aware of all this, and it moves me. It really does, and I can see that the strength of her reaction was proof that for her, also, books were powerful and words could be far-reaching, almost like spells. Still, I felt tremendous *shame* – and I still do, every time I remember how she treated me. Even after that silly perfume episode! My brain mixes the two up.'

A wash of self-hatred, nausea and nervousness, discomfort a live thing in her stomach. The desire to disappear.

'You felt you betrayed her?'

'Sometimes. She saw it that way. Saw me as a slut.'

'You weren't close again, after that?'

'There was no open fighting. I wasn't thrown out of the house. But she never called me *love* or *pet* again. Never again said, *Bless your heart*. Or *God bless*. Glen and I got married right out of school, so I left a few months later, anyway. I thought it was what I wanted. In retrospect, I was trying to purify myself in her eyes, and just get away, get myself to the city…'

'And how about your father?'

'If he was disappointed in me, he hid it. We talked that night.'

*

Her father is carrying the Raid, already uncapped.

'Watch out, I saw a cocky in here earlier. Big one. It was on the edge of the sink.'

Jan has just come out of her bedroom, after spending hours in there, trembly and tearful, though not actually crying. If she'd cried she would have been heard through the thin wall shared with her parents' bedroom.

In the piratey voice he does sometimes, he says, 'Where are you, you blighter? Come out, come out.'

The cocky isn't to be seen, but her father goes to town with the spray, anyway, as if spray-painting a large sign. For good measure, he does the same in the small segment of hallway that leads to the front door.

Jan coughs, breathing in the toxic fumes.

'Walk around the block?' her father suggests.

It's been ages since they followed this old evening ritual of theirs. Jan nods, relieved at the prospect of leaving the house for however short a time.

The sun is setting, the sky going the colour of ripe rockmelon. They start out in the direction of the pastel-green fibro place where a son, much too old to be living at home, still lives. *Poor things* or *Poor devil*, Betty comments, if this topic comes up. The pockets of air hovering over asphalt and concrete are still hot, while others drifting off soil or lawn recently hosed are blissfully cooler. A light, steamy haze surrounds one lusher portion of the verge that's wallowing in the luxury of a sprinkler. Walking as close to this as possible, Jan gets her left ankle sprayed; the shock and freshness are so lovely that for a moment the sensation overwhelms her.

'Just after you were born,' Morris says, 'there were some days when I had to take your brother, who was only a little bloke, with me to the factory.'

'I remember,' she replies, by which she means she knows this reminiscence.

He is talking about the textile factory on Parramatta Road where he still works, though this isn't the first factory on that road to employ him. (Earlier, there was a hat-making factory, where he hadn't lasted long because those were the days in which hats were going out of fashion. Earlier still, he'd tried – hating talking people into spending money they couldn't afford to be parted from – to sell encyclopaedias and insurance, door to door.) She remembers being in the car with him on Parramatta Road, stopped in the tetchy, stuffy heat of bumper-to-bumper traffic, steeping in smells of vinyl, exhaust fumes and the biscuity gusts from the Weston's factory.

Other times he has told her this anecdote, he has gone on to say something like, 'Bet wasn't very well then.'

She has started to have an inkling of how to interpret this, after overhearing one of her aunts, a wonderfully warm-natured woman who sings in the Salvos choir, make a brief mention of 'baby blues'. Betty herself has told Jan that she almost died giving birth to her brother, seeing – during one particularly touch-and-go stretch – a blue crucifix floating over the end of her hospital bed.

But he seems to be switching stories. 'Around that time, there was a Yugoslavian woman who worked with us.'

'Yes?'

'Her name was Anya.'

'Was she nice?' He likes to tell Jan about his co-workers, and usually does so with respect and a slightly poignant tone that makes her wonder if he wishes they were or had been more his friends than his colleagues. Has he felt the lack of a social life beyond the family?

'Good worker. Very efficient.'

Jan pictures her as a thin woman with an even thinner face, dirty-blonde hair, bargain-bin floral blouses, world-weary made-up eyes and great self-discipline that she has spent her life honing. She considers her father briefly then, asking herself why he has brought up Anya. They are passing the Italians' house. The robust cooking odours that come out of there often warrant a grimace from the sort of passers-by who'd refer to them as 'dagos' or 'wogs', as do the white statues of lions that frame their unusually grand front gate. There's a sense of: Who do they think they are, then? As Jan has grown older, she has been increasingly more intrigued than revolted by the smells and she often tries to get a glimpse of their yard. This is different from the other yards in which all you really see is a tree or two, a Hills Hoist, a barbecue, a shed, a gung-ho attempt at a lawn, a fence and maybe a view of the neighbouring yards. Whereas the Italians have a surprisingly big, leafy vegetable garden and a pergola that Jan imagines would provide some soothing shade. Are they achingly nostalgic for a place very different from here?

'One day she dropped a handkerchief – Anya did. I was walking behind her in the Dye Room. Of course, I picked it up and tried to give it back. Well, the strange thing was that she denied it was hers. And I'd seen her drop it, but I couldn't very well insist. I kept it because I didn't know what else to do with it.' He appears to be inspecting the street in front of them. 'It was perfumed. Of course, I never mentioned this to your mother.'

Reaching Fowler Road, Jan looks towards the library room of what was her primary school, the reflex producing a confusion of comfort and melancholy. She is still aware of the pressure of trying not to cry, like bands around her forehead, throat and chest – and of the conviction she has had all afternoon that a large and deep part of her life is ending. She needs to escape from there so badly and at the same time she fears that leaving will break her heart irreparably.

'Will we duck into the Top Shop?'

As they go in, Jan has the thought that she might not pass many more times through that multicoloured plastic strip curtain and find herself staring at the loaves of Tip Top on a white-painted shelf.

'Go on.' He gestures at the long freezer.

And how many more times will she hear that bird-like squawk of its hinge opening and peer through the icy mist rising into her face? She chooses a chocolate Paddle Pop and her father a lime ice block; when it's too late, she feels bad for not having made the same choice as his, which would have been cheaper.

'We'll take one for Bet, eh? We'll have to put it back in the freezer for a while when we get home.'

At ice-cream eating speed, they dawdle around the other side of the U of their street. Jan glances in passing at the place in the gutter where she can barely recall – a shiver of memory – the crumpled shape of a man and her father calmly explaining that there had been a car accident. She thinks that the way he is being with her now is a bit like how he was then, helping her get past a harrowing fact of life.

'Good ice block?'

'Nothing wrong with that.'

This is one of his classic phrases and Jan is never sure if she should take it as an awareness of mediocrity that he is endeavouring to make the best of, or just as his version of optimism, a glass-half-full kind of thing. She tries to focus on the sky and let the beauty of it be only that, and not entwine with her sadness. The lowest slice of the sunset has turned the light-through-stained-glass shade of raspberry jelly.

*

'I've wondered for how long he kept Anya's perfumed handkerchief and where,' Jan told the therapist. 'And also, if he shared that story with me because he thought I'd become mature enough to hear it. Did he mean to tell me that he'd been in love? That he'd desired her but not acted on that? That he understood there are times when you have to keep something to yourself, safely hidden? That he knew what it was like to get shut out of Betty's heart and imagine seeking solace elsewhere? But that longing has to be buried?'

19

CIRCULAR QUAY
10 November 1975

Stepping down onto the platform, Lorna wouldn't be dead for quids: the charge and thickness of the city around her, the sea edging in close. She smells dust, metal, machines, salty humidity and sexy perfume. So many people gadding about as they like, pleased with their own style, swinging their hips. She has a chuckle and pushes her teeth back in, thinking what a kick she'd get out of buying herself some new clobber. A polka-dot frock like one she sees going past that'd be worth a few bob, a flash scarf, any little thing – to look her best for Claude. Imagine choosing whatever she fancied at David Jones! That'd be the life. She wouldn't say no to a bit of finery. Spread the damn wealth around, eh?

She buys a pack of smokes, using her note; she'll have to go very easy with the dough. And then she wanders to where she can get an eyeful of the ferries coming and going but won't be in people's way. My word, the harbour is something, you can't deny it. Serious class. The fancy great New Yorky buildings on one side and the water on the other. Luna Park over there like a bit of rollicking they have to keep slightly out of reach. She lights up fast, gets a few quick puffs into her so then she can take her time with another scrumptious slower one. Oh there you go, that's the business. The smoke shimmies down to where she needs it and gets her vibrating nicely. While she finds a bench to sit on, a breeze plays with her blouse. She'll hear the sirens from here. Always, the waiting for messages, but the sea is made for keeping you company while you wait. Now she has a better gander.

Far off, the sea is less blue, more gunmetal, and the trees on the shore hug the land in a close, secretive way, like something out of a legend. It's strange, this feeling of things having been pushed over onto their side and stretched out, left to right and front to back, like the usual tight frame has been taken away. It's true that sometimes she suddenly starts seeing things differently, but this is new. She'd have liked to grow up with a sea view. Well, who wouldn't have?

He must know where she is and he'll be in touch soon. She could go to Glen and Jan while she's waiting, but the last time she did that, she got the impression she'd overstayed her welcome. Fair enough, a young couple is like that. And they're almost as strapped for cash as she is. They can't rescue her; she keeps hoping, but knows that salvation won't come from there.

The sun is starting to pack it in, but that won't be any letdown here. There won't be that sad, folding-up feeling of there being nothing much more to look forward to, now you'll just have to comfort yourself in the dark, kiddo. No, here by the sea, it won't be like that. See, the odd light is coming on and Gawd it's pretty and merry, like tinsel sparkling in the light from *It's a Wonderful Life* or *Holiday Inn* on the telly, when you're tipsy on rum and Coke. Lovely. Night-time can be so lovely. And, now that you mention it, she is hankering for a drink. If she has one or two somewhere, it might give Claude a chance to find her. That'll be his intention, she reckons. Yeah, for sure, he'd think running into each other at a pub by the sea was perfect. Couldn't she wait for him at the Fortune of War?

20

WESTMORELAND STREET

'You were telling me, a while back, about meeting Alicia. Is there anything you wanted to add to that?'

The therapist was dressed more casually than usual that day: she'd worn the black blazer before to their appointments, but not with jeans and a T-shirt. The mottled-grey T-shirt was Bonds, by the look of it. (Jan had a comfortable old white one in the same style.) The essential oil she could smell was possibly rosemary.

'After we left the pub, we headed up towards Glebe Point Road, along the edge of the park. I remember the feeling of the wine in my head. I was a bit sleepy and unsteady, like I was teaching myself to walk in someone else's shoes. Then she surprised me by asking if my parents were in love.'

'Why do you think the question was surprising?'

'Well, I wasn't used to that sort of directness. My parents would never have talked in terms like those – they'd have been too embarrassed. If they ever expressed anything like an endearment to each other or to us, it was usually in a slightly comic or a sheepish, gruff tone. Even when they kissed hello or goodbye, their faces would be half turned away. That's what you did, you either avoided talking about a feeling, or you went around it or came at it from an angle. My father telling me about Anya was something rare and whatever he intended to say about his own feelings was oblique. Open talk about feelings was new to me. I look back on the time I spent with Alicia as a kind of watershed between my parents' way of communicating, which had shaped me until then, and *this* – what we're doing now.'

'You mean the kind of talk that takes place during a therapy session?'

'Yes, exactly. The talk that wants to dig down through things, expose things, get to the heart of things. The way a lot of my generation …' She lifted her eyes to meet the therapist's and began again: 'The way our generation started to try to talk in the seventies, I guess. It became almost fashionable to ask searching questions, speak your mind, be "getting things off your chest" and so on – rather than being reserved or indirect as our parents, mine at least, considered it good manners to be.'

'I see. And how did you respond?'

'Huh?'

'To her question.'

*

1974

The light has taken on an orangey depth. Jan should be getting back home to Glen, who is often moody in the evenings.

'Yes, I think they were. Or they thought they were, in the beginning. They look pretty chuffed in the wedding photos. But maybe everyone does. Listen, I should be making tracks.'

'You don't want to come over to my place for a while? It's not that late.'

As well as being under the influence of the wine, Jan is curious about Alicia's house and the life that goes on in it.

'Maybe just for half an hour?'

'Good. What were we saying? Oh yes, and where did your parents meet?'

A pattern is forming, Alicia figuring out how to work her way through Jan's reticence with questions. Jan senses she is being seen as a specimen of the Western Suburbs – but it isn't like earlier with the rude boy at uni. Alicia doesn't make her defensive; she probes and listens as if the details of Jan's life are intriguing and worthy of reflection.

'At a dance. During their engagement, my father – who was living in a boarding house in the city – would ride his motorbike out to Canley Vale to visit her. He'd often be so tired on his way back that he'd fall asleep on the bike and be woken up when he swerved into the gutter.'

'Canley Vale,' Alicia repeats, as if this were a holiday destination she was dreaming over.

Jan would like to turn the questioning around and ask Alicia lots of things, and to just generally get her to explain herself.

She tries, 'Is your name Spanish?'

'Yes, but I was very young when we got here. I don't remember Spain.' The answer is almost snappish and Jan regrets having provoked lines that Alicia must have had to deliver countless times.

'Right,' says Jan, wondering if she is ruining this chance at friendship.

They walk in silence until they are passing Glebe Public School.

As if apologising for turning chilly, Alicia adds, 'My grandmother came here with us. She and my mother set up an import business, once they got here. It's done pretty well.' And a moment later, 'They learned English, but their accents are full-on.'

Jan waits, but there is nothing else.

So: a childhood of financial comfort, yet one in which her relatives were always asked about their accents and kids at school would have kept wanting to know where she and her name were *from*. It is evident that Alicia, who relishes talk, would much rather not talk about her own background. Jan is sorry, but she also thinks, Fair enough.

'Some of our neighbours are Aboriginal,' Alicia says, once they are on Westmoreland Street.

Jan is impressed by this and by the proud way Alicia has said it; passing certain houses, she'd like to stare at the short front yards and the verandahs with clapped-out sofas and armchairs on them, peer through half-open venetian blinds or screen doors veiling dim corridors, but she doesn't want to be nosey.

The place is single storey and long, like Jan's squat. She supposes that both houses would have been built in the 1880s or so, but this one has a pretty corrugated-iron-roofed verandah out the front and more style all around.

'This is so nice.'

'It's a bit derelict. When it rains, I have to put saucepans along the hallway to catch the leaks. No one will do any repairs.'

'Oh,' says Jan, following Alicia inside. 'Our place leaks too.'

They hear some sort of scramble, whining and a clatter of claws against floorboards.

Alicia kneels, dropping her overloaded string bag to the floor with a thump, and embraces what appears to be a Kelpie. 'This is Heidi. Hello beautiful.'

The dog is squealing now and trying to jump, delirious at the reunion. 'Shh, good girl. You don't need to wet yourself.'

Low bookshelves run the length of the hall. Jan wishes she had proper bookshelves like these, instead of just planks and bricks. And then she glimpses the living room, where there are even more, taller, handsome ones in heavy, dark wood, covering most of the wall space. There is a swerve in her mood, a quickening. This is the first book-filled house she has been in. In her half-drunken state, she feels as though she is standing on a shore washed by waves of books. It is exhilarating.

A movement makes her jump and then notice the man.

He is sitting on a sofa beside a vase of wattle, a notebook on his knee and a pen in his hand. His shirt is open to mid-chest and he is wearing velvet trousers. Alicia stands.

'Janet, this is Steve. Steve, Janet.'

'Good to meet you. What a book collection!'

It doesn't escape Jan that Alicia has greeted the dog with physical affection but not Steve. He looks a little older than they are and she guesses he would be considered attractive, but he has the sort of thick moustache she has always imagined would render kissing unpleasant; it makes her think of furry peach skin against the lips, a woollen jumper next to bare skin on a hot day.

'Well hello.' The pen still between his fingers, he waves, a gesture that some would deem feminine for a bloke.

Despite finding him somewhat off-putting, Jan also admires his nerve.

'I modestly call it my library,' he tells her. 'A lot of them are from the Third World Bookshop. And some are Alicia's, of course.'

'Janet's doing English with me at uni. Why don't I make us a snack?'

'Won't say no. And a drink?'

'We've already had a couple.'

'So?'

'Come with me into the kitchen?' Alicia asks Jan.

Jan nods, but says, 'I'll have to leave quite soon.'

The kitchen is dark, old and nicely worn. A hurricane lamp hanging from the ceiling makes it feel like the hull of a boat. A bowl of tomatoes, vividly red in the shadows, is like something out of a still life. Alicia, peeling a garlic clove, could herself be the subject of a painting. There is never any garlic in Jan's parents' house, because her father has trouble digesting it. The same goes for onions.

After putting several slices of handmade-looking bread to toast under the grill of the oven, Alicia carefully chooses and rinses tomatoes. Her arms are long and thin, and the back of her neck is visible when her plait moves. As she is setting out a bottle of oil with a dusky appearance, Steve appears in the doorway.

He serves himself wine from a bottle in the fridge. 'You won't be persuaded?'

'Oh go on, then,' Alicia gives in.

He raises his eyebrows at Jan.

'No, thanks. I really have to go soon.'

'Not even a wee one for the road?' His quiet, drawly voice strikes her as theatrical.

'No, ta, I'm good.'

It is strange to suddenly be with virtual strangers in their kitchen. Every so often, Heidi returns from a lap of the hall to lick Jan's hand, jump up on Steve, go to stand between Alicia's legs.

'What are you making?' Jan asks.

'Just *pan con tomate*.'

It sounds fantastically foreign. 'Oh?'

'Yes, come see, it's easy.'

Jan goes nervously to stand beside her.

'I cut the garlic in half, lengthwise – see? – and then rub the cut edge of the clove across the surface of the bread, like so.'

'And that's enough to flavour it?'

'Oh yes. It's a fairly subtle effect, but yes. Now, some people put the oil on the bread at this point, but I prefer to wait. Then you take your tomato, cut it, you get a cheese grater and, look, I'm just sort of grating it over the bread – so that I end up covering the bread with the pulp and the juice. You don't want the skin of the tomato.'

'No?'

It all seems mysteriously finicky, like a new language: Jan is amazed at the careful attention being given to each separate ingredient, its precise condition and role in relation to the others.

'You sprinkle some sea salt on top and finally, a trickle of oil. Have you tried proper olive oil?'

'Um, I don't think so,' admits Jan.

'Well, today your life will change. Here, try that.'

And Alicia is holding up a wedge of *pan con tomate* for her to bite. Steve appears to watch in amusement. Jan blushes as she tries to bite delicately. Mouth full, she nods and smiles at Alicia, who is waiting for her opinion. To concentrate, she has to briefly close her eyes. It's very different from any tomato sandwich she's ever had. The oil is strong, distinctive, not exactly rough, but the smell somehow goes right up her nose and also hangs thickly at the back of her throat. Self-consciously, she coughs. The tomato is *tomatoey* – a tomato at its most flavoursome and pure, the essence of a tomato.

'Alicia is obsessed with food,' Steve says.

Alicia pouts. 'Why wouldn't you be?' She is taking off her green shirt. The singlet she wears underneath it reveals an indentation, a vertical line over the top of her shoulder that must have been left by the merciless strap of her string bag.

He says, 'Whereas I'm the kind of barbarian who grew up on Coon cheese, Jatz crackers, Tip Top and cocktail onions – for special occasions. Iced VoVos or Fig Newtons with a cup of Horlicks for dessert.'

Doing her best to be friendly or maybe unthinkingly competing with him, Jan offers, 'Where I'm from, we're still getting over the shock of Kraft Parmesan. People say it's so pongy it makes them want to puke.'

'Damn wog food.' Alicia smiles.

'But I don't think like that,' Jan says awkwardly.

'I know, it's okay,' Alicia assures her. 'She's from the Western Suburbs,' she tells Steve.

'Ah,' he notes, leaning back and taking in this information that might explain a lot.

Jan wishes she could convey that one of the things she finds thrilling about Sydney is learning – even if she hasn't been able to afford much takeaway – that pleasure in food isn't necessarily to do with familiar comfort. It can ruffle you.

She says, 'For example, I really love Lebanese food.'

'Where's your favourite Lebanese?' asks Alicia.

'I like Abdul's, which is …'

'On Elizabeth Street, Surry Hills. They do the best baba ganoush.'

They eat in the front room. Jan would have preferred to be alone in there, at her leisure to explore the shelves. As it is, she only gets the odd glance at a spine or two. *Howl*. *The Flowers of Evil*. What a house, what people! It's like she's found her way into some magnificent alternate reality.

'So you're doing English?' asks Steve.

'Yes, but majoring in social work. And you're a poet?'

He nods, apparently without any irony or self-deprecation. Imagine, Jan thinks, having the self-confidence to call yourself a poet, to think you could be one! Asking people to pay attention to you like that, knowing full well they might want to take the piss out of you because you thought you were so good – something like an aristocrat, even though you weren't. Like a friend of Virginia Woolf or something. Jan notices a kind of two-pronged reaction even in herself, who is attracted to poetry, if not particularly at ease with it. Alongside her admiration, she feels a little threatened, as if he were judging her as his inferior. And a kind of thought spasm: Is he a bit of a wanker?

After they've finished eating, Alicia and Steve drink wine. Steve's arm is draped along the back of the sofa, his fingers moving occasionally against Alicia's shoulder.

Jan says, 'I really have to get home to Glen.'

They come with her into the hallway, Heidi hysterically guessing she is going for a walk.

'Janet's a swimmer,' Alicia says. 'We should all go to the beach together.'

'My husband isn't all that keen on beaches.' Jan doesn't add that she isn't either.

'Just the three of us, then. Give me a call.'

'Okay, and thanks for the bread with the tomato,' she says at the door.

Alicia smiles, holding back the trembling Heidi, and Steve, already retreating across age-battered floorboards, gives one of his airy waves.

Walking alone down their street, Jan stops to bend over some jasmine that is lolling over a paling fence. The perfume mirrors the infatuation she is feeling, fine and heady. But she also feels something more wistful. Envious? Of their sensuous house and life? Maybe of Steve and his male poet's assertiveness.

21

FORTUNE OF WAR

10 November 1975

A chap beside her at the bar is giving her the glad eye. He must be getting her from a good angle. She is still relaxing into the feeling of arriving at the pub: the cheerful, hoppy air, the falling towards the bar like into a net held out to catch her. And suddenly, her hand filled with a nice, damp schooner and the flavour spreading through her and smoothing her out. Warmth, a bit like finding yourself in pleasant, restful company.

The fellow is moving across his coaster and his drink, shifting over. He's not bad looking, really. Tallish, solidish, decent smile. She isn't that fussy and it's not that she wouldn't consider him, even if just for a flirt, if it wasn't for Claude, who she is hoping won't take too much longer to find her.

'Evening.'

She nods. Raises her glass. 'I'm waiting for my boyfriend,'

she says, to get things straight from the get-go. 'But would you fancy a hand of euchre, to pass the time?'

He wasn't expecting that. He is well-dressed, with a proper shirt and tie that he's loosened after work. He will probably underestimate her.

'Okay, if the next round's my shout.'

'Deal.'

They move to a table, like people with meaningful business to see to.

'Are we playing for money?'

'Too right we are.' She takes her deck out of her handbag.

'Fiver?'

'Tenner.'

He smiles. 'She's a sharp one.'

'You bet.' And he's a bourgeois who hasn't been around the block as much as he reckons he has.

Afterwards, she's putting her new note away when he asks tiredly, 'You've played in competitions?'

She smiles. 'One or two. RSL clubs.'

He's been losing interest, like most men do, once it's not about winning anymore. Claude isn't like that. She hopes he doesn't mind about this bloke. But she needed the money and, well, you get a bit lonely, don't you? One of the miraculous things about Claude is the politeness of him. He's the kind of man who'll say, *Sugar*, and look bashful. Whereas she and the other people she knows say things like: *Fucking hell, fuck me, fuck all, cold enough to freeze the balls on your dog, piss-poor, cat's cock hair*. And she is also used to being scared of certain people suddenly letting their anger out like a fire-eater's blaze. With Claude, though, you wait for the sarcastic comeback, the piss-take, the first jagged rise of a temper – and nothing. He's gentle for real, not just unpredictably. Gentle all the way down through the layers of him. There doesn't seem to be any need to punish or bully or get revenge skulking around anywhere. It's amazing. And completely new for her to be excited by someone who also makes her feel safe.

But he still isn't showing up and there have been no clear messages for a while. A bit buzzy after her win and craving him, any sign from him, she heads out by herself into a warm night on George Street. She's also a touch peckish and she wouldn't have said no to, say, some rockmelon with Pauls vanilla ice cream. Rolls-Royce of a dessert, that. But for now, a Winfield will have to do her. And she's going to need somewhere not too iffy to kip.

22

MANLY
1974

Her stomach is queasy with butterflies when she sees Alicia and Steve at Circular Quay. His arm is around her waist. They appear happy and relaxed and Jan guesses – the thought making her an interloper – they have made love that morning. Alicia is in a jade-green dress (understandably, she favours green, a colour so striking against her dark hair and skin), Steve in white pants and a billowy mauve shirt. He presents himself as a dandy or a rock star, Jan thinks. In the sharp white light, she sees that the lines at the outer edges of his squinting pale-blue eyes are deeply etched, and on his forehead there is a marked vertical furrow between his eyebrows. He belongs to a different generation from theirs.

They wait like herded cattle to be allowed onto the ferry, gulls screeching, the smell of seawater haunting, and this impression of having given up control unsettles Jan. She shouldn't have come.

She dithered a great deal over whether or not to. Knowing he'd refuse to join them, she invited Glen. Apart from not liking swimming, he's suffering over an assignment that's due soon and he's pining for his guitar, which he's hocked again. He once played for so many hours in a row that a couple of his fingers cracked and bled, and he was proud of the calluses that formed afterwards. When he is strumming 'Sisters of Mercy', 'Famous Blue Raincoat' or 'The Banks of the Condamine' by candlelight, it is better between them; sometimes almost as if they were new lovers again, adventurous bohemians, runaway kids who have just romantically got the hell out of the Western Suburbs. As she left the squat that morning, he was sitting in a gloomy pool of amber light and dust motes. She couldn't tell if she felt more the bad wife or relieved to be going.

Still, boarding the undulating ferry, Jan very much wishes she'd stayed at home. Steve leads them to the front of the boat. She would have preferred to sit securely inside. While he and Alicia stand at the railing, she quickly sits on a bench and holds it firmly with one hand.

She barely looks around her for the first minutes of the ride, the view too dramatic to take in. She doesn't feel trained for or maybe deserving of this sort of staggering beauty, not like someone brought up with it would; she doesn't know how to accept the harbour casually, as they seem to be doing. She has that sense she gets from time to time of not entirely being where she is, of being an impostor pretending to be a normal person, some kind of ghost.

And now a deep roll as they catch the oceanic current coming through the Heads, fear shocking her like a light turned on accidentally in the middle of the night. That's the Pacific Ocean out there, Jan tells herself, staring at the openness she can't relate to. The backs of her knees are sweaty.

Alicia must have noticed her tension, because she comes and sits beside her.

'Did you go to the beach much, growing up?'

'Almost never.'

'Oh?' That enquiring face.

'Well, of course, we were inland.' Jan would like to explain that she loves the idea of the sea, adores reading about and imagining the Mediterranean, say, or Cornwall, but she has never learned to feel at home with beaches. 'I'm a suburban girl.' She is playing the Westie again for Alicia – or just being one? 'Public pools are where I swim.' God, they will expect her to be a cocky, athletic ocean swimmer, that kind of proper Australian. And they'll see she is ridiculously frightened.

Steve, still standing, appears to be watching the seagulls flying alongside the ferry and diving every so often for a fish.

'No beach holidays when you were a kid?' Alicia is inviting Jan to go lower, fall down a shaft of intimacy.

Rather overwhelmed by this level of attention, Jan makes an effort. 'My parents did rent a cabin by a beach a couple of times, when my brother and I were little. In a place called Tuross Head, where my father got taken as a kid.' Alicia nods and waits. 'What I remember most about those holidays was Dad warning us about everything – stitches, sharks, riptides, rough seas. He hardly swam, and my mother didn't at all. I got rolled quite badly once.' She smiles, wanting to make herself into an entertaining story. 'I suppose I've been a chicken ever since.'

'That's completely understandable.' Alicia has mastered the tone she will use with her future clients. 'And yet you've turned into a strong swimmer.'

The ferry jolts to a stop and their legs touch. They have arrived.

'What about you?' Jan asks. 'Did you go to the beach much, growing up?'

'Oh, not really.'

They drink wine as a light breeze picks up. The tangy, nearly fetid smell of salt water, familiar and unfamiliar, is stirring, as is the sound of the waves, but Jan remains conscious of being observed and disoriented by the odd seaside pine trees and the beach atmosphere – gaiety and lassitude, slow hypnosis.

Steve says, 'On the ferry, you two were talking about childhood fears?'

He was listening to their conversation, then.

'Oh. Something like that,' Jan replies awkwardly.

'You got spooked swimming in the surf when you were a kid?'

'Something like that,' she repeats.

'You know, you've got to turn things that freak you out into an adventure, feed off them. Otherwise they shut you down, they define you.'

'Good philosophy,' Jan says, finding him insistent and patronising. Though maybe to some extent he is right; maybe a few lucky people manage that.

'I know what I'm talking about. When I was nine, I experienced an accident, an accident involving a boat. A bad one. I could easily never have gone near water again.' After a moment: 'Poetry saved me. And meditation. Allow me to recommend both.'

It's intriguing to hear a man suggesting his own delicacy, referring to emotion and the psyche as things to explore.

He continues, 'We could do some breathing exercises together now.'

'Ah, thanks, but no.' She pictures herself failing to meditate. 'I might not go into the water today, anyway.'

'Oh but you *have* to.'

A sudden panic, like she was back in primary school and a bossy boy has decided to make a game of her. Will he try to force her into the sea, relishing her embarrassment? The idea of some public initiation ritual is repugnant and this is what makes her firmly decide – though she intended to swim with them – that she won't, she can't.

'You two go in. I'm enjoying just sitting here.'

'We have to convince her, don't we, Lish?'

Jan doesn't like the nickname. He has stood up and started to strip off. There is virtually no hair on his very white chest.

'No, she should only swim if she wants to.' Alicia's voice is muffled by the dress she is pulling off over her head.

The taut thinness of Alicia's thighs makes Jan even more determined not to expose her own body. Anyone would consider her fat and slobby in comparison to her impeccably slender new friend. Growing up, Jan was spoken of as 'big-boned', and for sure her thighs are chubby. She is also comparing Alicia's sleek black costume, its straps stylishly crossed over in the back, to the saggy, threadbare Lycra of her old Speedo. She tries to not watch the couple undressing, but can't help catching flashes of legs and hips. The quiver of Alicia's contracting stomach muscles.

'You're sure you don't want to come in, Janet?'

The gentle way of saying her name almost persuades her. 'No, I'm good, thanks. I'll have a bit of a walk and keep my eye on your clothes. You two go and have fun.' She rolls up the legs of her jeans a tad to show that she isn't entirely rejecting fun.

'Oh come on!' Steve holds out his hands towards both women.

Alicia takes one and says, 'Leave her alone.'

He keeps reaching towards Jan, though she is dressed and shaking her head. There is a rush of heat to her face.

'She's stubborn!'

'Good for her.'

He's right: she might be excruciatingly shy, but her will is strong. Jan wonders uncomfortably if it's her mother's stubbornness. She watches them run in, Alicia's body like a patch of deep shade alongside the colourless sunlight of his. He prances, the more childlike of the two, while she is lighter on her feet, suppler. Once they are wet, shocked by the cold, their voices rise in pitch.

He turns and beckons one last time to Jan. He is stubborn, too. When they wade in deeper, she walks along the beach, relieved but also feeling limited, deprived and mocked. There is some curmudgeonly consolation in the solitude that lets her concentrate on the absolute smoothness of the moist sand. Tipping her head back, she sees that the sky is like a second seashore: a creamy, bubbly edge against a great watery sweep.

Soon, she turns to search for their silhouettes. It is obvious even at a distance that they aren't serious swimmers. They paddle, stand and jump, do a little body surfing. Remembering her promise to watch their things, she starts back and is already close enough to them to catch a couple of the half-screamed words they are tossing to one another, when she steps on the bluebottle.

She understands what has happened and doesn't. It is intense and warm. After a first glance at the loose bluish shape, afraid to look down again, she takes a step into the water and shakes her affected foot around in the froth of a broken wave. The sensation scratches and sparkles.

Alicia approaches with a disorderly, smiling breaststroke. Her hair is plastered to her skull, and when she stands beside Jan her chest is heaving, her collarbones and ribs surprisingly evident.

'Everything okay?'

Jan would prefer to pretend that nothing has happened, but she is behaving strangely and has wet her jeans to above the knees. Her feet are sinking into sand that she can feel rearranging itself around her, and she thinks she'll lose her balance.

'I just stood on a bluebottle.'

'Oh shit … Bluebottle,' Alicia calls to Steve, who is coming over to them.

'It's fine,' Jan says. 'I can hardly feel it.' Why does pain have to be embarrassing?

'Where?'

'Back there. You two be careful, in case there are more.'

Later, on the beach, he says, 'Show us.'

'No, really, it's fine.'

'Show us.'

He studies the splotchy red trail across the top of her foot. 'I've got just the ticket for that.'

And quickly, without checking to see if anyone is watching, he lowers his costume.

Alicia, who has been working her way back into her dress, snickers uneasily. 'God, you should have asked her permission.'

'Fisherman's remedy,' he protests, apparently preparing to urinate.

It is the second penis Jan has seen in her life – third, if you count her brother's when they were very young. She does her best to keep her eyes averted, without seeming like a prude.

'Shy, isn't she? Well?'

'Oh, okay.' She waits for it to be over.

'Better?'

'Yes,' she says, to please him, though the impression of burning remains.

*

'Steve made you uncomfortable?' the therapist asked.

'Yes. But it was confusing. There were things about him that I appreciated. He was very different from other men I'd known, and then there was the conundrum of Alicia's feelings for him. If she was with him, he had to be special. And I wanted him to like me, for her.'

*

After the afternoon at Manly, Jan's thoughts circle Alicia and Steve more and more. She wonders what balancing acts their relationship involves and if they are happy together. Are they living a great passion, love that matches their fantasies –

what they imagined romantic love could be when they were children and teenagers, the visions they comfort themselves with when they dance alone to music or let their minds wander while waiting to fall asleep? It is increasingly difficult for Jan to convince herself that her marriage to Glen fits any of her own fantasies.

23

HYDE PARK
10–11 November 1975

She decides to start off on one of the benches that go around the fountain. Safer here? It can be hard to know when it's better to be out in the open and by the same token maybe visible to the cops. She is reassured by the bloke sleeping rough on the bench to her left: he's long-term, organised, with folded boxes and even some sort of chequered blanket. He won't give her any trouble. He'll be all right, probably. A great load of bats go over, like a dark cloud that's alive. It's funny how nature can make you happy and frightened pretty much at the same time.

'Ah, bloody religion,' she says aloud, her eyes falling to the silhouette of the cathedral. They've sometimes made a decent building – of course, that's been part of their game, knowing how to come across as elegant and soothing when it suits them. Couples pass her, heading out for the night, fun and lust coming off them. Girls in skirts nearly showing their knickers.

Quite a few blokes are making for the men's toilets down by the station. And looking a bit more interested in going for a leak than you might expect. Good luck to them – she hopes they won't find themselves in any trouble.

Thankfully, it isn't cold and she's got her cardigan on. Still, she wouldn't have said no to a blanket. Or just a pillow, or even a rolled-up jumper to put under that bit of the neck that prefers to have some cushioning. But it's definitely nicer to be outdoors than under a roof you don't want to be under, nicer than in a single bed in a dormitory. Jesus Christ, the misery of adults lined up in single beds – like bloody nuns or kids at some boarding school where they lord it over you and get a kick out of your suffering. You've got to keep reminding yourself that what matters are freedom and justice.

Once it's getting to be seriously night and quieter, with fewer people out and about, she lies down as best she can, her bag under her head and her arm through the strap. They'll have to really give her a walloping, if they want that. She hasn't heard many sirens and she hasn't been sure that the ones she's heard have been for her, not one hundred per cent. She doesn't know why Claude is taking so long, but he'll have his reasons. He must have been far away and he's had to deal with God only knows what. She worries for him, sometimes.

She jerks awake, discovering that she's chilled and seized up and less sure than before about the bloke on the bench beside hers. Time to shoot through.

She gets up slyly and tries to walk away as if she's got somewhere to go. Down a pathway that's a corridor made of trees. If you'd grown up in a forest, the feeling of trees all around you in the dark would be normal. The great big figs make her think of filigree brooches, the odd star or streetlight appearing between the branches like diamantes come adrift. A rat runs just in front of her shoe and she says, 'Jesus.' The walking is warming her up a bit. Something nearby glitters and she stops to make sense of it. What do you know, it's a possum – sitting up there like Jackie, regarding her earnestly. Eyes like costume garnets. Hello. He seems to be asking, *What are you about? What's your story?* All the bad stuff there is in life, all the stuff so terrible you can hardly admit it's real, hardly survive it, and then this little present.

It makes her remember, as she often does when she is in the mood for wrapping herself up in something warm, something cosy and bed-snug, how they found each other.

He did garden chores for people in the neighbourhood – that's how it started. She isn't certain if it was before or after the second time she was in hospital that her husband first had Claude come over to do the lawn. Her mind was smudged around that time, smeary glass she couldn't always see through. Claude also had been in a psych ward, apparently, and was living then in a halfway house. Big bloke, preferring to nod than to say much. Greeny-brown eyes, silty-river eyes.

*

While her husband loafs around watching footy on the telly, she sits on the bed she has shared with her daughter, Debbie, for all the months since the rot in the marriage couldn't be denied anymore. The heart can't forgive what it can't forgive. Smoking, she listens to the wireless, to a blowy knocking itself over and over against a fly screen, and especially to the mower. A neighbour mowing might have got her goat, but knowing it's him is pretty nice. It pushes other things out of her mind. And it's surprising how aware she is of what he's up to, if he's behind the house or in front or around the side or getting closer or farther away. It's not just on account of the noise that stops and starts and sometimes stops for so long that she's afraid he might be finishing up and on the verge of clearing off.

At one point, she looks out the window and there he is, about to have a go at the hedge with some shears. She can tell he's being careful, even though there isn't all that much to trim. She likes how he works, paying attention, giving it a burl, calm and steady. It matters to him to do a proper job and make things nice. Some people have a talent for that and you can't entirely see how they do it – making ugly things nice, almost just by being there. There is a reek of petrol from the mower. The thing leaks a fair amount and today she quite likes the scandalous smell of it.

He comes closer, right up under her window, so that she has to step backwards fast. Practically winded, she moves forward again, but keeping to one side of the window and peeking on a slant through the curtain that gives a bit of privacy but still lets the light in. He is examining a geranium that isn't exactly the picture of health. The yard has bugger all in the way of flowers, just that. She isn't going to say anything, she's only watching while she finishes a smoke. Her hair isn't combed and her face isn't on, not even a bit of powder or lippy. Little curls in the hair on his chest escape from his singlet. His pale shoulders are freckled. She feels flushed and giddy.

She is hiking the curtain out of the way. You startle yourself, sometimes.

Through the fly screen, she says: 'Not in great nick, eh?' Softly, because her husband is probably asleep on the lounge.

The air is thick with heat, petrol and mown lawn – like something golden-green has exploded and is flowing everywhere.

'Nah, it's the soil.' Her voice hasn't shocked him. It's like he has sensed where she was, too. 'Dry.'

'Yeah, and don't take your shoes off because the grass is full of bindis.'

'Wasn't planning on taking me shoes off.' He smiles.

It's the kind of hesitant, true smile that sends your mood in the good direction. His teeth are real by the look of it, also, which makes her feel worse about her own. She wishes he'd seen the teeth she had before the gum infection that got them all yanked out. How she wept when she lost her lovely teeth. But that's an old sadness and now she holds her cigarette in front of her face, going for a bit of Bacall.

'I'd offer you a smoke, but I couldn't get it through the screen.'

'You're right. Thanks, anyway.'

It's sad that some people might get the wrong end of the stick and think he is slow in the head. She can tell that this isn't the case. He's leisurely, that's all, and not a gift-of-the-gab type. Which actually she finds is a relief, because she has learned that there's usually something on the other side of a good talker that the talk is hiding, like a mat over a bit of crook flooring. You probably don't want to peek behind it.

'Your name's Claude – that right?'

He nods.

'Is that a French name?'

'I'm not French but.'

'Well it's still a nice name.'

He seems pleased. She hasn't flirted in, Christ, donkey's years, but this would appear to be one of those things that come back to you once you start doing them. No wedding ring, she sees, wondering what the story is there.

He says, 'I'm in the sheltered workshop.'

'I heard that.'

'I met your husband.'

'I know.'

'Has he got a job?'

'Just a pension. He buggered his back when he was twelve, carrying sacks of wheat at Peek Freans biscuit factory. He was real bright – had a scholarship to go to high school, but he dropped out because, he says, he didn't have any school shoes and he only had one exercise book for all the subjects. Later, after the war, he had a job in the army. Now he's talking about racing greyhounds.'

She's prattling on because she's nervous. Well, it's been a long time since someone was interested in her the way he is. She wants to add, *We're not in love anymore, if that concerns you.* She thinks he will understand this.

To give him a clue, she adds, 'It's not much of a yard.'

'I've seen worse.'

'I bet you have.'

He smiles.

Her heart going like the clappers, she imagines stroking those curls of hair on his chest. And the roundness of his shoulder under her lips. She is tipsy but also sober. Already, her mind is less fogged up, turning transparent and edgeless.

24

WESTMORELAND STREET
1974–1975

The bluebottle sting rises into a slight uneven welt on the side of Jan's foot. The skin peels, but a reddish-brown discolouration remains, like a fading burn. Glen reckons you can't see anything there: it's her imagination. Though the evidence is clear to her, he still makes her doubt herself.

A week or so after the afternoon at Manly, Jan runs into Alicia as they are leaving their English exam and they make a plan for the two couples to go to the movies together.

They go to see *The Discreet Charm of the Bourgeoisie.* Outside the Union, the women introduce the men and Glen extends his arm for a handshake. The gesture belongs to their fathers, strained and out of place in its virile politeness. Steve hesitates, possibly amused, and then shakes the waiting hand crisply.

During the movie, Jan can feel that Glen isn't relaxed or enjoying himself, whereas the others seem to have settled in to its absurd, aimless spirit. Alicia keeps passing her a bag of Jaffas and she eats more than she should, gorging herself on orangey chocolate. She finds it endearing that Alicia – despite her serious gourmet attitude to food – should have a sweet tooth and a soft spot for Australian lollies. Afterwards, they are invited back to Westmoreland Street.

Getting home, Steve disappears for a few minutes and returns wearing a sarong. Jan senses Glen thinking, *What's with him?*

Steve proceeds to put on a Miles Davis album, *Sketches of Spain*, lowering the needle to the record with extreme slowness. He then serves wine, lights a joint and asks Glen, with a kind of posed intensity, 'You a Borges man?'

Glen doesn't know what he is referring to, and Jan can see him taking the question as a test he's been set up to fail. 'Wouldn't say that.'

It isn't that Glen doesn't read or isn't clever. He did well at their high school and hated the anti-intellectual mood of much of the place as much as Jan did; that was something that had brought them together. He is proud to read the *Herald* and watch the ABC news, and he goes through phases in which he reads novels – but there haven't been many of those since the early days of their relationship, when she found his reading attractive and imagined it would remain essential to him. During the last year, all he has read are textbooks and *Zen and the Art of Motorcycle Maintenance*, because people were talking about it. Whereas Jan feels she is living an inferior version of her life unless she is reading a novel or two. If she doesn't have any on the go, she is anxiously waiting until she will have and feeling like she isn't breathing deeply enough, isn't looking far enough into the distance or carefully enough at herself.

Next, Steve asks Glen if he likes jazz.

Oh shit, Jan thinks.

After a drag on the joint, Glen replies that he isn't too familiar with it. He says he has mainly been listening to Leonard Cohen and Hendrix, as well as to a bit of old blues. Lightnin' Hopkins, Howlin' Wolf…

Steve nods, switching quickly to the topic of movies. 'What other Buñuel have you seen? And what about Fellini?'

Glen accompanies Jan to the odd art movie, and tends to find them interesting, but Steve's experty, rather pedagogical tone – as if his knowledge was a series of rare objects he'd discerningly collected and felt obliged to tour you around – intimidates him and he lets Jan work at the conversation alone. Listening to the others, face closed, he pats Heidi; he is more patient with dogs than he is with people. After less than an hour, he squeezes her elbow to let her know they should get going, mentioning that he has to hit the books early the next day. Jan is sure that Steve and Alicia have found them disappointing and uninspired.

They walk home under a mass of strangely bright cloud.

'I thought the movie would never end,' Glen says. 'All the posh people saying empty things, one person's dream, and then another one's, and they keep going along that road in the middle of nowhere, God.'

Jan makes an understanding sound. But in fact, the European feel of it appealed to her and all the unending disorientation rang true somehow.

'So – Alicia and Steve – they're against monogamy, are they?'

The comment surprises Jan, who has forgotten having told him this. She wouldn't have expected him to remember it.

Glen goes on, 'Well, I mean, it probably *is* artificial. It certainly doesn't seem to make people happy, does it?'

'Do you think Alicia and Steve are happy?'

'I don't know. At least they look like they're having fun.'

She has suspected that he is bitter about having missed out on the promiscuous hippie good times he might have enjoyed – had he been a bit older and not married to her. This is the closest he has come to admitting he is dissatisfied with their relationship. A rim of moon is lifting above cloud and they are passing a Moreton Bay fig that is half silvered and half shadows, the opening in its trunk like an oval window into an obscure realm.

At home, as soon as they are inside, Glen kisses her against the uneven bricks beside the door. They make love, if that's what it is, as they haven't in long months, both of them ready. She knows he is seeing Alicia in his head. The next day, she discovers she has grazed her knuckles and bruised her hip.

No one proposes again that the four of them socialise together. Alicia invites Jan to go to Westmoreland Street whenever she wants to, so they can help each other study. Jan goes a couple of times and they sit out in the backyard in the ripening hot weather, peacefully reading and drinking tea. Those hours are so much more pleasant than the rest of Jan's life. She adores them. So it is a relief when, after the exams are over, the ritual of the two of them meeting once or twice a week to read alongside one another in that garden continues.

*

'I think I realised even then that I'd always remember the time we spent together in her backyard.'

'Why might that have been?' asked the therapist.

'I don't know. It felt so cosy and private, but exciting, too. Like we were hidden at the centre of important things, of books and reveries and the city.'

*

Jan is on a wicker chair set in the shade between a glossy India rubber tree and a paper bark that is shedding pallid layers as soft as a woman's skin. Beyond the shade, the light is a white gold that in the late afternoon takes on the warmer tones of sandstone. A breeze gives away the presence of nearby jasmine. Alicia is opposite Jan on a recliner, in the mint-green sarong she likes to wear around the house, an enamel camping mug of tea usually balanced between her thighs, her bare feet to either side of Heidi on mossy bricks. There is the luxurious blitheness of exams finished and heavy summer air. Jan is getting high on *One Hundred Years of Solitude*, Alicia flitting between Freud, Doris Lessing, Ursula Le Guin and Peter Carey (an Australian who has recently published his first book of short stories, which she has described to Jan as clever and nicely bizarre).

Here, time turns edgeless, transparent. Reading all afternoon isn't some kind of self-coddling cop-out. It's not only reasonable to read as if your life depended on it: it is a calling, sacred. The yearning and sadness Jan is often aware of, her sense of watching time pass, an almost-painful tugging and tautness in her chest, have not disappeared – but they are interwoven with wellbeing, with feeling, if not exactly *at home*, then in the right place. Where she wants to be.

Every so often, one of them speaks, comments on what she has just read, says, 'God this is good. Listen to this …' Or, 'I wonder what the cognitive therapy approach to this would be …' Or something simple and fanciful, like: 'That cloud looks like a boat.' To which the other might reply, 'It absolutely does.'

For longer conversations, Alicia's preferred topic remains Jan's childhood.

One day she asks, 'What's your mother's favourite music?'

'Um, God … She doesn't really listen to music. I mean, my parents never put the radio on for music. Only for news. They have an old record player that they never use.' Jan thinks some more. 'I do remember, when I was little, her sometimes humming "You Are My Sunshine".'

Playing the role of exotic wildlife, a mystery of Australianness Alicia is studying and determined to fathom, has come to feel more or less natural. Welcome, even, because Alicia's attention – so focused and thorough – is addictive.

'And what about you?'

'Huh?'

'What music did your mother listen to?'

'Classical.'

Jan waits. 'Did you enjoy it?'

Alicia shrugs. 'Some of it.'

Nothing more.

Jan tries, 'What was the house you grew up in like?'

'An apartment, in Double Bay.'

And that's it. Jan pictures a lot of white, gold-plated fixtures and marble, a balcony, maybe a pretty view.

'Did you like it?'

'There's heaps of Lladró in it, which gives me the creeps.'

'What's that?'

'A Spanish brand of porcelain figurines. You know, like a farm girl with a basket full of wheat, two ballerinas dancing together – that sort of thing. I had the job of dusting them, which I hated. I was always warned not to break them, so I was always nervous about it. And my grandmother has lots of old photos in her room of people I never knew.'

Imagining the musty atmosphere surrounding those photos, how their foreign intimacies in old-fashioned black and white could have unsettled a child, Jan leans forward without thinking and reaches for Alicia. But she quickly withdraws the gesture.

'That sounds kind of bleak?'

'It was!'

Soon after this, Alicia vanishes inside for a long while, Jan resuming reading. Birdsong rises and falls. Her stomach starts to rumble and she remembers she skipped lunch. Lost in her book again, she is startled by Alicia returning with a tray.

'I went and got us some tucker.'

Alicia has recently started adopting some of Jan's expressions, *tucker* among them. She also sometimes uses *ta* for thank you and *tea* for the evening meal. Jan is touched by the learned words and by this gift of food that is much too generous. It is a Lebanese spread from Abdul's: houmous, baba ganoush, tabouleh, falafel, vine leaves, voluptuous ladies' fingers. At the squat, they've been down to austere variations on bubble and squeak for a few days, so this is surreally sumptuous, a king's banquet.

'Gosh, thank you! You shouldn't have. Steve's not eating with us?'

'He's got a friend over. I took them some.'

'Oh.'

Then, they don't speak much. They are concentrating on the flavours, the lavish satisfaction of hunger, having all that you need and more. Triangles of bread exquisitely soft and bendy with freshness; houmous splotched with paprika and oil, lightly granular and decadent with tahini; the tabouleh crisp, minty and lemony; the smoky char-grilled tang of the baba ganoush virtually stinging the tongue.

'I should be getting home.' Jan seems to be always saying this. 'I don't even know what I'll make for tea.' The treat over, she is already feeling guilty that Glen's meal will be so much more frugal than what she has just enjoyed and she won't have any appetite for it.

Alicia makes a face. 'Oh stay a bit longer. I was about to put the kettle on. And I'll send you off with Lebanese leftovers, anyway.'

She often suggests one last cup of tea or wine. And Jan, always sorry to leave that house, generally accepts. It has occurred to her that perhaps Alicia was lonely as an only child. Neither she nor Alicia has a sister and it is possible that, not accustomed to being intimate with other girls, their time together is novel and important for both of them.

They carry their plates inside, Heidi frisky in the lead. The dog suddenly doubles back, nearly causing Alicia to trip. They laugh and Jan takes hold of one side of the precarious tray. They hear music, jazz by the sound of it, contemplative and rousing. Listening with Alicia in the shadows of a Glebe hallway on a summer afternoon, giggling a little and wondering if the tray will fall and everything will break, Jan feels happy as she rarely does.

'I'll take it.'

'You sure?'

'I think so.'

A woman's voice is abruptly, briefly audible. Taking over the tray, Jan tries to read Alicia's eyes.

'That's Anita, Steve's friend,' Alicia explains. 'They're having a meeting, for the magazine.'

'Oh, right.'

'Listen, do you want a bath?'

'What?'

'Why don't I run you a bath? You can take your book in.' She proposes this with the tone of a child hatching an irresistible plan. 'There's nothing better than reading in the bath. Not much, anyway.'

Being offered a bath at someone else's house is outlandish, isn't it? Has Alicia proposed this because she doesn't want to be left alone with Steve and Anita? Puzzled, Jan ends up agreeing – to prolong the afternoon's happiness and to support Alicia, if she is being asked to do so.

Waiting for the bathtub to fill, she investigates the bathroom. She has been in there before, but rushing because the latch on the door is broken. Now she has time to notice that their toothpaste is Indian and they have a tub of Lucas' Papaw ointment. Do they rub that into cuts or dry lips? She opens the small window, letting in air that smells somehow both earthy and almost seaweedy. There is a long, flat stone on the windowsill, a fossil. With her fingertip, Jan traces the chalk-white outline of a fern, suddenly feeling she is looking down from an upper floor into a sort of impossibly steep stairwell at the bottom of which lies a Sydney of rainforest and Aboriginal walking trails.

Alicia knocks. 'Decent?'

'Yes, come in.'

Plaintive music enters with her. She puts the cup on the corner of the bath between the tap and the wall, and then tests the water with her hand, approving.

Jan wants to say, *You give me too much.* Her throat is tight and she only manages a flat: 'Thank you. What's that music?'

'Coltrane, *A Love Supreme.* I'll leave a towel for you here. Got everything you need?'

'More.'

'Good. I'll get back to my Freud. It'll be nice knowing you're here. Do you like it?'

'What?'

'The music.'

'Very much.'

Leaving the room, Alicia grazes Jan's shoulder with her hand. Jan thinks this might have been accidental, but wanting to reciprocate in case it wasn't, she tries to touch Alicia's arm. What she actually touches, though, is her hip. The surprise of bone projecting through soft fabric. Then Alicia closes the bathroom door behind her and Jan hears her footsteps and Heidi's nails pattering along the hall.

There is a Turkish delight on the saucer beside the teacup. She gobbles it, revelling in the taste of rosewater that she still finds rather astonishing, the fineness of that floral perfume in her mouth.

Some time later, when she is warm and loose in the water and her reading, there is a knock.

'Yes?'

Her back to the door, she thinks it is Alicia coming in, till Steve says, 'Having a nice time?'

One of her legs is hooked over the side of the tub. She wants to move it but feels paralysed as she hears him unzip and begin to urinate.

After a strange, suspended moment, leg still stiffly raised, she leans forward to hide herself as best she can.

'Don't mind me,' he says.

This is nothing, Jan tells herself. This is the sort of thing that happens in a big city, in the house of a psychology student and a poet, brilliant, open-minded people. I'm only inhibited because of my hang-ups, my Anglican suburban upbringing.

'This isn't the first time you've done that in my presence,' she says, wanting to be casual like they are, a hip Sydney person. And remembering, in spite of herself, what she saw the other time: the greyish-pink skin and his business-like way of handling himself, how easy it was for him to be watched.

'True. I'm making a habit of it.'

He flushes the toilet and washes his hands, but doesn't leave. Worrying that her leg will cramp, she keeps her arms folded across her chest and stares down into the water.

*

'I didn't tell him to get out,' she said to the therapist. 'I was even worried that he wouldn't find me attractive! I hate that as a woman, there's *always* the question of am I being attractive? Am I being seen from a flattering angle?

'A year or so later, when I was living in a share house, that sort of situation probably wouldn't have shocked me. I got used to people wandering out of their bedrooms naked or in their undies, and constant talk about sex and bodies and how important it was to be natural and liberated from all the shame our parents had taught us, et cetera. It was the era, of course.

'But Steve threw me.'

*

He asks, 'What's your star sign? Not that we believe in that.'

His voice is even slower and quieter than usual. Jan can't tell if he is teasing her. In her parents' house they occasionally read each other their horoscopes, but she wouldn't have suspected he would put any faith in such things. Steve is interesting because it's hard to tell if he is tongue in cheek or for real, cynical or some kind of innocent.

'Scorpio.'

'Ah, so we are perhaps quite similar to each other.' He doesn't explain what he means. After a hesitation, he goes on, 'You should think of submitting something. I haven't asked you if you write. Do you?'

'Submitting what?'

'To *The Source*.'

'The source?'

'My poetry magazine.'

'Oh no, I don't write poetry.' She is thinking: I bet the girl he is having the meeting with is an aspiring poet. He appeals to girls' fragile, barely confessable hopes.

'What made me a writer was an accident that happened when I was a kid. It killed my mother. I wrote my first poems during the months after she died.'

'Oh God.'

'Yeah, she got knocked off a boat into the sea and drowned. She'd gone out on a yacht, with another man, as they say. She had a taste for boating, but my father didn't have the budget for that. Is this where the creature got you?'

'Huh?'

He is pointing to her foot that is over the side of the bath. When he kneels beside her, she catches the odour of dope, like dense undergrowth in stagnant water in a heat wave. Along with the story about his mother, it seems to turn the air in the room darker, thicker, more private, as if they have just woken up together in a fusty bed.

'It branded you.'

'That must have been so hard, unbelievably hard for you, as a child. The shock of that.'

He takes advantage of the lowered guard of her sympathy to touch her foot. She jerks.

'You don't have to be so shy, you know.'

His finger starts to move back and forth, and panic makes her laugh. As if to stop the laughter, he takes a firm hold of her foot, pushing his thumb into the tender spot in the middle of the sole.

'One of my lesser known but not lesser talents is as a masseur. If you know how to give a foot massage, you will never lack a friend.'

Trying to extricate her foot from his grip, Jan leans back in the tub and makes a kicking motion. But it is too weak to achieve anything. She is afraid to use force, not wanting to be seen as the girl with no sense of humour; she is reminded of her dreams in which she gets attacked and is unable to scream.

'You carry a lot of tension,' he says.

'In my foot?'

'Yes, among other places. You really should consider writing poetry. You could start by keeping a diary – that can sort of open up the floodgates. You'll see. Anyway, if the floodgates do open, I'd be happy to read something for you.' He lets this sit, appraising her body, probably finding her legs to be on the solid side. Her bent leg starts to shake. I am being silly, she tries to calm herself. This is like something out of a movie or a book or something that would happen at the Chelsea Hotel.

'And you're beautiful,' he says, releasing her foot that hovers before she pulls it back towards her. 'Don't you realise? Thank you.'

He stands and leaves. She isn't sure what has occurred. Thank you for what? And what has Alicia been doing all this time – talking to the other girl? Jan's book is in the bath, floating beneath the surface, bloated with water. She'll have to pay a library fine.

That night, she dreams she is talking to Helen, after school.

Her teacher is saying, 'Hope is so important, because sooner or later, it's justified. It's like we are living in utopia now. Maybe you'll be part of some third wave of feminism, Jan. You're the woman of the future.'

The plovers dive-bomb them as they run past the oval. It is eerie and familiar.

Waking to see the paper blind on her window glowing like a lantern, Jan thinks that maybe she will start keeping a diary again, after all. A dream diary? Abruptly, things seem simple. What she feels for Alicia is less complicated than friendship. She has a clear, bright longing to be up against her skin, to travel far inside her mind, her perceptions, her superior manner of being.

She loves her.

She is in love.

While Jan is preparing breakfast for herself and Glen, guilt and shame – the suspicion that she must be a treacherous, twisted person – start washing up against the beautiful certainty. Guilt, shame and fear bleeding into each other. Guilty fear and also luscious fear, her stomach nervily expecting joy. But she knows that she can't go back to Westmoreland Street again.

Some weeks later, one day that she has forgotten to take the pill, Glen wants sex and she goes along with it.

25

ALEXANDER'S

11 November 1975

Lorna is famished, craves an egg flip with a wee kick of something fun in it. The sunrise sort of sidles into the room and then starts running the show. Things have opened up: she can see and hear and feel far. Crikey, the birds are loud. And the green of those parrots. Strong buggers, the seagulls. If there were something in reincarnation, she wouldn't mind coming back as that, as a hardy traveller. Even the sound of church bells excites her that morning. Couldn't be him? No, Claude's not a churchy man, that wouldn't be his style.

She is stiff and it takes some limbering up to get herself walking normally and down to the toilets by the station. She has a piddle, washes the old face and dries it as best she can with dunny paper. Wanting to be ready for her big day, she combs her hair, dabs on some powder and next pouts for a long time – cheeks hollowed right out, eyes vain and knowing and slightly amused – as the maroon lippy glides on and she studies the effect. Not half bad. She hopes her knee-highs aren't laddered. Tea is now very much in order, or one of those *cuppa-cinos*. She likes those, too.

The feeling of joining the smart crowd coming out of the station and heading importantly into the city, stepping out on the town! For a moment, she imagines her hair is done properly and she is looking like a slick chick, a real bobby dazzler. She is passing DJs, but it's too early for the tea room, where she has an idea that Claude might go to find her, later on. The afternoon is more when you go there, she fancies.

She turns onto George Street, peering towards the Town Hall steps and remembering how bubbly with pride and jubilation she feels when she is marching here for the workers on May Day, on her birthday. She decides to stop in at Alexander's. Not for a full hot spread or anything, just something to take the edge off, maybe some toast with her cuppa. It's cosy in there and adventurous, like it were a boat about to set sail, make for open water. And there's a nice comradely feeling of jostling shoulders with other people who are comforting themselves as best they can with basic pleasures – a hot cup, something that'll stick to their ribs – before a day of work. She'd have liked to have a job in town, like a girl in a picture set in New York, living in a flat with her best girlfriend. She is a bit weepy, but not unpleasantly. Will Claude be having his breakfast now? Weet-Bix, toast, soft-boiled egg? She waits and listens.

She loses track of time in an arcade that she finds somewhat mysterious. There are several floors and dinky little shops selling odd things you wouldn't necessarily expect they'd have a shop for – like miniature soldiers. One shop has filmy frocks you'd seriously need a petticoat under, and you wouldn't believe the prices, Lord have mercy. In a place like that, it's always good to take advantage of the toilets because the ones there are proper, top quality, posh. They have one of those extra rooms with comfortable chairs to rest on and mirrors with lights around them, like you were the leading lady in your nice dressing room at a theatre. It's peaceful and safe there. She washes her face with hot water and even has a very decent sleep.

In the tea room at DJs, her sense of expectation almost hurts, is almost too much. Any minute now, he could come in. He'll be shy in a place like this, but she'll smile to reassure him, maybe even hold his hand and, anyway, together they won't care what anyone else thinks, will they?

She tried to save some milk for him. But now there is none left in the midget pot. There was barely enough for one person who doesn't take much milk in their tea. Why do they do that? Why would you even make a milk pot like that? Stingy.

26

GLEBE POINT ROAD TO THE CITY

11 November 1975

Exam nerves making her antsy and unhappy with herself, Alicia has been trying to relax with *Johnno* under a Moreton Bay fig in Foley Park. She admires her lecturer's novel, which makes her feel she knows Brisbane, though she doesn't. In fact, it makes her long for Brisbane in a sad sort of way, as if she'd grown up there and had no choice but to leave. It means a lot to her somehow that in the novel there are fig trees similar to the one she is sitting under. She looks up at the inside of the tree, awed by it as an explorer might have been, attempting to sketch it in a notebook of botanical discoveries; vast and sinuous, it seems to belong to a more majestic dinosaur-inhabited past.

But Alicia feels guilty for having briefly let herself be dreamy. She should really be studying at Fisher Library, or doing a food shop. Deciding on the latter, she sighs, puts her book away and heads to Galluzzo's for fruit and veg.

The sight of Janet is a shock. She recognises her from behind, despite an unfamiliar dress, some big purple Indian thing made more vivid by her auburn hair. It is unquestionably her – that cautious way of considering something while leaning slightly back, arms protectively folded across her chest.

Alicia wants to run away, but she is already inside the shop and she realises that she would also like to rectify what went wrong. Her memory of the last time they saw each other, months and months before, is tainted with regret.

*

Bridge Road coursing with a sudden wild downpour. Alicia is on her way to visit Janet and, having no umbrella, she has to run the last stretch, visibility turning into pearly swaths of water. She'd have put the saucepans out at home, had she expected it would rain; she hopes Steve will remember to do it and doubts that he will. Though she has checked the street directory before leaving, she still has to wander – thoroughly soaked now, corduroy jeans heavy and adherent with water, rivulets running into her eyes – for a couple of minutes searching for the right number. Then she finds it.

The front of the little terrace is hidden by feral bamboo that, as she distinguishes it within the watery air, makes her think of an island glimpsed during a storm at sea. It is the first time she has been invited here and she can tell from Janet's slightly hangdog face, when she opens the door, that she is shy about Alicia seeing the place. She remembers that when Janet made the invitation, she talked the squat down, calling it 'a bit of a dump', evidently meaning to lower any expectations.

'You think I'm some kind of bourgeois?' she tried to joke, hurt to suppose her friend must see her that way.

She has also been disappointed by the fact that Janet hasn't come over for one of their reading-in-the-yard afternoons in ages; she has often remembered their convivial conversations and silences.

'Is this what you call a flash flood? I'll leave my boots outside.'

'Don't worry about that. It couldn't be any damper in here. The leather might go mouldy, that's all.' She chuckles.

In the hallway the light is low, dove grey. Even with the door closed and the rain beating on a portion of the roof that must be corrugated iron, they hear with surprising clarity a truck tackling the hill up to Glebe Point Road. There are smells of Nag Champa incense and cooked rice.

'God, you're wet. I'm sorry to make you come out in this!'

'How could you have known? Anyway, I love rain like this. It's so subtropical.'

'Come and I'll get you a towel.'

Following Janet down the hall over dodgy floorboards, carefully avoiding a baking tray left out to catch drips, they pass two small rooms and Alicia gets an impression of bareness, rough bricks, wood that might be untrustworthy with splinters, slapdash carpeting. She wonders who lived in these worker's digs before Janet and Glen. She is moved to catch a glimpse of the milk crates for bedside tables, with a large pile of books on one of them topped with a folded *Herald*. And she notices that the bookshelves in the mini living room at the back of the house have been assembled with bricks and planks. Their table, probably all-purpose, isn't much larger than a card table, and it has been embellished with an old Vegemite jar holding frangipani flowers, their umbrellas half open. There are also sprouts germinating on a windowsill. Glen doesn't seem to be at home.

The bathroom is a skinny space containing just a tub and a sink. Janet's swimming costume, cap and goggles hang over the towel rail.

'Use this towel and I'll go and get you something dry to put on.'

Janet has to squash herself into the wall in order to leave the bathroom without bumping into Alicia. She half closes the door, and Alicia peels down her wet jeans with difficulty.

A moment later, Janet says, 'I'll just leave this here.'

Alicia turns, feeling childish in her underpants, and sees Janet awkwardly reaching around the door to hang a tracksuit from the handle.

Janet's face appears as she tries to grab the tracksuit that is slipping to the floor. 'Sorry!' She averts her eyes and is gone, calling, 'I'll put the kettle on.'

'Thanks.' Alicia is still slightly breathless from her run and the flap of arriving at a house for the first time drenched.

Coming out of the bathroom, she stops to admire a cloudy but handsome mirror with a scalloped border into which art postcards have been stuck.

Janet says, 'I found that, one garbage night. Opposite Wentworth Park. It was a beautiful night, the moon looked *too* full and there were so many bats flying over. Have you seen the fig tree in the park there, I don't know what kind it is, with all the bits hanging off it? Like a fringed curtain? You feel like you could walk under it and vanish. Anyway, someone had left that mirror out the front of their house. I couldn't believe my luck. Deco, do you reckon?'

That eagerness of hers.

'Yeah, I do. It's lovely.'

Janet sees life in the inner city as an adventure, which makes being in her company somehow adventurous. When they are together, the excitement of things is more obvious; Alicia even feels exciting herself. And she loves drawing folkloric stories out of Janet.

'It's amazing what people throw away. And what you can get for next to nothing. Like this teapot.' It is Willow pattern, dark red. 'I found it at Vinnies.' The lid falls off while she pours the tea. 'Oh, sorry, that happens sometimes. Did the noise scare you? It's nice though, isn't it?' When she puts the lid back on, Alicia notices a neat lightning-bolt crack across it.

'Very nice.'

'Remind me to show you something, later. It's outside – but close by. A little cave. The sandstone is magnificent, like dark old gold. You wouldn't think there'd be a cave around here, would you?'

Of course, Janet was very nervous early in their friendship, but Alicia thought they were past that. It's true that being in the squat is a bit like waiting in a corridor. But the scruffiness verging on disreputable and something improvised reminiscent of camping – this sort of thing is Glebe's romance. No Lladró figurines to be religiously dusted here. Alicia is drawn to the sense of being on an edge, hovering on the brink of chaos. For her, Glebe is all edges – the edge of the sea, of the city, of the university, of social categories and identities. She has chosen to live there among edge-dwellers like Janet and it makes her, the immigrant, feel more legitimate, maybe even more authentically Australian than she has done before.

A large cockroach runs across the wall above the table, darting down to hide behind *Tassajara Cooking*, which is propped on a ledge beside the album cover of *Songs from a Room* and a box of index cards.

'Sorry,' her friend apologises.

'For God's sake, I live in fucking Sydney, too. Please never apologise to me for anything. Ever again. You offend me.'

Janet pours more milk and then more tea for them both, the lid falling off the pot again. 'Bloody thing.'

Alicia doesn't usually take her tea with milk, but Janet's nervousness is making her nervous and she says nothing. And actually, the tea is satisfying with it, substantial and bitter enough so that the milk is welcome rather than sickening. The tea she makes herself isn't this intense and good. Janet is fiddling with the strainer.

'Listen, are you okay?'

'I think I have to leave uni.'

'What! Why?'

'I'm pregnant.'

Alicia only just stops herself from saying something chilling in its speed and irreversible cruelty, like a snake's tongue darting out, something her mother would say. *You silly girl.*

The problem is she doesn't think that Janet is remotely silly. In fact, she is one of the most intelligent, perceptive people she has met at university and Alicia has frequently thought that she'd be capable of an impressive career as a therapist, of anything really. Something original. She *could have* done *anything*. And with her class background, she isn't going to take advantage of what their government has done for someone like her? She's going to squander the absolute gift and glorious justice of free university tuition?

She can't fake enthusiasm. 'You're nineteen. There are alternatives, of course. You're sure you want it?'

A helpless shrug.

'How old was your mother when she had her first child?' Sometimes Alicia is afraid she is drawn to gentle people because she isn't gentle herself.

Janet has flinched. 'Eighteen.' She looks like she might cry.

And Alicia is stunned by the strength of her own rising grief. Janet is a tragedy, splendid in the flower of her youth that will wither so soon now. About to lose whatever suppleness her life has, so much of her energy for daydreaming and adventures. She is falling into the gap between traditional womanhood and the new ways of being that she can't fully seize. From this point on, Janet and Alicia will belong more than ever to different worlds.

'Where is your toilet?' She finds she can hardly speak.

'It's outside. Sorry – I'll show you.'

'It's okay. I'll find it.'

'Watch out for the leopard slugs on the path. There'll be a lot now.' Still that galling apologetic tone, as if the slugs were an unsightly aspect of herself.

Alicia rushes outside, disoriented to see that the rain has stopped. She nonetheless remembers to watch out for the swollen glistening slugs that both impress and make her shiver with revulsion. The air is steamy and misty but clearing. There is an astringent scent of eucalyptus. The door of the dingy old dunny closed behind her, she feels the dreaded wave of warm tears. She closes her eyes and pushes her fingers against her tear ducts, squashing them down. Who is she to judge Janet's choices? Is she seeing her friend from her mother's perspective, through the lens of immigrant ambition, that ruthless compensatory drive? But it seems unbearably sad that it should only be possible to live one version of a life. For the first time deeply, she feels how a woman's body is tied to reproduction and time.

She has herself more or less under control when she comes out, though she is embarrassed by the coldness she displayed. Over a ghost-grey fence four o'clocks droop, hiding their violet linings. Through a gap in the palings, sunlight cascades onto a banana tree. This modest scene is surprisingly lush, and Alicia finds herself imagining it as a painting or an illustration in an old children's book – the radiance shown with white space and thin black lines. She thinks: I will forget having seen this serene loveliness.

She turns and Janet is standing by the open back door. 'Everything okay?'

'All good. Which way is the cave you were telling me about?'

Janet smiles and points, but she has apparently forgotten her offer to show it to Alicia. She says, 'I finished *Girls in Their Married Bliss*. Remind me to give it back to you.'

And their talk shifts to books.

Walking home in wet boots and a borrowed tracksuit, Alicia wonders why she wasn't able to be comforting. Should she even have tried to touch Janet? Or maybe offered to go to Family Planning with her? She is already looking back on the afternoon, as she will do for many years, as a missed opportunity – of what sort she isn't quite sure. However, Alicia will not forget the sunlight that followed a storm streaming through the gap in a weather-bleached paling fence.

*

Janet turns, her face blank. And then she smiles uncertainly. Gosh, she is pregnant, very clearly now. Statuesque and pink-cheeked, also, but perhaps slightly haunted – or is Alicia projecting? She realises, seeing her friend holding the greenish bunch of bananas she has just bought, that she has missed her a great deal and felt betrayed by her not getting in touch.

'Only bananas?'

She is immediately sorry for the thoughtless comment: it could be that Janet couldn't afford anything else. She has seen her pay for things by painstakingly counting out a quantity of coins from a drawstring purse full of small change. She tries to imagine what it would be like to go to a fruit shop and have to ignore everything succulent and exotic; it's hard to sustain the feeling of confinement and drabness, but she strives to for a moment.

On the footpath in front of Galluzzo's, she says, 'Janet, look at you.'

'I know. Like the side of a house, as my mother would say.'

Her voice has become strange to Alicia again, like a known voice on a recording can sound. Not unfamiliar but disconcerting – as if shown from a new angle or spied upon. Alicia often feels like a spy.

'No. You look wonderful.'

Janet's gaze veers away. 'Thanks,' she replies miserably.

It is a battle to compliment her. The air feels like damp silk.

'How much longer?' she asks awkwardly.

'A couple of months.'

'God.' She has again reacted as if to dire news. 'Oh, and … where are you off to now – the pool?'

'No, I'm hoping to find my mother-in-law.'

'Your mother-in-law? Where do you expect her to be?'

'Glen's dad heard from the hospital that she went AWOL yesterday. We're not sure she's in Sydney, but she usually comes here when she does that. Sometimes she comes to our place, but she didn't last night or this morning.'

'What's her condition?'

'Schizophrenic.'

Alicia tries to picture things she has trouble picturing – forced hospitalisation, electroconvulsive therapy – but it is as if she can only see outlines, or vague scenes from Janet Frame. Sometimes she wonders if she wants to be a therapist because it will force her to imagine horrifying experiences like she was living them herself. She has also noticed that she can be insatiable for information about people's pasts, especially difficult ones and ones involving muddy, complex motivations. Is it because hearing about other people makes her feel less strange? Or because her mother and grandmother have always been so reluctant to talk to her about the important parts of their lives in Spain? She reassures herself that she isn't closed in the way they are. It's just that she always prefers to tilt the mirror, as it were, so as not to be reflected in it. She likes to think all this was fated, predestining her to be a psychologist.

'Where might she go?'

'I've already tried the lounge of the AB pub, which was one possibility. There are a couple of other places that are worth a shot. She likes to go to the tea room at David Jones. There's not much chance I'll run into her, but I'd rather be out than sitting around at home waiting.'

'I could come with you, if you don't mind some company.'

'You don't need to be studying?'

'I don't think I can take Fisher today. And Steve's having a meeting with Anita at home.'

They start strolling.

'You don't mind?'

'Huh?'

'All the … meetings?'

In the beginning, she had been able to calm Steve. He'd be fidgety and then she'd go and sit beside him or put her arm around him in bed, and he'd quieten: some internal feedback loop would be interrupted and the tension would leave his body. But her calming effect appears to be wearing off and his restlessness comes on more often than before, like the twitchy, ill-tempered hankering for a drug. Having a fresh female audience is what seems to work best for this. It makes him more leisurely again, somehow allowing him to play the mellow, philosophical older man.

'Steve requires a lot of attention to feel he exists. He liked it when you came around, for example. It put him in a good mood.' It put Alicia in a good mood, too.

'Really?'

Alicia would like to explain that Steve is the course of treatment she is following while she convalesces from her childhood; he helped her escape a household of tough women.

It was his softness she was drawn to, the fact that he was so different from the women she grew up with and to the kind of Australian man who frightened her. With his dog and his homey, book-bolstered house and its cosy, bushy yard, his vaguely mystical ideas, his delicate ways and voice. Even if she is less sure than she used to be that his gentleness is necessarily the same as trustworthiness. But it would be much more relaxing to fall back into her old habit of asking Janet questions. Is that still possible?

She tries, 'See *Picnic at Hanging Rock*?'

Janet nods. 'You?'

'Yeah. What did you make of it?'

She gives this some thought. 'It was like being inside a refined daydream. A nightmarish, refined daydream.'

'Wasn't it? Mirandaaaa,' Alicia calls out for one of the missing girls in the movie and Janet smiles.

Reaching Parramatta Road, they are about to turn towards Broadway and she has the impression that Janet has avoided looking in the direction of the university's turrets.

'Do you want to get a bus?'

'No, I sort of feel like a big walk.'

'It won't be too much for you?'

'I don't think so. Not if we take our time.'

The flow of people around them makes remaining silent easier. They pass the man she has seen before who wears a careful arrangement of tinfoil over a cap. She likes that Janet neither ignores nor stares at him.

A while later, Janet gestures at a church. 'Glen's parents grew up in a housing development that was set up by the minister of that church in the thirties.'

'St Barnabas – Anglican?'

'Yeah. But they're both atheists, very much so.'

'That was where?'

'Southwest, Liverpool. Place called Hammondville. For destitute families who'd been evicted from the inner city. The father had to have been out of work for at least ten years.'

This stuff is good, bringing them back to the conversations they used to have, taking Alicia out of herself and into Janet's Australia, her way of seeing. Getting the first whiff of yeasty air coming off the brewery, she comments, 'That smell makes me imagine fields and industrial towns in the north of England. Sometimes it annoys me that I compare Australia to other places like that – places I've never been to.'

'I do it, too. Maybe it's inevitable in a country where so many of us come from elsewhere or descend from people who do. We can't just see it as itself.'

It is sheltering, this use of *us* and *we*, balmy, as if they are walking arm in arm. They are starting to feel the pull of Central Station's force field, though the Clock Tower isn't visible yet. The sense of acceleration and imminence has a contradictory effect on Alicia, making her feel both keyed up and relieved, like she is finally going somewhere. Janet's skin has a moist sheen.

'You okay? We're not going too fast?'

Her friend's hand goes to her lower back. Her stride might be a little slower than it was, but she still gives an impression of strength, with her broad, muscular swimmer's shoulders and her newly solid body.

'No, I'm good. I like train stations.'

They can see the Clock Tower now, its comforting old bricks and cupola a sort of anchor.

'I was just thinking that, too.'

'I was remembering how excited I used to be as a kid when Dad brought us into the city for the Easter Show.'

Alicia has never been to the Easter Show. 'Was it fun?'

'I waited for it like it was Christmas – the whole carnival atmosphere, the smell of the animals, the sweet baby ones, the show bags, the rides. Though I was always scared of the rides. All except for the Ferris Wheel. To be honest, even the Ferris Wheel – but I forced myself to go on that. My brother teased me pitilessly.' She glances at Alicia. 'You see that I've always been a scaredy-cat.'

'Did your father grow up in Sydney?' she asks after a pause, to keep Janet talking.

'No, in rural New South Wales, the South West Slopes.'

Alicia tries to look as if this means something to her. But actually it does, because she is visualising it. 'On a farm?'

'Yes, a fruit orchard.'

'What kind of fruit?'

'Cherries. Young – that's the name of the town – likes to think of itself as the *Cherry Capital.*'

'Ah, no less?'

'No less, and in fact my grandfather created a variety of cherry that he named after my father's brother, Harold. Harold's Cherry. I always wondered if Dad wasn't offended not to have had a cherry named after him, too. I always felt a bit sad that there wasn't a Morris's Cherry.'

'From now on I'll think of cherries, all cherries, as *Morris's.*' They smile at each other, Janet's face something like merry for the first time that day. 'Your dad worked on the farm?'

'Until he was sixteen, when he left home to come here. Do you know where your father was raised?'

'Spain, Asturias. He buggered off soon after I was born, so I don't know much more than that.' About to tilt the mirror again, Alicia makes an uncharacteristic effort: 'My grandfather died in the Civil War. My mother and grandmother don't talk about it. I know so little about how it was for them in Spain. Only a few random things – for example, my mother hates certain vegetables, so I wonder if she had to eat a lot of them over there.'

There is a silence and then Janet says, 'Thanks for telling me that.' As a therapist might.

Alicia goes on quickly, 'It's funny to think of your dad being younger than us now, walking these streets.'

'Yeah, isn't it? I suppose his mother had told him about Sydney. She worked as a servant here, in someone's house, before she was married.'

'Oh that's interesting. Do you know where exactly she worked?'

'No, unfortunately. Or where my dad lived – just that it was in a boarding house. I imagine a cramped upstairs room, with a bathroom down a creaky hall.'

'Everyone noticing when you came and went.'

'Exactly.'

'Did he like Sydney?'

'I think he was in awe of it. He was a shy boy from the country suddenly in the Big Smoke.'

'It must have been pretty overwhelming to start with.'

'Yeah, I reckon. For five years, he was taking night classes at tech so he could get his diploma and work as a dyer. Do you know where the TAFE is in Ultimo, a bit back there?' She turns and points. 'It used to be Sydney Technical College.'

There is a hiatus, Alicia trying to imagine Janet's father's life in Sydney in the forties. She is also thinking: This is the Indian summer of our closeness.

Eventually, Janet says, 'He often stopped to look in this window.'

'Your dad?'

'He liked looking at the shaving sets, aftershave and stuff like that. The sorts of things a British gentleman would own, I suppose. Does your mum come into the city much?'

'Not really. She prefers going to Bondi Junction to shop. My grandmother comes in from time to time for Cyril's Delicatessen – over that way. She goes with a couple of friends who call themselves the Old Jews. To buy duck-liver pâté and so on. Wanna go up Sussex or Dixon, instead of George? It's more fun.'

'Good idea.'

Alicia adores walking through Chinatown and infers from her friend's face that Janet enjoys it, too. Glimpses of wildly colourful signs down alleys that could exist in detective novels set in San Francisco. Shops selling things whose purposes you have to guess at. Fantastically pungent odours that you struggle to describe to yourself: fishy and fungal, cured, fermented. Even a lettuce in a gutter, a rat making haste, gusts of unusual garbage smells are satisfyingly exotic, somewhere between faintly disturbing and erotic. The wonder of finding yourself in a fresh pocket of reality.

'Dad saw some men playing Two Up around here, back in the day.'

They are picturing the scene. Is this why their friendship has felt significant? They take each other's intellect seriously – there's that. And for both of them, imagining is an essential part of reasoning and understanding, at least as important as everything else.

They make their way back to George Street via Liverpool Street. The sky seems to be very far above them and it is pleasant to walk in the cool shade cast by blocks of buildings. Alicia is refreshed by the feeling she gets in the inner city of being neither quite outdoors nor indoors, at the same time here and nowhere, camouflaged.

Passing the Spanish Club, Janet asks, 'Ever go there?'

'Once, a long time ago. My grandmother said she overheard a conversation there between some Franco supporters, so she never wanted to go back.'

Nine days later, Franco will die, and when Alicia's mother and grandmother hear the news, they get drunk. It will be the only time Alicia will ever see them like that. Fiendishly determined – which isn't new, but the floppiness is, the disregard for appearances. Even then, they won't evoke the past, at least not to her. Some years after that, Alicia will reflect that, though their trauma was not hers, she spent her childhood and teenage years straining to see what was inside the bare outlines within which they'd worked to contain it. Then the time beyond that offering to the very few who, like Janet, invited her to reveal herself, more stark outlines.

27

THE TEA ROOM AT DAVID JONES

11 November 1975

It is disorienting to go into DJs with someone who knows how to show the right self-assured detachment in a place like that. If Alicia was attracted to one of those luxurious handbags or scarves, for example, it wouldn't be in a make-believe way, with a wistful sense of impossibility. She moves like she can buy anything that takes her fancy.

A glossily made-up girl in a suit asks them if they would care to try some Shalimar. Alicia accepts automatically and then Jan nods timidly and offers her wrists. Like in the Van Morrison song, she is thinking. The girl with the perfume will be noticing she is a pregnant Westie in a cheap Indian dress that is faded because she accidentally washed it in hot water; she is a bludger living in a squat, who maybe even secretly wants to steal something from a swanky department store. Her heart rate has risen like she is a child about to get in trouble.

On the escalator, she feels heavy and dizzy. When they get off, she holds on to a coat rack for support. 'Wait.' The texture of the coats is surprisingly soft.

'You all right?'

'Yes, but I might have to go to the bathroom. Sorry.' Her bladder is painful. She has been holding it in since Central.

'You *might* have to go? Of course. Jesus, remember you are forbidden from apologising for things.'

She just, barely, stops herself from doing it again.

*

'Do you find it interesting that you still remember those feelings you had at David Jones so clearly, all these years later, when you're much better off than you were?'

Jan thought, Yeah, now that I'm living the life of Riley as a single mother on a social worker's salary. It was true, though, that she felt rich in comparison to how she once was, and she was grateful for that. A bit guilty, too, perversely. The therapist's childhood must have been securely middle class, like Alicia's. And of course, a psychologist earned more than a social worker: that old hierarchical relationship, the psychologist gazing down from up above as if from a private box at the theatre. Jan has noticed the elegant cut and supple leather of her R.M. Williams boots that are in perfect nick.

'I don't know if you would understand,' she tried to explain. 'Going to the tea room at DJs was seen as a high-class thing to do when you went into the city for "a day in town". It was a kind of symbol. Even if you could hardly afford anything there.

'To someone from out west, Grace Brothers was fancy and DJs was even more for the hoity-toity. When you went there you tried to make yourself look as posh as you could, like you deserved to be there, you were good enough. I guess that to our mothers, it was how they imagined department stores in London or New York might be, something out of a movie. It was glamorous to me, too.'

'*Maybe* I would understand,' the therapist said. Was she annoyed or amused? 'Do you know the Cossington Smith painting of it?'

'Of what?'

'The tea room at David Jones.'

'She did one of that? I've seen the ones of hers they've got at the Art Gallery of New South Wales. I love those, the gorgeous warm colours … But I don't think I know that one. What's it like?'

There was a silence. The questions didn't usually go in this direction.

'Can you describe it to me?' Jan insisted.

Another hesitation. 'Red chairs, does that ring a bell?'

'Um, maybe. Tell me more.'

'How can I describe it? Quite modernist? You see a café interior, vaguely between the wars. Some people, rather ghostly, are sitting in their coats having refreshments. What you mainly notice are the chairs, which are those ones with the rounded backs with the rungs going down from them. Scarlet chairs. And bottle-green tabletops. Anyway, you'd have to see it. I can't describe art.'

'Yes, you can. And I have seen it – or I feel like I have from your description.' Jan smiled.

The therapist did too, a rare occurrence, half of her mouth lifting and the other remaining anchored to some solemnity or uncertainty. This hesitant, true smile helped Jan forget for a moment the queasy feeling that had been intensifying as she laboured to bring back the day from long ago.

She sighed. 'Thank you, Carole.'

The therapist looked down at her notes. 'For … what? Trying to describe the painting?'

'Yes, and just in general.'

'Oh.' Another little smile, as if in spite of herself. 'So, where were we?'

*

The comforting smells of hot tea, coffee and toasted sandwiches.

'She'll be off her meds. If we find her,' Jan whispers.

Alicia nods, taking this in her stride.

She won't be here, Jan thinks. But she is. In a corner. Her milky-green leatherette handbag on the table next to a teapot. She is staring into the distance, not seeing them.

'She's here.'

Lorna's expression is distracted and she is rocking herself back and forth, as she does. But she isn't dishevelled: her short coppery hair has been recently combed. Her colouring is good.

Jan goes over to her. 'Lorna, it's me.' There is a pause. 'Glen's wife, Jan. And this is my friend, Alicia.'

'Glen's wife,' she repeats, mulling this over as if the fact were a slippery object she was doing her best to grasp.

Kissing her on the cheek, Jan is moved by the sight of her earlobe – slightly puckered around a piercing with no earring in it – and by her odour that is reminiscent of the inside of an old closet, lavender sachets and the faint musty sweetness of aged leather.

'Great to see you.'

'You're pregnant.' She puts a hand on Jan's stomach.

'Yeah, you're telling me.'

Lorna has taken hold of Jan's dress and is slowly lifting it, examining her legs; when it rises above the knees, Jan pulls away, trying to laugh.

'Can we join you for a cuppa?'

'I haven't got much money left.'

Alicia says, 'Who fancies a Devonshire tea, my shout?'

'Devonshire tea!' Lorna is impressed.

'You sure?' Jan asks.

'Completely.'

Once they have ordered, Jan says, 'Done a runner, eh?'

'Yeah.' Lorna beams festively.

It is a relief to see her more cheeky than darkly suspicious.

'Are you a communist?' Lorna asks Alicia matter-of-factly.

'I think I probably agree with most of the ideas. Maybe I'm a socialist?'

'You're for the workers, but?'

'Definitely. I'm definitely a leftie.'

'May Day is my birthday. I march every time I can.'

'Good for you. How wonderful.'

The food makes them jolly and playful, like kids wagging school for a lark. The cream is deluxe and the jam the kind with little clumps of dimpled strawberry in it. Jan, who for what seems like ages has been constantly somewhere between peckish and nauseated, eats with enjoyment. She feels she is in a gentle British fantasy, at an Enid Blyton picnic.

'Doesn't she have a big bust?' Lorna comments to Alicia, studying Jan's swollen breasts.

'Just right, I'd say.' Alicia winks at Jan.

Jan blushes.

Alicia asks a waitress, 'Could we have some more milk, please? We're going to need quite a bit more. You wouldn't have a larger jug?'

Lorna tells Alicia, 'You're very thin, watch out for that. If you're on the bony side, as you get older, you can start looking scrawny. But you've got a terrific head of hair.'

'Thank you. I like your hair, too.'

'My hair is one of my best features. Is that Jan? Fancy meeting you here. Jan, listen … Hear that?'

'What?'

'Listen.' Lorna's eyes are lost and expectant. 'Can you hear that?'

There is a pause. They listen, Jan glancing at Alicia, before nodding.

Outside the air feels denser than it did before, nearly Western-Suburbs hot. They discuss where they'll catch the 431 – Town Hall Station or Museum Station, deciding on the latter. They are already waiting on Castlereagh Street when Jan sees Glen. He is about to cross the street towards them and the thought strikes her clearly: The party is over. He must have just finished his shift, which she remembers was somewhere in the CBD. There is a flatness to his body language, she thinks, feeling guilty because he has to do such hard work. He tried other jobs before: he was a 'male nurse', and then he drove a delivery van for Australia Post. Construction is heavier but more flexible; he claims it makes him feel freer than those other jobs did. But his ears have been funny since he spent a full shift with a jackhammer. They will be funny for the rest of his life.

'There's Glen.'

'Glen?' Lorna is surprised. 'That's my son. He goes to New South Wales University. They're having a baby.'

He doesn't see them waving till Jan shouts. She can tell, waiting for him to cross the road, that he isn't particularly pleased to see them. He often goes leery and cringing around Lorna.

As soon as Glen sees his mother, he is skewered by relief and its opposite, the old fright-or-flight response.

When he joins them, he kisses her, aiming for her cheek as she offers her lips. 'There you are.'

His eyes drop to the sight of her tragically cheap navy-blue court shoes, the ones she wears to look smart in, his heart burdened with the responsibility that seems to make him both a weary old man and a hypervigilant child. He registers the presence of Alicia.

'Work okay?' Jan asks.

He doesn't reply. 'You haven't heard.'

'Heard what?'

'They're getting rid of Gough!'

'What do you mean?'

'They're kicking him out. Someone heard it on the radio at the site.'

'What!'

'How?'

'What's that about Gough?' Lorna demands to know.

Glen puts his hand to the bulk of the Marlboros in his back pocket. He doesn't really have the money to spare for cigarettes and it's not that he even enjoys smoking that much, but he needs to know the ritual of a release is waiting for him.

'He's out. They've dissolved the Parliament. The Governor-General did.'

'How can that happen?'

'Apparently, it's happening.'

'Where's Gough gone?' Lorna enquires.

Alicia feels she is in an absurdist play, everything strangely encoded and foreboding. They get on the bus like children being taken on a school trip they don't want to go on, only able to follow orders that might turn out to be sadistic. She and Glen sit opposite Jan and Lorna.

'He's out?' Lorna is asking. 'What general?'

'The *Governor*-General, the representative of the queen.'

'What queen?'

'Jesus Christ. Of bloody England, Mum. I know it's unbelievable.'

'The Pom?'

'Yeah.'

'But …'

'I know. Fucking hell, eh?'

Looking for ripples of amazement in the people around them, Alicia isn't sure if she is seeing anything but her own shock. She says, 'They'll try to undo all the important things. The Medibank. The free uni tuition. The progress for Aboriginal rights.' Glen's shoulder is resting against hers, and she imagines him judging her as someone who won't feel the impact of this in her bones, as they do – the ones without any financial cushion. And she supposes that to some extent, he would be right. But she does empathise with suffering, labouring at that like a vocation, and she knows racism in ways they never could. She leans into him briefly, in an attempt at solidarity. 'God.'

Her son isn't happy. No one is anymore. And they were just in the tea room having scones and a lovely time. What's going on? Lorna tries to listen again for the sirens and is frightened not to hear any. Has Claude been scared off? Her heart is going fast then slow. Euchred, shafted, rooted by the Pommy queen? Surely not. How could they possibly get away with that? Of course, the powerful out-and-out bastards have their ways of getting the knife in you, and somehow they've done it to Gough. The angle has changed. Where is the bloody bus even going?

Jan feels pressure on her pelvis, on her lower back, and the sort of seasickness she used to get on buses when she was a child. She has been telling herself that she'd go back to uni sometime after the baby is born, because she must have something for herself; or something to help her escape herself. Guilt and a sense of waste. Has she blown her chance at university forever? Is that all over for the likes of her? And for the likes of her baby? She has assumed she would be the first in a series of people in her family to be able to depend on going to university, if they wanted to.

Lorna says, 'Gawd, I'd love a drink.'

'You and me both,' Alicia seconds. 'Why don't you all come back to our place and we'll have a few?'

Jan sees Glen put his hand on Alicia's arm and say, 'That'd be great.'

He wasn't looking forward to returning home with his mum and her, to the three of them sitting around, confined in the squat, trying to make conversation and pretending to not know that Lorna would have to be escorted back to where she hates being. They don't have much food in, either, and Jan doesn't know what she could make them for tea – what she tries to think of romantically as her 'peasant-style' spaghetti? Since Alicia put her on to olive oil, she makes it with that instead of margarine, and she crushes the garlic cloves instead of cutting them and has learned to not burn them.

'What will happen to the benefits?' Glen asks.

Jan hears his fear. The bus lurches and the baby inside her with it. I must stay calm, she reminds herself as she has been doing frequently. But now there is a new vibration of alarm, a new halo of precariousness around things. The misery of the past weeks suddenly appears less undeniable, more crucial, and so does the distance separating her from Alicia, who doesn't know what it is to live on the minimum. She wouldn't think that people who get handouts are bludgers, would she? We really are of different species, Jan reflects. Just as I am of a different species from someone who is truly poor, or who has always been and will always be poor. But I grew up nervous about money, among underdogs and battlers and those who were almost that – and had to live fearing the descent.

She remembers Mrs Forsythe, Helen, saying during a lesson: 'In British novels, class is always the thing.'

Even then, Jan thought, Is there somewhere where it's not, then?

First, Jan sees the front gate open. And next, Steve: he is on his haunches at the edge of the road.

'Oh,' Alicia says, like she doesn't have enough air. She drops her bag and runs.

Something brown. Heidi.

Jan tells Glen, 'Stay here with your mum.' She picks up the discarded bag and walks slowly towards Alicia, who has gone down on her knees.

Steve is justifying, 'Only for a minute. You know what she's like.'

His feet are bare on the footpath and his T-shirt is inside out. 'Madame George' can be heard through the front door, almost unbearable with nostalgia. Jan remembers the Shalimar that was sprayed on their wrists earlier that day at DJs, in what now feels like a former existence. She looks down enough to see there is an angle to Heidi that is plain wrong and around which Alicia's hands are hopeless. It's over.

'Why was the gate open?' Alicia asks.

'I was distracted, I just heard about Gough … Is it true?'

He smells of dope, reminding Jan of the day he watched her in his bathtub. She tries to touch Alicia's shoulder, but doesn't know how to and takes her hand away.

'Oh God,' Jan says. 'What can I do?'

Alicia makes a short, pained sound that hardly seems to have come from her.

'I'm sorry, Lish,' Steve tells her.

Alicia finally stands and folds her arms across her chest as if she were cold. She says, 'I want to take her to Glebe Point. Bury her there, I mean.'

Though it is the brittle voice of someone who has decided she won't cry, Jan sees tears on her face. Alicia is looking at Steve with anger and this clarifies Jan's anger towards him. He doesn't give the impression of having understood the dog's death; this could be the dope, the shock, or their interaction.

'We'll come with you,' Jan announces.

Lorna is keenly awaiting a couple of drinks. Everything is confused and jumpy. They are out the front of what looks like a decent place, in a city way, not exactly posh but not shoddy, either. Nice and comfy. She doesn't fully get what they are doing there. The men are acting guilty and the women are sad. The poor dog is dead, but it's not just that. You can tell when the love is good with a couple, and with these two it's not. She recognises the squirmy, uneasy-tummy feeling of this from childhood, how it was around her parents: like the milk in the house is off, it isn't so easy to breathe, there's a sort of riddle you haven't been able to solve. Very bad thing, though, losing a dog. Tommy was hit by a car, too, and you never saw a sweeter creature. They thought he might even have had some Pomeranian in him. But she doesn't want to think about Tommy or about Gough. Jesus Christ.

Across the street, in a house with an old lounge on its verandah, a woman moves in the doorway and then draws back into a hallway. That woman – unfortunately, Lorna couldn't really see her face or smile at her – has probably been through a lot, too: they might have tried to hide her away, shut her up and make her sleepy, done worse.

Glen is tired and irritated and feels dirty – his filthy King Gee's and boots being the least of it. Standing like a boy by his mother again and watching the pregnant Jan from a distance that has come to seem as inevitable as an incurable illness, he is aware that it is too late for so much.

He notices it's turning into a summery night, before helping Lorna into the back of Steve's brown Datsun; he and Jan get in on the other side, Glen offering to scoot over and sit in the middle. He is reminded of that old sense of a back seat being some combination of prison and refuge, and of how important it is to get the fuck away from such situations.

Alicia tells Steve that she'll drive, because – this is pointed – *she* isn't stoned.

Lorna asks, 'Will we be having dinner?'

'Oh,' Alicia responds. 'Do you like Lebanese?'

'I do, yeah.'

'Leb always does the trick,' Steve comments superfluously.

Alicia turns to Jan. 'It's a bit of a detour, but I think this calls for Abdul's. Don't you?'

Jan smiles.

'Good. We'll take a picnic. Send off Heidi and Gough properly.'

Shortly after, Glen hits his head on the roof. The suspension is stuffed.

They double-park on Elizabeth Street and Alicia and Steve go in for the food.

Glen asks Jan, 'You okay?'

It annoys him that he sounds contrite. He also sounds uninvolved with the question and he can see her, as he has been able to do for many, many days now, considering herself invisible to him. How well has she been watching him, though? Does she ever imagine his thoughts?

'Yeah.'

He reaches across Lorna to roll the window down a crack.

At the bottle-o on Glebe Point Road, Jan goes in for a cask of wine and some cans of Pilsners for Lorna; they can't really afford all that, but they'll cross the bridge of being broke when they get to it. As she opens the door to get back in, he breathes in the sweet, exhaust-fumy smell of the inner city and it's good – it relaxes him a bit, helping him to feel more anonymous and exhale with a sigh. This is one of the best things about the city, the feeling it can suddenly give you of being capable of evading the people who know you, of nearly dissolving.

28

BLACKWATTLE BAY

Alicia carries the bundle wrapped in green fabric. There is brine on the air and the pacifying sense of land about to give way to water.

Eventually, she says, 'Here.'

'Here?' Steve asks.

'Yes, she liked nosing around this tree, after we'd been to the little beach.'

'Okay. I can do it.'

'No, I want to do it.'

'You've only got a garden shovel. It's not the right tool.'

She shrugs. 'I'm doing it. What you can do is put out the picnic blanket, make sure everyone has food and drink.'

'You'll tell me if I can help?' Jan asks, once he's out of earshot.

She shakes her head but adds, 'I don't want you to tire yourself out.'

'I'll bring you a drink, at least.'

'A very large wine would be perfect. Please?'

Jan hands Alicia a wine that is almost overflowing and sees that she starts drinking the way Lorna does – a couple of speedy sips, getting it into her.

Jan bends over and touches the green fabric self-consciously. 'I really liked that sarong.' The past tense, because it isn't a sarong anymore. It's a shroud. She sees Alicia wearing it in her backyard – a book on her green lap, bare calves with Heidi between them – and feels tearful. 'I'm so sorry.'

'She liked it, too.'

Alicia is not an easy person to comfort. Jan goes to sit on the edge of the picnic blanket closest to her. Not hungry, she doesn't eat and only follows the others' talk on and off.

'Where did Gough go again?' Lorna asks.

'Nowhere,' Glen replies wearily. 'He hasn't disappeared.'

'Was he arrested? We might get arrested, too.'

'I doubt it. Don't worry about that now.'

'Is there a ferry from here?'

'I don't think one leaves from here, exactly.'

'Where are we again?'

'Blackwattle Bay.'

'Don't pull the wool over my eyes.'

'I'm not.'

There is a long lull in which all Jan really hears is Alicia working with her shovel. The night has fallen properly, the darkness abruptly thick, if not complete. The city around them exudes some light and Alicia has propped a torch beside her to illuminate her work. Jan's eyes keep drifting as if on a current to the shine of the water. Every so often, she catches herself wondering when Heidi will join them. Poor Alicia will be doing that, too, for God knows how long.

Squatting at the end of the mound, Alicia is resting or thinking. She seems to have finished. The men are dispiritedly nibbling, drinking and talking. Lorna smokes, a look of hibernation to her. Jan gets up slowly, her back achy, and goes over to stand beside Alicia. She is riding an adrenaline rush like the ones that overtook her at uni, as she got up her courage to answer a question, in front of everyone, that the teacher had asked. Worse than that. A large clump of hair has fallen out of Alicia's plait and partially covers her face; Jan has never seen her unkempt before. With difficulty, she lowers herself onto her knees. 'I probably won't be able to get up again.'

'I didn't dig all that deep – I hope it'll be enough. So, that's done.'

Jan is aware of Alicia's heat and her own. She is sweaty from their long walk and the day's shocks. And she is always hot now. Her overly full body pulsates, ticks like a bomb. She has an almost overpowering impulse to somehow take away the other girl's suffering, plunge her hands into that disordered hair, hold her head, collapse into her. It alarms her that she might be about to make her confession. Irreversible.

Alicia says, 'I wasn't allowed to have a dog at home. My mother thought it wasn't right to have dogs in the city.'

'No?'

'No. I wonder if she had a dog in Spain.' Realising then how much of her hair has slipped from its plait, she removes the elastic that was holding it. 'One of my grandmother's friends told me once that my mother and my grandmother tried to leave the country during the Civil War. They were in a camp for a while in the South of France. But they left and went back to Spain, because it was so awful. Apparently, hundreds were dying every day and the sanitary conditions were horrifying. I was thinking about that while I was digging. All those bodies and how they buried them. I try to imagine it, but I can't, not really.' She finishes her third large glass of wine. 'Are you afraid of having the baby?'

Jan understands that she shouldn't say anything about Spain, not yet. And though speaking of her own concerns seems selfish now, she must try to be honest.

'Terrified.' She doesn't add that she is frightened, not just of what the experience will be like, the pain and whether she'll die in childbirth like in the olden days. But also and even more than that, she is afraid she won't be able to hide the pain enough – she'll scream, be messy. Why does so much of her thinking involve shame and embarrassment?

'I would be too.'

Jan waits, sensations hitting her with great clarity, as if she had to learn them by heart because this is a farewell. Smells of the sea, freshly exposed earth, sweet musk. The light sting of a mosquito bite that she resists scratching. The somehow familiar unfamiliarity of seeing Alicia's divinely dark hair loose and voluminous, her rolled-up shirtsleeves, their shoulders almost touching, the extreme nature of what was said a couple of minutes earlier and the recent calamities – all of it placing them together at the lip of a drop.

Alicia continues, 'It's like we're in a different world now, we've entered a nightmare.'

Jan isn't sure if she means Heidi, the government or something else. Maybe the lot. She says, 'The mozzies are eating us alive.'

'Oh? Yes, you're right.' Alicia scratches herself savagely.

Jan winces and, without thinking, goes to move Alicia's hair out of her eyes. Stopping herself before she does it. 'I can smell the perfume.'

'Huh?'

'What they sprayed on us at DJs.'

'I'd forgotten about that.' Alicia lifts her wrist to her face. 'I'm not sure if I like it. What do you think?'

Now she offers the wrist to Jan. Is the gesture automatic or tender? It is hard to interpret body language in the dark: even more than usual, you don't know if what you are seeing is only what you are imagining. On the other hand, tones of voice are especially revealing and Alicia's is intimate – vulnerable, at least. They have never been so close. Jan is dizzy with emotion and the thought of resting her mouth on the inside of Alicia's wrist. She bends over the shadowy arm, a fall into musky sweetness.

Steve says, 'You've finished? Come and have a drink with us. Jan, shall I help you up?'

He is standing behind them.

*

'Take your time,' the therapist said.

*

Even unsteady with drink and sadness, Alicia has a provoking air of *So what's your fucking problem, then?* As he watches her from the opposite side of the picnic blanket, slightly pissed and stoned himself, Glen finds this more arousing than annoying.

Jan has a certain allure tonight, too. Oddly, this tends to be the case when she appears most separate from him. He gets a brief flash, as he almost never does anymore, of their hitchhiking honeymoon to The Entrance, her embroidered blouse and the way she looked at him, like he was unchained and legendary, like they were about to be photographed for an album cover. (Even during those first days together as husband and wife, there were moments when she eluded him, when he wasn't undoing her in the ways he'd anticipated and the mood was spoiled.) Earlier still: her centre part, plaits, school blazer and that hint beneath her seriousness of a muffled smile and considerable warmth. The smell of chlorine on her skin and the stimulation of their jitters. The shiver in witnessing her girlishness almost but not quite melting into maturity, the first time he saw her take out her plaits.

Unfortunately, he will be able to retrieve such images for most of the rest of his life, especially at times of instability or change. One night in Newtown, kohl around his eyes, newly broken-in cherry-red Docs on his feet, he'll be walking down King Street from a gig at the Sando that people actually showed up for – the envelope of cash for his performance snug and proud against his thigh – and everything will appear to be at long fucking last open to him: the pubs and crowds and record shops, the cinemas and takeaway restaurants, the possibility of a midnight kebab in Camperdown Cemetery followed by a future rich in travel and sex and reading newspapers with coffee and cigarettes in the shade of unimaginable trees under which he might meet passionate foreign women. And he'll suddenly be forced to consider that those women might not love him right, either, not enough, in the right way, the way he has felt is offered in dreams and songs. Those women might come to see him as Jan does now, no longer searching for something she has given up hope of finding. Lorna looked at him like that today, also. He thinks she is sleeping; she is lying on her side, head on her handbag. It is essential that he get away from them both.

Alicia stands up and wanders over, glass in hand, to visit the dog's grave.

Steve asks Jan, 'So did you start keeping a diary?'

It irks Glen that this is the continuation of a conversation begun without him. He himself doesn't feel capable of talking to Jan, though.

'No,' she replies. 'But I did think about starting a dream diary.'

'Excellent idea. Do you ever dream of the sea?'

'Um. Sometimes I have a nightmare – about a tidal wave.'

'A recurring dream? And what happens in it?'

'Oh the usual, I guess, a wall of water bearing down on me. A giant wall. And I go under, or I'm about to.'

Glen gets up, mumbling about going for a smoke.

They are vaguely watching Alicia, who is leaning against the tree that Heidi liked, sipping wine. Glen is heading over to her, maybe to offer her a cigarette; the two start to talk. What they are saying can't be discerned.

In that moment, it is clear to Steve that he still needs Alicia, but – he doesn't quite know how to formulate this – he has begun to wake up from the dream of her foreignness. He understands, slightly uneasily, that it has flattered his vanity to be with someone so rare. Her curiosity, her magnificent skin and general elegance, her rigorous worship of food, the safety in her steady supply of cash and all the other ways she has made his home and daily existence more reliably pleasant. And she is entangled with his cheaply predictable visions of what he thinks of as her country, even though he has learned that for her nowhere is that as much as Australia is. The eccentric intensity of Lorca, Picasso and Dalí, arrogant flamenco twirls, bullish bullfighting, Moorish arches predestined in their perfection, landscapes of barely survivable arid majesty, *Sketches of Spain*. He supposes that's what love is, inevitably, your dream of the other person's foreignness. And naturally, as the dream is lived it ceases to be the muddle of exotic charm – the unfulfilled longing – that it was, leaving you struggling to sustain an illusion you have seen through. He is reminded of when his father told him Santa Claus wasn't real and how for a couple of years more he tried to pretend he couldn't believe this, because he wasn't ready to let go of that idea of magic or of his own innocence; though he then had to live with the sickly knowledge that these were compromised, that believing in magic was being hoodwinked and shown up as a fool. Often, it appears to him that he was never innocent, never an authentic child, always a cynic and a fool.

Speaking languidly, like one far removed from things, he says: 'My father was that stamp of man who throws his son into the deep end to teach him to swim.'

Jan observes, 'It's interesting that you say *son* rather than *me*.'

'I guess it is.'

He is thinking, Yes, funny how language can both reveal and obscure. Of course, he believes in language as he believes in almost nothing else. He definitely feels he is at one with a movement of thinkers who intend to create a new openness – perhaps ultimately a renewed society, at least some adventurous and original subcultures – through a fresh, more honest use of language. But he does realise that at least as often as words bring him clarity, they don't. And despite his love of metaphor, he sometimes catches himself, as he goes to describe one thing by comparing it to another, moving away from that thing and up to more secure higher ground.

'Did you think you were going to drown when he did that?'

'Strangely, I can't remember. Where does such a memory go?'

He sees that Jan sort of buys him and sort of doesn't. She is smart, by which he means: accustomed to ambiguity, disenchantment and compromise. (Smart or unlucky – is there a difference?) Still, she very much needs to be brought out of herself, beyond the inferiority complex, the cultural cringe and all the fragilely middle-class, suburban confinements. He is coming to consider her the kind of locked-in, tied-up person who could be interesting as she is liberated. It is evident that, notwithstanding her marriage and the child she will only too soon have, she herself wants to play. She is fairly begging for that. Like him, she feels how wrong it is to say no when life offers you something you want. And maybe how futile are our attempts to suppress the anarchic uprisings of the nervous system.

Her head moves sharply and he looks to see why.

His girlfriend and the boy, embracing.

It could just be friendly, but it isn't. He can tell from the wilted flower of her abandoned head, and oh how melded with lust they are.

Jealousy or humiliation? Either way, it is unexpected because he has hoped Alicia would get to this, to validating his freedom by exploring her own along paths he has tried to teach her. Even so, the turn of events is necessary and opportune.

'To think of destiny as singular is tragic.' He wanted this to be an optimistic message, but it hangs between them sorrowfully.

'I think I'll go for a swim,' she says, her voice entirely different from how it was just a couple of minutes before, clotted. She seems quite affected by what's going on. Poor thing, with her worldview she will probably take it hard. 'I've been craving being in water all day.'

It is true that heat is coming off her like she has a high fever.

'Here?'

'Yeah.' She is unlacing her shoes.

'Skinny-dipping?'

'No, underwear will do the job.'

'And what about the big bad ocean?'

Ignoring this, she stands up slowly. She is in pain and is bent on inflicting more pain on herself. There is something so beyond control about a pregnant woman, so fatal, so sensual. Has he said this, or just thought it? Even before the pregnancy, Jan was rather strapping, a fleshy beauty.

Jan checks on Lorna, who lolls on her side, handbag for a pillow, but doesn't look at Alicia and Glen again before walking to the water. She is conscious for the first time of being relieved to take the baby away from Glen, to put distance between him and her child. This thought spreading through her like a cool filigree.

'Wait up.' Steve has followed. 'I feel really bad about Heidi. Lish will never forgive me.'

'You reckon?' She stares straight ahead as she speaks.

'No. But I loved her, too. I got her from the RSPCA – they were going to put her down. I suspect she was mistreated as a puppy, that's why she was so manic.'

'Kelpies can be like that. She was lovable.'

They are nearing the edge of the water and Jan is enticed by the mild sound of it stirring. How polluted is it? She shivers. The reflections of distant lights on the nearly waveless surface are shimmery and slippery, reds and blues. Things feel so contaminated and corrupted. But there are also plentiful stars, hulking Moreton Bay figs and the tantalising, heartbreaking open-ended dream of a port by night.

'Christ, what a fucking day,' he says. 'Now anything can happen. The trees behind us could go up in flames.'

'I know.'

'It reminds me of how I felt on the night of my mother's accident. That *nothing* was solid. Maybe nothing would ever be solid again.'

'I can imagine.'

Is his mother's accident a technique for shortcutting to a confidential mood by signalling his sensitivity and knowledge of pain? And is she really going in? Could there be rips? Sharks?

'*Blackwattle* is a beautiful name for a bay,' he goes on. 'It's important to realise that all we get of happiness is fragments, so if we come across one it's our duty to seize it because who knows when the next one will come. Sometimes it's a word, when it's the right word. Overwhelming enough. Like Blackwattle …'

He is playing the poet for the purposes of seduction, but if she concentrates on the word it does indeed encase her mind, a cobweb of dusky blossoms.

As Jan steps into the water, somewhat breathless, she asks, 'Does black wattle actually have black flowers?'

'Wouldn't have a clue. Doesn't matter. The idea of them is enough.'

It isn't really cold, but there is nonetheless an element of surprise, a transition to undergo. This is what she needs. She advances till she is knee-deep, her mind closing when she starts to see Glen and Alicia together: she can't, can't at all. The downside of love is the down, the plummeting from the crest of your fantasy of it. Shattered euphoria, dark adrenaline, sadness unfurling.

'Sydney is too beautiful. One doesn't know how to handle it,' she says, sounding like an unworldly outsider and also noticing the pomposity of *one* the way a Westie would, her own brain mocking her for being a poseur; she can't win. The water is at her waist. 'Okay, it's now or never.'

Watching her go, Steve thinks that a challenge with women is leading them to their desires or perhaps encouraging their diffuse minds to focus on yours. He is a little all over the place himself, with that anxiety he gets every so often, like he has just become aware of a void below him. Although he is excited by Jan and that excitement is, as usual, making him feel powerfully tingly in his perceptions, this is not going quite as smoothly as he might have expected. There's a sense that he won't get the reward for being a good, clever boy, that things are somehow spoiled.

He tries some yogic breathing, which sometimes works, bringing back the presence of his grandmother, who taught him how to do it. He misses her tonight, her poignant lordly air of the former beauty and the formerly well-to-do. He particularly misses the soothing hours they spent in her bedroom. The misty scalloped glass of the sconces, the wine-coloured carpet to which cat fur adhered in swirls, the windows open onto the yard that looked – if you didn't turn your head too far in either direction – like a beguiling secret garden. The cloisonné hair combs laid out on the dresser waiting for an elusive special occasion, as were the lamé handbags stored in pristine cardboard boxes in a drawer. In bed beside her, propped against worn sateen pillowslips smelling of violet cologne and Nivea cream, he listened to her itemise her history of admirers. Or they read together. The safe wilderness of Keats, Emily Dickinson, Jane Austen and the permission she gave him to be womanly. It is too easy to blame his father for him never having been particularly at ease with other men. But come on – how could he not? His father was a fire-eater, startling his son at a certain point with the blaze of rage he couldn't any longer conceal within. It had seemed to reassure the man to release it and be able to watch the child or whoever else was around him recoil in fear; the catharsis refreshed him, briefly, before embarrassment set in, also briefly. How could this not have left Steve suspicious and shifty when it came to blokes? *Australian* ones? He has sometimes wondered if, had he lived in France, for example, he'd have had some dear bookish male friends, who kissed each other in greeting and sensitively discussed their romantic and literary obsessions over aperitifs. His grandmother's bedroom had been that sort of closeness, a drawn-out European cocktail hour of genial words.

Lorna has been listening and listening and not hearing what she needs to hear. When she thinks his signal might have gone dead, she is distraught like a puppy left all by itself. She must believe that though she can't hear him, he is nearby, like when he was working on the yard. But to be honest, she is more and more worried that the business with Gough has thrown him badly. Somewhere on the other side of a curtain of grog, she is thrown too. The only thing entirely clear to her is that she's not going back to that hellhole. And just as she is thinking this and realising that she is alone on the picnic blanket, she hears them. Doesn't she?

Definitely.

Yes, oh at long last.

Saying, Come to me.

The rising tide of pleasure. She is already much stronger and prouder and on her knees. Standing now, look, that's the way, and only a trifle wonky. She is off to take her chance, follow his bright trail through the dark, picking her way to the riverbank. A pause to remove her knee-highs and slacks. This takes some time. She is seeing herself in a white negligée like that one Grace Kelly wears in *Dial M for Murder.* If it wasn't night or she wasn't a tad pissed, the water would probably be a lovely greenish brown. She has imagined that when they meet up, he'll ask if she's paid attention to his messages and she'll reply, *You know I did.*

Lorna has never really been able to picture the journey down Parramatta River to Sydney Harbour. Will she see willows on the banks? Will it be like how she imagined the Mississippi, when her sister told her about Huck Finn? And what if you were to carry on from Sydney to Glasgow, her grandparents' voyage the other way around? Wading, she can't tell if the water is hot or cold. She is filling herself with the thought of him, going as far outside of herself and as far into him as possible.

Jan's belly is lighter in here. She begins with breaststroke, jerking up in panic to breathe each time her head surfaces. In a pool, she knows she can swim strongly for at least an hour, but in open water her endurance is questionable, still to be proven. She shifts to freestyle, which is smoother and more efficient, her neck relaxing a little, spine and arm movements lengthening. Quickly, though, her hair winds around her face and, with her eyes closed, she is dizzied by the rolling of her body within the rippling of gentle waves. She swallows some seawater. A peculiar intrusion, that salt entering her system. Her terror is confused with weightlessness and smoothness and no longer knowing if she is on a straight line. Her heart is going very hard, her whole self throbbing with blood, the possibility of suffocation, the desire to dissolve.

Steve waits at the edge. 'You're a strong swimmer. You were in for a long time. You did it.'

She rests on her knees, squeezing water out of her hair, chest heaving.

Touching her shoulder, he says, 'You're cold.'

He half lifts and then leads her. For a moment, the ground beneath them oscillates or she does; she doesn't quite have her land legs. She can't make out the others at all, luckily. Alicia and Glen. She is shaking and wishes that would stop, wishes this night was over. Sand between her toes. Alicia.

And now he helps her to sit down, moving behind her, saying, 'We'll warm you up.'

He begins by rubbing her back. His hands are firm and her eyes are running; maybe she is crying. The heat of his mouth on her neck is a shock and her head twists sharply away from him. Wanting to say something, but once more there before her are Alicia and Glen; her mind is buckling and so is the ground. A tumble, the grass as bristly as his moustache. There is pain and a sort of nothingness, a deserted white road.

When it is over, she has to focus to recognise where she is, who she is. She separates herself from him and stands slowly.

And drifts. Could she just return home alone? She imagines the asphalt of Glebe Point Road, some of the day's heat stored in it, against the soles of her feet and the comfort of walking along that familiar road. But no, she couldn't, not dressed in underwear, and anyway she doesn't have her keys.

She is thinking this as she becomes aware of a bulky shape breaking the water's surface, not far away. She approaches it.

Lorna.

29

GLEEBOOKS

'You thought she was dead?' the therapist asked.

'Yes. It took me a while to find her pulse.'

Jan glanced at the hedge through the window, dimming as it always did around that time, and then at the woman asking questions. There was something different about Carole's eyes today.

'By the time we got her to Prince Alfred, she was unconscious. The coma lasted a week or so. In some ways, it was over for her, anyhow. There were no more escapes and escapades after that, no more May Day marches, no more energy for rebellion.'

'Was that the last time you saw Alicia?'

'No, I ran into her again. But years later. For so long, I thought I'd run into her somewhere, sooner or later, and I didn't. Then I saw her again, when I'd given up on it.'

*

1975–1987

Jan doesn't run into Alicia during the last foggy year spent at Bridge Road or the following ones in a share house on Arundel Street. She is trying to go back to university, working various part-time jobs, and she and Glen are sporadically, despondently still seeing if they can make a go of it. They can't. Jan feels a lot like her own ghost, like she's bizarrely survived herself, continuing but in a new paler form, as Lorna does. Weary with sadness, she often catches herself staring at objects. Her son David's ratty Fat Cat fallen from his little bed. Someone's child's Stormtrooper figurine on a windowsill or permanently deflated lightsaber in the backyard. A bong, a saucer used as an ashtray, a bottle of gin. *Sesame Street* on the telly. Someone's coffee-mug-ringed *The Joy of Sex* or *Babar* book. Someone's meditation cushion that doubles as a pouf. The white box containing a diaphragm. A jar of forgotten miso at the back of the fridge.

Among David's memories of the house on Arundel Street will be: a light bulb on the ceiling seen through the circular bottom of a rice-paper shade, a sticker representing a rainbow on a grimy segment of window, snakes of Vegemite and margarine escaping through the holes in sandwiched Vita-Weat crackers, lumps of Blu Tack from off the back of a poster of Marilyn Monroe with her dress blowing up, the salty taste of Play-Doh, being bathed with other people's blond children he doesn't feel close to, walking in on a couple having sex in the kitchen, a Joan Armatrading album cover leaning against the wall in a sort of glum dusk that may have been partly conjured up by the music, waking worried and melancholy from naps, trying to imagine death while sitting in the dark under a blanket.

They will both remember, one day they are returning from a walk to Forest Lodge, finding some fluffy toys in a hollow of a Moreton Bay fig – like a doorway into magic – and this appearing to be a sign that life could unexpectedly offer gifts. Jan has the irrational feeling that it is a message from Alicia. Alicia is remembering her, right then, maybe living some intense emotion she wishes she could share with Jan. (Sometimes Jan comforts herself with the thought that they are like Laura and Voss in Patrick White's novel: separated but connected and communicating in profound ways.) She and David might even be about to run into Alicia in the flesh. But of course that doesn't happen.

And Jan doesn't ever see Alicia while she is getting takeaway from Abdul's or Rowda Ya-Habibi, a new restaurant on King Street she favours, or the rare times she goes to the Art Gallery of New South Wales or the Academy Twin cinema. She is especially convinced she will encounter Alicia at a bookshop on Glebe Point Road, such an Alicia kind of place. Jan pops in there often, even when she is as usual broke, just to browse and be inside the air that is rich with the incense and beeswax candles they also sell and library-sweet from the second-hand books alongside the fresh new ones. Just to meander between readings past and future, walking a threshold of private pleasure and discoveries. With the nervy possibility that Alicia could be on the other side of a shelf, easing out the elegant orange-and-white spine of a Penguin Classic, lifting it to her face so that – eyes half closing – she can sink into the visceral contentment of the scent of printed pages. Bittersweet expectancy. Alicia is never there.

Jan feels her absence so strongly, so physically, some days, on the streets of Glebe or Newtown or in Victoria Park, it is virtually a presence, a feeling that surely will have to soon materialise into the real Alicia. She stares at any woman of approximately the right age and build she passes. Sometimes, she whirls around with the worry that she might be losing her chance, failing to see her because she is looking the wrong way.

During the six months Jan and David spend in Tasmania, after it is definitively over with Glen, at least for Jan, it is obvious that there will be no accidental running into Alicia. This is an awareness that pervades every day. But slowly, Jan becomes capable of thinking more widely: of all the lives that must be studded with missed encounters and the unfathomable ramifications of those non-meetings.

Next, still never crossing paths with Alicia, they are in Balmain for a time and then they move to the Blue Mountains – for another attempt to flee the poisonous end of the marriage and hopefully avoid a court case; for the cheaper rent and the ideal of greater peace in an almost rural life that in some ways echoes the imagined green and pleasant land, with mountains so eroded by age they can give the impression of hills and fireplace-heated tea rooms; for a little grandmotherly or New Agey goodwill at a remove from the more cynical city.

When Jan thinks of Glebe and her life there in the seventies and early eighties, it is with longing and regret: as you think of someone you loved, never really stopped loving, who was not able to fully return your feelings.

After the move to the Mountains, she ventures to the city only every so often. At first, because she is unemployed and distracted by hunting for work while getting by as a single parent on the dole. Then she becomes busy in new ways with the job as a counsellor at a community centre that she manages to swing, despite never having finished her degree. But a few times a year, she and David make an adventure of going down. To the Easter Show, for example, from which they return show-bag-laden, David with a lime-green glow-in-the-dark plastic necklace wrapped around his wrist. And maybe once a year, when he is with her parents or Glen, with some money she has put aside for the splurge, Jan makes that train trip by herself. She never goes with a friend, never quite having learned the trick of friendship.

Blackheath to Central, two and a half hours or so. Passing through Medlow Bath, she gazes at the Hydro Majestic Hotel, where she has taken David a couple of times for a hugely expensive cappuccino and slice of cake to share, and felt – against the backdrop of French-gypsy mood music and valley splotched royal blue with cloud shadows – an impostor, at best a spy. Then more valleys and bush, houses cottagey and villa-like, pretty weatherboards and ugly bricks. Katoomba, Leura, Wentworth Falls, Bullaburra, Lawson, Hazelbrook, Woodford, Linden, Faulconbridge, Springwood, Valley Heights … The houses gradually getting closer together and more suburban, getting Western Suburbsy in a way that makes her stomach contract and stops her from looking out the window so much. She tries to concentrate on whatever book she has on the go, but that doesn't last long because the city's approach is building in her like a storm. The old sense of counting down to an event, being on the verge of something uncontainable and not entirely knowing who she will be when she discovers it. Blacktown, Westmead, Parramatta, Strathfield …

Next stop: Central.

Her days in the city can be rather lonely and empty, but as she gets older these qualities seem to hurt less. It is precious just to be on her own and relatively free in places that attract and interest her. Sometimes she goes to the Art Gallery of New South Wales because she tends to feel peaceful there and she doesn't have to spend any money if she lingers over the permanent collection. Once, she finds herself standing for an amount of time impossible to measure – with a sense of recognition, almost of rediscovering a forgotten dream – in front of a painting entitled *The Flood in the Darling*. Had Alicia been there beside her, Jan could have said, *See? That's what you did to me. You drenched me, ruptured my banks, took possession, changed the order of things. See what you did to the light in me. You made it glossy, made it into mother-of-pearl. You unmade … You made …* It is probably much better that Alicia isn't there to hear this gibberish.

After the gallery, Jan often wanders in the ridiculously spectacular Botanic Gardens or crosses Hyde Park, thinking of Lorna and where she might have slept rough. She considers going to the tea room at David Jones, deciding against it, going instead to the one upstairs at Dymocks Bookshop. A pot of Earl Grey for one, which she uses to anchor a novel open.

But usually, eventually, she can't resist the pull of Glebe and she makes a big walk of it, listening to an album on her Walkman as she heads on up from Central, past Railway Square and Broadway, eyes bouncing off the turrets of Sydney University to search over Victoria Park for the dazzle of light flashing off the pool. Sometimes she half considers a swim there, hankering for it, imagining herself moving through the turnstile and inhaling chlorinated air and baby oil, before stripping off nonchalantly in the change room amid clouds of Rexona spray deodorant and loose swimmers' camaraderie. But she is no longer much of a swimmer, that baton has been passed to David, so she simply turns onto Glebe Point Road.

Where, the day she will actually run into Alicia, she goes to Badde Manors Cafe to kill time before the movie she plans to see at the Valhalla. Ensconcing herself in a small booth facing a single chair, with the *Herald* and a metal teapot of chai. The aroma of cloves and cardamom like ancient forest medicine, the honeyed heat of cinnamon and ginger.

Her head is still full of the movie some hours after this as she makes her way towards Gleebooks. She is singing to herself the Tom Waits track that opens it and seeing the loving happiness of the couple in their rural idyll at the end. Jan passes studenty types who look younger than she can remember ever feeling. The music in her stride and that street also deep in her body, in her hips and her heart, it occurs to her that she is at home there. At least, less of an impostor there than she is or will be anywhere else.

That welcome-back scent, already, of incense and libraries, while she studies the window display at Gleebooks. *The Waste Land*, *Kiss Kiss*, *The Harp in the South*, *The Hitchhiker's Guide to the Galaxy*, *The Man Who Loved Children*, *The Archetypes and the Collective Unconscious*, *The Vivisector*.

And in she goes, deciding that maybe she can afford a treat. She is not sure what sort of thing would match her mood.

'Janet?'

Of course. This apparition, when she has given up hope. A surge of happiness and fear.

'Janet? It's Alicia.'

'Oh, wow.'

They had no habit of touching each other, so they just stand there, smiling and stunned.

At last, Alicia holds out her hand and Jan takes it briefly, formally. Alicia's hand is cold, and beneath a black linen dress that is hardly creased she appears to be even thinner than she used to be. Her hair is in some sort of chignon, its length concealed. The years passed are not immediately obvious in her face. Perhaps now she looks a little more whittled, somehow more concentrated.

'It's great to see you.'

'You too.' Jan's chest and stomach feel compressed. 'Are you a fancy psychologist now?'

'Ha, yes, absolutely. You?'

'Counsellor.'

'Same difference.'

'Not quite.'

'But that's wonderful, that you went back to uni.'

Jan doesn't clarify that she never finished her degree.

There is a pause. Then Alicia says, 'Lorna?'

'The last I heard, she was in a halfway house in Summer Hill, or somewhere like that.'

'Poor thing …'

'Yeah.'

'So, you and Glen …'

'No, not for yonks.'

'And your son?'

She knows I had a boy, Jan notes, wondering who would have told her.

'He's almost in high school already, if you can believe it.'

'Gosh.'

'I know. And … you?'

'Kids, no.'

Jan sees the ring and, pointing at it, tries to joke, 'Oh no, you're not really married?' The words provoke a flutter of déjà vu, as if the present moment were a false bottom hiding a deeper, truer moment.

Alicia smiles. 'I know, I know.'

'Not Steve?' Jan is almost certain it won't be Steve. A few years back at the State Library, she tried to track down some of his poetry but couldn't find any. The librarian thought that *The Source* hadn't existed for a long time.

'Jesus, no.'

Jan stares at a birthday card on display: crimson paisley edged with gold.

Alicia begins, 'I'm sorry …'

Their eyes meet, Jan returning a questioning look with her own.

Alicia goes on, 'I've imagined apologising to you so many times and now I'm doing a shithouse job of it.' She presses a place between her strong eyebrows as if her head ached, exhales and then speaks quickly. 'I was incredibly sorry about how things turned out. That was the *last* thing I'd have wanted … All I can say, which is so feeble, is that I wasn't tremendously stable at that age.'

Jan, noting Alicia's use of the word *shithouse*, tries a smile. 'Yeah, who was?'

'It was mad. I'm so sorry.'

They move out of the way of a dignified woman with elaborate dreads, floaty velvet and a pungent aura of sandalwood.

'Well, it was a mad day. And you'd lost Heidi and we were young, weren't we?' She is thinking, though, that she and Alicia had seen through youth well before then. Also, that there is no question of the heart forgiving what it can't forgive, even if it wants to. 'I feel guilty about it, too.'

'Guilty for what?'

*

'Yes, guilty for what?' the therapist asked.

Jan shrugged. 'That's how I'm put together.'

'Or trained?'

'Or trained.'

*

Not answering, Jan is faintly reassured to glimpse *Wuthering Heights* on a shelf: just the idea of moors and someone else's hopeless passion to be lived snugly inside reading.

'On a different topic, my mother moved back to Spain a couple of years ago, And we're leaving tomorrow.'

'You're leaving for Spain tomorrow!'

'Maybe not forever – we'll see. I don't know if I'll feel at home there, but I want to try it.'

Jan says, 'That's brilliant. Listen, I'm sorry to rush off, but I have a train to catch. Up the Mountains.'

'The Mountains? Nice. I should go too. I'll come out with you.'

'You didn't want to buy something?'

'No, I don't know, I was just looking … But I've still got packing to do. It's really time for me to go get a cab.'

Jan won't let herself ask or even picture where and to whom she is getting the cab. On the footpath, she tells Alicia, 'I remember, that night, you saying we'd entered a different world. You were right. Well.' She has already composed her face and taken a step back.

'Give us a hug? After all this time.'

'All this time,' Jan echoes, not making a move but feeling her grip slipping.

Alicia pulls her in close, into a smell like custard and mandarin. Jan has the impression she is being throttled in the heart and desire shocks her, after so long. It is all extreme and enfolding. She starts to move away.

'Not so fast. I've missed you.'

Obediently, Jan links her arms around Alicia again and somehow collides with her cheekbone. She ducks her head, so that her mouth is on Alicia's throat, barely, but enough to detect the twitching of her pulse. She gasps or sighs, afraid to move again. It is abruptly clear to Jan that Alicia is not surprised by what she may only now be fully comprehending. From the tension in that slight body, the tightness of her arms and her minimal breathing, it seems plausible that she is waiting for something. But Jan isn't certain. What she is certain of is that her own energy for self-torture is limited and she does not want what cannot be freely given.

She lifts her head and, opening her eyes, sees a taxi in the distance over Alicia's shoulder. 'Cab.' She extricates herself and waves at it. 'He's stopping.'

'Janet, can we keep in touch?'

Alicia is looking for something in her Filofax, handing over her card. But Jan will not promise anything and she foresees how thinking of Alicia any more than strictly necessary would be foolish. She will not learn to imagine her husband; him, wrapping a foulard around her neck, his hand on her thigh … Already, a wash of jealousy as warm and shameful as wetting the bed as a child. She refuses this regression.

'Go now,' she says.

*

'At least, that's what I like to tell myself I said. I'm not positive, though. Honestly, I probably wasn't that clear.'

'That's okay. You can tell it like you want to tell it.'

What was different about Carole's eyes today, Jan realised, was that there was no foundation beneath them. So she could see the shadowed skin that was ordinarily concealed, the flecks of inky violet.

*

About to close the cab door, Alicia calls, 'Janet!'

She is holding out her hand through the window. Jan runs over, thinking she might say, *No one else ever called me Janet*, but she can't speak. She takes the hand, not formally this time.

The movement of the cab separates their interlaced fingers, jolting Jan's shoulder.

In the taxi, it occurs to Alicia that she should also have apologised for never returning the tracksuit Janet once lent her. It's odd that she remembers this now because, though she still has the tracksuit, she had practically forgotten it used to belong to Janet. Much faded, for years it has been her most comfortable, softest thing to wear around the house, and even now that the elastic in the waist has all but given up, she still wears those old trackies every so often if she is ill or glum and sure no one will see her.

'Where are we off to?' asks the driver and there is an interval of blankness: she doesn't know.

The cab finally out of sight, Jan sinks down onto the footpath, her feet in the gutter. Some time later, an elderly woman asks, 'You all right, love?'

She nods and this is when she begins to cry, yet she can more or less keep it down until the woman has walked on. How the sweetness of strangers can undo you. She doesn't cry for long. Her grief is more efficient than it once was, more a simmer than a boil. It has to be. She wants it to be.

(One morning many years later, going to visit David and her new grandchild, she will pass this place where she sat in the gutter, weeping, and remember.)

She gets to her feet, wipes her eyes and, instead of walking to Central, heads the other way. The wine bar she passes tempts her, but she keeps walking, wondering if she will ever be over the broken heart of the seventies. She pauses to fish her Walkman out of her backpack and change the cassette, slotting in *Remain in Light*, which is poised at the start of a favourite track. Ear buds in. Play.

When she gets to Glebe Point, she stands leaning against the graceful strength of a Moreton Bay fig. She turns off the music to concentrate better on the spreading branches, tough sheltering foliage, buttress roots like the fortified walls of a fantastical miniature city. Time begins to feel roomier as she inhales warm bark and sweetish trampled fruit, hints of industry and boats on watery air. Lorna, waiting here for Claude, might have felt something like this, waves of pain and need, slivers of joy, gratitude for the messages received.

The music starts up once more and she sets off at a brisk clip back in the other direction through the jungly jumble of the Inner West. The portside dreaminess, the rough inner-city cosiness, the scraping by, the restless and world-weary university students, the spunky, bouncy ones on the make, the poor crazy buggers in tinfoil-covered headgear to prevent their minds being read, the skinhead fascist that people recognise from demos, Armani and patchouli oil, fashion and its irrelevance, the ones into religions and no religion, skin and faces and gazes, choices apparent and real, desperation, the uncertainty about belonging, the everlasting guilt and sorrow of colonialism and genocide, colossal sunlight and skies so softly blue, the love affair with multiculturalism, the rosewater and cashews and sugar in your favourite baklava, the perfumed kick of that coffee you were so hanging out for, all the addicts and hedonists, rain coming and going like storms at sea, nights falling on streets overflowing with four o'clocks and jasmine, eucalypts and wattle and frangipani and fig trees like grand doors left ajar in time, savage nostalgia, bottomless want, the sex and closeness and love that it might only be possible to find in books and songs and movies and paintings and delirium and faraway places you'll never set foot in or not till it's too late, the swell, the heart in the ears listening for the sirens, the bright trails.

Acknowledgements

The Australia Council for the Arts generously supported the writing of this novel, with an international residency in Rome.

Heartfelt thanks to my publisher and first editor, Catherine Milne. *Grazie mille* to Scott Forbes; thank you to Alexandra Nahlous, Pam Dunne, Lisa White and the rest of the team at HarperCollins. *Un grand merci* to my agent, Jeanne Ryckmans.

Memories of my parents and grandparents, and of their stories, have fed and been transformed in this novel; I am extremely grateful to Gary Thornell, Terry Cameron, Isabel Cameron (Grumley), Jack Grumley, Rose Bailey (Thornell), and Hal Thornell.

Muchas gracias a Miguel Alonso.